To my parents, Sila and Bibhuti Dutta Roy.

Ranjita Dutta Roy

SEE YOU IN EZRA STREET

AUSTIN MACAULEY PUBLISHERS

LONDON ∗ CAMBRIDGE ∗ NEW YORK ∗ SHARJAH

A CIP catalogue record for this title is available from the British Library.

ISBN 9781528989008 (Paperback)
ISBN 9781528989015 (ePub e-book)

www.austinmacauley.com

First Published 2022
Austin Macauley Publishers Ltd®
1 Canada Square
Canary Wharf
London
E14 5AA

My initial gratitude goes to Valerie Loh, who has been my mentor and has seen this project grow, since 2016. I am also grateful to Daniela Saleth, Cesc Canet, and Sila Dutta Roy, for reading through the final drafts. I would like to thank Calcutta based Jael Silliman, for reading and commenting on earlier manuscripts. A special thanks goes to Kate Lyons (Standout Books) for reading two early manuscripts. My gratitude also goes to Somdyuti Datta Ray and Smita Dutta Roy for reading two chapters, and my teacher Jack Adler (Writer's Digest University).

Part I

Chapter 1

Tanushree Roy Chowdhury turned her gaze towards the cobblestones at the doorstep to her Berlin apartment house in Prenzlauer Berg, which were interspersed with golden tiles. Her cold fingers trembled and stripes of uncombed hair covered her sunken face, making it difficult to turn the key. As she closed the green heavy wooden front door behind her, she wondered what the fate had been of the people those tiles commemorated. She carefully stepped forward on the orange-and-black tiled floor, took a firm grip of the banister, and slowly climbed up the four flights of stairs of the Altbau building. As she entered the flat on the top floor, she slumped down on her red sofa-bed. Rays of sun shone on the whitewashed walls opposite her and reflected back on her face. For a moment, she closed her eyes and longed to be in the comfort of her parental home on the Swedish west coast.

When she opened her eyes again, the room was full of thick fog. White heavy layers had formed under the ceiling and were spreading like a billowing curtain of milk against the walls of the room. They slowly moved towards the sofa-bed where she was lying. *Get up!* a far-away voice commanded inside of her, but her petrified body had turned into a sandbag, sunken into the red cushions beneath her. Her eyes rolled back and forth, her gaze trying to penetrate the creeping swathes around her. Somewhere deep inside, she felt a glimpse of recognition, as if she had the power to stop this. But it was too late already. The fog was now all around, wrapping her into its density. For a moment, she felt suffocated, and to calm her rising panic, Tanushree tried to draw deep breaths. Immediately, the stench of burnt rubber filled her nostrils, and a metallic taste invaded her mouth. *Gas!* she thought and began to tremble heavily while flashes of shaved heads, bony bare shoulder blades and dark opened eyes and mouths attacked her consciousness. She could hear screams, sharp orders and the rattling sound of a helicopter propeller. It was like she was in the middle of a roaring war. The golden tiles had reminded her of that day in her life when she had first been brought to light about the unfathomable treatment in the concentration camps. She saw the face of the man who had told her about the atrocities of Auschwitz. She was thirteen and surrounded by her classmates in the high ceiling assembly hall of the school. It was a morning session, but the slender elderly man caught her attention from the moment he stepped on the stage. He began to tell them what inhumane behaviour he had endured and little by little disclosed the pain of losing one's own at a tender age. She remembered how gloomy the hall had suddenly felt and the heavy rain which fell outside. At the end of the morning session, the old man signed her book, and as he turned his arm she saw the tattooed number again. Then he looked up at her face.

"Your eyes look like my granddaughter's," he said. Tanushree sat up on her bed with eyes closed and fists clutching the bed linen. In her head, were pictures of a half-bombed Calcutta. She saw flashes from the streets of Dacca, a city she had not even visited. There were dead bodies everywhere. She began thinking about the people who had lost their lives around the time of the Partition of India. She observed a street scene from the Japanese bombings in Rangoon, another city she had not even been to. What had happened to her family during those years? She trembled, overwhelmed by the flashes. Tears rolled down her eyes, still sitting on the bed with her eyes closed.

She got up to call her parents and tell them that there was no need to worry. She promised to come home by the next flight to Sweden. Her words were troubled and incoherent.

"One died on a South Calcutta rail track, one in an open street in Dacca, another one in the Japanese bombings of Rangoon and my grandfather left this earth before I was even born. Why did I not have the luck to meet them?" Her mother cried on the phone, but Tanushree hung up the receiver after uttering those words.

She went to the kitchen to boil some water. The sleep deprivation had played around with the neurotransmitters in her brain and she had begun getting illusions. She took a sip of the lemon infusion, but the tartness made her retch, so she ran to the toilet and vomited into the bowl. She closed her eyes and lay down on the tiled bathroom floor. Tears gushed out and after a while, exhausted, she fell asleep. The gas had slowly disappeared. It had only been a nightmare…

The same evening, Tanushree admitted herself to the hospital. She needed to explain to someone, but every time she brought up the nightmare, she was asked to rest. The ward nurses gave her mood-stabilizing and sleeping pills, and she slept like a log the first five days she was admitted. On the sixth day, she met an in-house psychologist.

"Could you tell me what happened, in your own words please?" the young soft-spoken female psychologist asked her. She had chestnut brown hair, blue eyes and a six-feet-tall plump body. The room was as sterile as a room can be, without a single painting on the white walls, and it smelled of hospital soap.

She told her the whole story of her sleep deprivation, associations, illusions, family, but it was hard to explain in words. She decided to try to tell her the story about the Partition.

"So, in the 1940s there was a partition of India, which was accompanied by conflicts between Hindus and Muslims…" The psychologist gaped at her as if she was wondering why she brought it up. She seemed to have made up her mind about her patient's background.

"Right. Now tell me a bit about your own family. I know how uncommon it is for people in your home country to become highly educated. I suppose that causes clashes between you and your parents."

The moment the psychologist uttered those words, she knew she was expecting a story about a family who could hardly afford their daily bread and had been saved by the Swedish state. Tanushree wanted to tell it to her face that she was wrong and should get a reality-check. How often did those families afford to move from India to Europe in the 1960s?

"I mean, after all, in Northern Europe, every other person is highly educated." Tanushree knew her kind. She was the sort of person who cared about titles, but never for the knowledge people retained. She just knew it and was sure she walked around with prejudice and opinions, which were never challenged. The only time she left her safe bubble at home, she probably went to a resort in Thailand, where she never even brushed shoulders with locals, let alone went out to experience their daily lives.

"I'm not sure what you mean, but of course we have differences in opinions! I only think that's healthy in a relationship," she replied, crossing her arms over her chest. The last thing she could connect her mental state to were differences in education level. Her parents had passed on to her their cultural interests and love for political discussions. They taught her everything she knew about Indian history that her Swedish schooling had not provided her. They had made her mind wander and explore. If she wanted to hear about her family, why was she not open to discussing the Partition and why Tanushree had fallen ill in the first place?

"My family was expropriated in the wake of the Partition and some of them lost their lives during those years," she said. The psychologist began listening, but it made Tanushree sad how misery had caught her attention more than anything else.

"I still don't know all the details, but my mind painted vivid pictures of events and family members I had never met." After some time, Tanushree knew the psychologist had lost interest because her gaze had turned to the window. She could not make the connection she was trying to make clear.

"What I was trying to say is that your country must be very different from this city, where half of the population is highly educated," she repeated.

It annoyed Tanushree that when the young woman asked her questions, she never dug deeper. It was as if she followed a standard recipe and paid no heed to anything her patient had to say. She referred to herself as highly educated, but knew nothing about the history of the second most populated country in the world. Were psychologists not supposed to be open-minded and analytical? Tanushree sighed and thought about how little people knew about their surrounding world and how distorted their pictures were because of their need to generalize. They never consider how cultures may have changed over the course of the years. She had been haunted by that kind of attitudes since her childhood days. She looked into the eyes of her psychologist again. Should she tell her about the ancient universities of Nalanda, or the way the British had brought western higher learning to India two centuries ago. Tired of constantly having to fight ignorance when she knew the next second the person she had talked to would fall back into old patterns of reasoning, she decided to do neither!

The psychologist looked down at her watch. "Oh, time's up. Nice meeting you today, Tanushree,"

They shook hands, but Tanushree was not happy. She was not convinced this was the accurate path to take. While she walked out from the sterile room, she wondered if she was just obsessing over the past. She recalled how her friends sometimes told her that she immersed herself too deeply into subjects that were of interest to her, as if it were a crime, but as she walked up

Friedrichstrasse, she was slightly abashed at the thought that she had judged her psychologist, perhaps wrongly.

After climbing up the stairs to her apartment, Tanushree sat down on the sofa, exhausted from the past few months of too much work, and too little sleep. She leaned her head back with her eyes closed. In only a month, she had to hand in her PhD thesis to the examination board at the university. The thesis, which lay half-finished on her desk, was her attempt to marry Western classical music to Indian classical music. The thin shoulder straps of her white linen dress were almost cutting into her skin. Three months ago, she had been able to wear the dress, without any part of her body bulging out. But she had given up her twice-a-week running routine, and her meals of late had consisted of ample amounts of those treacherous carbohydrates she craved for when she was stressed. As a result, she had nightmares and was suffering from an obsession over her family history.

She took a deep breath, opened her eyes again, stood up and turned her face towards the window in the living room. It was gloomy outside, just like it had been in the dream. Then she turned her face towards the wall. For a good few minutes, Tanushree stood in front of the black-and-white picture of her paternal grandfather, which was a copy of the one in her parental home on the Swedish coastal city. The man from the last century stood leaning on an ornate pillar with carefully carved flower petals. He looked like a proud young fellow with his clean-shaven face and the shawl wrapped around his black raw silk suit. He stood with one foot steady on the marble floor and the other leg crossed over it.

She walked to the desk and opened the top drawer, where she had kept an original picture of her paternal grandparents together at old age. It was taken many decades after the single photo of the youthful, Debendranath Roy Chowdhury. His hair was grey and his body was much thinner. She turned her gaze towards his face and noticed his eyes were sunken and fatigued just like her grandmother's. His eyes were turned to the floor as if he was staring into thin air and his bottom lip jutted out slightly and she could see the lines of his cheekbones. There was no sign of the proud man of his youth. She knew the picture was taken in Calcutta a few years before he passed away, because on the back, in fine handwriting, was the name of the studio and in cursive writing 'December 1966'. Her grandparents had sent it as a thirtieth birthday gift to her father, Alokesh, while he still lived in West Berlin.

Tanushree finally looked at the photo of her family village home in East Bengal before the Partition of India in 1947. It was a two-storey marble palace. At the front, there were four ornate pillars like the one her grandfather leaned on in the first photograph. The image of the house reflected itself in the pond in front of it. Tanushree had been surprised to know that her grandfather was a partial owner of a palace, which was rightfully her family's heirloom.

Standing still by the copy of the canvas painting of the palace, she recalled how hurtful it had been to be called a working-class child. Her mother, a former vocal singing teacher of a high calibre in Calcutta, had succumbed to becoming a day care nurse in Sweden. Her father had spent years specializing in electrical engineering but had attracted intellectual inertia at an early stage. It still annoyed her how the foreign academic degrees and training of her parents had been disparaged in the country they had chosen to live in. She was reminded of her mothers' muffled cry that she pretended not to hear as a teenager. Then she turned her head towards the window and thought about her childhood home in Sweden. It was a green wooden townhouse with double-glazed latticed windows parted in the middle and framed in white paint. The houses in the neighbourhood had been built purposefully for the workers at a famous ball-bearing company almost eight decades earlier. The roofs of the 'Egnahem' houses, were made of slanting orange tiles and each house had its own chimney. While she stood there and thought about the apple tree she used to climb when she was a child, she could not help but think about that time when she and her childhood friend had decorated the whole street with buckets of garden-picked dandelions. The grown-ups had been furious with the children that evening. She walked back to the painting and reminded herself how the grandparents of her childhood friends had built their houses themselves, and how she had never told them her own father had spent his childhood summers in the marble mansion in the painting. She thought about how her grandfather had paid for some of his children to study abroad, while the parents of many of her friends had never even done higher studies. After a moment's thought, it dawned on her how much this double identity had taught her about the workings of the human mind. How stressful it was the few times she told them the truth and people assumed she lied because to them, being an immigrant meant being from a poor and uneducated background. Had her grandfather felt something similar after he lost his property and family members in East Bengal – when there was no more evidence, and he had been forced into a new existence? Was that the reason for the disillusion in his eyes – or did something else happen? Then she looked into the moonstones of her grandmother.

"At least, he spent most of his life side by side with someone to whom he could express his sorrows and setbacks," she said to herself and sighed. Her child-loving grandmother, Chandramukhi, had been her playmate the first two times she had visited India. One day when she was four, only a few months after her family had returned from a visit to Calcutta, came the bad news. She remembered her father had cried the whole night, and she had tried to console him by saying, "We all have to leave one day."

Little did she know that evening in late May 2017 that her emotions would soon be answered by a century-old correspondence between her own grandfather and the man with whom he had shared a seven-decade long friendship, which began in Colonial Calcutta in 1905. The universes of four young students collided, because they were children of the same presidency. Decades later, they would find themselves suffering from fear, agony and endless sorrow due to a line drawn on a map by Cyril Radcliffe.

Chapter 2

Forty-two years before the line was drawn by Cyril Radcliffe, the stout young gentleman came out from the lecture hall with his gaze at Isiah Cohen. The two youngsters, whom he noted his classmate had already befriended, were standing outside the lecture hall in the mass of students on the veranda of the first floor. Isiah knew the only reason his classmate directed his attention to him was because of what he had said at class that October afternoon in 1905. He could not help but let his own eyes linger on him as he approached. The young man wore brown loafers and an elegant dark suit covered with a white shawl. As he came nearer, Isiah could smell his cologne. The fellow student stretched out his hand.

"I'm Debendranath Roy Chowdhury." His handshake was firm and his gaze steady.

"Nice to meet you, Mr Roy Chowdhury. I'm Isiah Cohen," he replied.

"Please call me Debu. That's the name everyone knows me by. I quite appreciated your remark in there about the possible ways of making home rule possible."

They had just come out from one of their first lectures in Political Science at Presidency College in Calcutta. The professor, a young Bengali gentleman, had asked his class whether they considered independence from the British Crown plausible. At first, Isiah had wondered to himself whether it was even allowed to raise such questions at a university class in the city, which was still the capital of British India. But he had read about the Irish Home Rule movement and felt encouraged to speak, so he raised his hand.

"I think an initial step would be to manufacture commodities like food and clothes locally. We also must build up the infrastructure," he had said in his mellow voice, after which the professor had nodded his head in appreciation.

Debendranath introduced the two other classmates who were in his company. One wore a *topi* cap and had large dark brown glowing eyes, which looked at Isiah with warmth. His eyes and nose crinkled as he smiled towards him. On the contrary, the other young man had a contempt in his eyes, and Isiah did not know what he had done to earn such a welcome. For a second, he noticed Debu glancing at the man with the fierce eyes whom he later found out was Jyotish Ganguly. The man with the topi cap stretched out his hand to him.

"I'm Abdul Huq," he said in a deep voice.

"Jyotish and Abdul are both born-and-bred Calcuttans, but I have my roots in East Bengal." Isiah could not help but hear Debu's loud emphasis on East Bengal. He looked around him. They were still standing upstairs outside the lecture hall of the concrete building with long arched and open verandas. In a few places along the veranda, were busts of previous students and teachers of prominence. He always thought his classmates looked precocious to be eighteen-year-olds who had just begun senior college. The students were almost always properly dressed.

After a long day, Isiah Cohen and his newly found friends Jyotish Ganguly, Abdul Huq and Debendranath Roy Chowdhury walked out through the high gates of the academic institution to find a place to have their evening snacks. Nine decades earlier, their college had been one of the first western institutes for higher learning in the country. This afternoon the streets were full of pupils from the neighbouring Hare School. They zigzagged over College Street, the back alleys by the park and past the yellow stately building of Sanskrit College. In those days, the streets were not busy with cars, but rather horse-drawn or cow-drawn vehicles and rickshaws. Isiah noticed Debendranath glancing up at Albert Hall as they passed by. He later learnt it was the building where his friend used to meet with his party comrades. Debu was a stout gentleman in those days, newly matriculated into Presidency College with his aim at the Department of Law. As was often the case with the enthusiastic young man, he had participated actively in the class discussions and Isiah had paid attention to his words the same way he had done the past few weeks before they were introduced. He felt exhausted after a long day. On top of this, times were turbulent. Many things nudged to get out of the back of his mind.

"How do you feel about the partition of Bengal, Debu?" Jyotish Ganguly asked and sat down on the wooden stool on the pavement and sipped his tea. It was simple powder tea, but Isiah's stomach had craved for it during the whole Political Science class. In fact, he was a bit of a tea addict. Isiah saw wrinkles on the forehead of the man who was otherwise so jovial and optimistic. He

19

would soon find out the political stir in Bengal Presidency had coloured his friend's past months. Around the same time as he had moved back to Calcutta to attend senior college, the first partition of Bengal had begun. Some people said it was done by the British in order to calm down the riotous Bengalis and to create tension between Muslims and Hindus, which would take away the focus on resistance against the Crown.

"Well, it means that my childhood home is in one province and my whereabouts in another. The thought of it certainly makes me torn," Debu replied.

There was a moment's silence as a horse-drawn vehicle passed by on Harrison Road and the dust rose from the ground like smoke.

"Do you think it may be time to move over to Calcutta?" asked Jyotish Ganguly.

"After all, you belong to a minority in East Bengal."

"I don't know what will happen to our estates if we leave it behind. Besides, we have lived side by side with our Muslim brothers and sisters for generations, and I see no reason why that should not be the case in the future."

Debendranath was the son of a Hindu Zamindar and headmaster of a school in Vikrampur. The estates had belonged to his grandmother's family for many generations. He soon confided in Isiah that despite having spent much time in their home in Dacca town, the estates in Vikrampur was where his heart was. There were the meadows he used to fly kites in as a child and the pond where he was taught how to swim. There was the home where he met his cousins during the holidays. So many memories had been made in East Bengal that the thought of leaving felt heavy on his heart.

"I certainly hope you are right my friend."

Jyotish Ganguly put an end to the conversation as he noticed his classmate's distress.

"You will all see what a gem East Bengal is when you come for my wedding," said the young student. His eyes looked dreamy.

"Have you decided on a bride Debu?" asked Abdul.

"Yes, we have. She's a young girl of 16, very musical and quite intellectual if I may say so. Her father brings her home works of Wordsworth and Keats, and she has learnt the sitar from an early age. Her face is one of the most beautiful and innocent I have ever seen."

The others looked at each other and smiled at the comment of the lovestruck man.

"Will she be living with you in Calcutta?" asked Abdul.

"Yes, I plan to take her back here with me after the wedding. I also hope to get her matriculated into a college. She's far too intelligent to sit at home. Besides, I would be bored if I had to live with someone who cooks and takes care of the household all day. What would we talk about? I need a wife who speaks my vernacular."

Isiah had just learned that Debendranath lived in the college hostel during weekdays, and in the family's old bungalow in Tollygunge, on weekends. His older brother had recently finished his Law studies in Calcutta, whereas the youngest brother, Narendranath, had joined Debendranath in the city to finish intermediate school, and to eventually pursue his MBBS at the Calcutta Medical College. Isiah was looking forward to visiting the family coming Sunday when they were going to study at the home of Roy Chowdhury. After sitting silently and observing his classmate, he finally opened his mouth.

"Yes, I hear Bengalis from the other side of the Padma River are very engaged in the education of their daughters. Wasn't British India's first female physician from a Barisali family?" Debu's eyes sparked upon hearing his sentence and he lifted his head.

"Yes, that is right my friend, and it has already been two decades since she graduated. Raja Ram Mohan Roy left us with a task. How much longer shall we bear this inequality between men and women? Our task is now to seek independence from the crown and equality, between genders, between castes, and between socioeconomic layers of our country. Equality comes from education, the right to practice the same professions and right to land ownership," said Debendranath.

He later confided in Isiah he had been taught the art of oration from an early age. Debu knew he often spoke confidently and triumphantly, which stirred up mingled feelings in other people, but it had also made him involved in politics at a young age. Abdul Huq and Jyotish Ganguly both glanced at each other sceptically. Jyotish rolled his eyes, but Isiah glanced at his zealous classmate and gave a coy smile in agreement to his newly found friend's refreshing thoughts.

"Do you really think our womenfolk are made to sit on school benches all day, cramming their heads with the knowledge they will never retain?" asked

Jyotish provocatively. His lips were pressed tightly together and his eyes squinting.

"Yes, I think it would do them good to have access to higher education," Debu replied. "I see no reason why women should not be able to learn and remember the same way as men do."

"I can't think of a single discipline their brains are suited for. Law requires fast thinking and decisive minds, and decisiveness is definitely something women lack. Medicine requires physical work. The Natural sciences and Mathematics require a sense of logic. Women are far too emotional and feeble to excel in such fields. Maybe Literature could suit their temper, but then again how much use would they be to society?" Jyotish paused to let his classmate speak.

"You are obviously wrong, Jyotish, considering the world has already seen a sheer number of female mathematicians, physicians, lawyers and natural scientists. But if we let our daughters go out in a world where people live with similar convictions to yours, they will, of course, feel discouraged," Debendranath said with a flushed face.

"Let's say we assume that some of our womenfolk are indeed suited for these traditionally male professions Debu, would you really like your daughters to study and work side by side with men? We all know women cannot control their emotions and such a setting would encourage all kinds of immoral behaviour." Isiah watched Debu's eyes become narrow, while he listened to Jyotish's words.

"No, Jyotish, I do not agree that women are animals that need to be tamed. The ones I know are highly self-restrained and have a very high sense of morality." He almost yelled at his classmate now. With this quarrel began a seven-decade long love–hate relationship between Jyotish Ganguly and Debendranath Roy Chowdhury. They were both of the same faith and brought up in the same era, but with completely different outlooks on life. At the same time, a deep understanding arose between Isiah and Debendranath. What Debu did not know then was that the conversation also planted a seed in the head of Abdul Huq who would four decades later find himself suffering from the same fear and agony as his East Bengali classmate.

Isiah gave the elderly Chinese man a silver coin as he handed over the plate with freshly made momos to his younger sister Hannah.

"Here you go. See you next Sunday," the vendor said in his Indian English accent.

The man was middle-aged and wore a half-sleeved shirt and linen pants, where he sat in Sun Yat-Sen Street. The morning air was fresh. It was 5:30 a.m. and late October. They had to wait in queue for almost twenty minutes to taste the delicacies the man fried in the big metal pan. Isiah could smell the fried dough from the hawker's stalls. For the past four years, Hannah and he had made it into their mission to wake up early every Sunday morning and walk over to Tiretti Bazar, which was just a twenty-minute walk from their parents' flat in Marquis Street. He watched his sister as she bit into the white dumpling with her eyes closed. He loved how the taste of it brought a smile to her light pink lips. Sometimes he was scared a young man would get smitten by her beauty. His two-year younger sister was the only confidante he had in this world, and he could not bear losing her, not quite yet. Around them at the market were elderly Chinese men and women sitting on low stools and cooking everything from momos, soup with fish balls, chow Mein and woks. They walked a bit farther down the street to where the dessert stalls were. Hannah rubbed her palms against each other. The siblings chose rice balls covered by sesame seeds. He did not know if he was allowed to feel this euphoric about something so trivial as food, but he still relished it. There was a long silence of munching, biting into rice balls and lip-smacking.

"So, he's not from around here then?" said his sister.

He had told Hannah about his charismatic newly found friend.

"No, he's from East Bengal, and he seems very proud of it," he answered.

"How very exciting. I've always wondered what they're like."

"He's quite a character, and he has no problem questioning our lecturers, I've noticed. Judging by his confidence I would never have guessed he's merely eighteen," he said.

They had walked to the crossing of Vander Burg Lane and Tiretti Bazar Street. A horse cart came in their direction, but otherwise, the streets were unusually calm. When they had both finished their rice balls, Isiah walked Hannah home. At this time, Calcutta was home to a mere million inhabitants, but on Sunday mornings this area was busy. After walking Hannah home to their flat in Marquis Street, he set off to the study session of the day with his classmates. He was quite excited to see what Debu's weekend dwelling looked like.

At the electric tram stop at the Esplanade, Isiah met Abdul Huq.

"Is this the closest route for you?" he asked after greeting him as he knew Abdul's family lived in Park Circus.

"Well, I was out on a walk in the morning. I went to the mosque to pray, so I thought I might as well take the tram to Tollygunge from here."

Abdul Huq was a quiet young man with a deep voice, and one could see in his eyes he was always in deep thoughts, a bit like Isiah himself. On the trip to Tollygunge, few words were exchanged between them, but Isiah had no problem sharing a moment of silence with his classmate. He was the kind of man who made him comfortable in his company no matter if words were exchanged or not.

They got off the tram and walked through the lush suburb to the Roy Chowdhury bungalow. In those days, this part of town was still a southern suburb of the city, where people had their weekend getaways. So was also the case for the Roy Chowdhury family, even though Debu used to live in the hostel of the Presidency College during weekdays. They knocked on the door and a young man opened the door and let them in.

"Welcome to our simple abode," Debu exclaimed, as he came walking towards them in the living room. "This is my younger brother, Narendranath." The young man with the moustache smiled towards them. Isiah looked down and noted the floor was of black and white mosaic, similar to their floor at home. At the opposite wall was a wooden sofa with carvings and brown cushions. On a table next to it was a gramophone. Isiah had never seen one before, but he knew very well what they looked like. The light yellow walls were decorated with a mixture of Kalighat paintings and old Mughal motives. From the far end of the living room, a flight of stairs led up to the first floor. Debu guided them through an arched doorway from the living room to the dining space with a dark wooden table with six chairs around it. The aroma of toasted bread and freshly brewed tea oozed out from the kitchen.

Isiah's life had been perfectly fine void of any romantic interest before she came down the stairs that Sunday morning. He immediately noticed her unblemished face. It looked innocent, but her kohl-rimmed eyes marked the prominent light brown irises, and her lips were coloured with pink lipstick. Judging from her childlike features, she was probably not older than sixteen, but there was something about her that allured him. Even though she was most likely not more than two years younger than him, she was far more stylish than

24

any Bengali woman he had seen before. She was beautiful in her deep blue silk sari with golden leaf patterns, and she wore it with grace as her feet stepped downstairs.

"This is my younger sister Debapriya. She's quite a sleepyhead," said Debu jokingly while looking down at his pocket watch, and then smiling towards his sister. Her face burst out in a broad smile. Isiah forced himself to look away from her, so the others would not notice he was drawn to her.

"I assume you are my brother's classmates. I'm very pleased to meet you all," she said halfway down the stairs.

"Hello," they burst out almost all at the same time.

Her unblemished cheeks blushed. Then she looked down and snuck into the kitchen to prepare her breakfast. But Isiah caught himself peeping over in her direction many times that morning.

Chapter 3

112 years after Debendranath Roy Chowdhury and Isiah Cohen first made acquaintance with each other, Tanushree's fork pierced through the thin piece of herring on her plate. It was the summer evening of the Friday Tanushree arrived in London to celebrate midsummer with her cousin's family. The mixed sweet and savoury taste, and the next to raw texture of the herring reminded her palette of the many midsummer dinners at home in Sweden. She flushed it down with water. They sat in the living room of her cousin Rohini's home in Harrow. She had promised her cousin's children to treat them to a Swedish midsummer lunch, so after arriving at St Pancras station, she had spent her afternoon in the Swedish grocery shop carefully picking out the items for dinner.

Tanushree clinked on a glass, and they looked up the next 'snaps' song on the sheet of paper next to their plates. At the end of the song, she took a sip of the strong akvavit she had bought for the adults. For the children, she had chosen elderflower squash, but the liquids had the same colour. On Midsummer's Day when she celebrated the summer solstice and the old heathen traditions at home, she often drank this. It burned as it slid down her throat and she sat quietly to herself and observed the others. They seemed to be so happy together, but she was self-controlled, almost a bit withdrawn and barely talked to the others. She could feel it.

"What are you thinking about, Tanu?"

Rohini stood behind and touched her shoulder with her hand. Tanushree turned around and smiled.

"I'm thinking I would love to be more like your family, and be able to open up like you."

"Yes, I was watching you from the other end of the table and you have been kind of quiet. You look so sad sometimes, and you seem to spend a lot of time on your own…"

It was obvious her parents had talked to her cousin, who put down her glass on the oval wooden table and sat down beside her. Tanushree decided to be very honest with her.

"Would you like to go on a walk with me?" she asked.

"Sure, let me just go upstairs and get my shawl," Rohini replied.

Through the glass door, Tanushree saw her hurrying down the stairs with her shawl resting on the shoulders, and she stood and left the table to go and meet her. They closed the front door to the house behind them as they set off to the little hill in the forest at the back of Rohini's place.

"I had a manic episode in Berlin. That's why I've taken some time off. I overworked and stopped sleeping for some time, and I began getting flashes of people and family members I had never met; people who passed away during the Indian Partition and World War II," Tanushree explained. It was just easier to get things off the chest at once. She was so relieved that for once she did not have to explain every single word to someone.

"Yes, you looked absent-minded just now, when we were sitting at the table. That's a horrible nightmare to have. I know it sounds like a cliché, but I think we have such bad dreams for a reason. Maybe your subconscious is trying to tell you something." Tanushree nodded.

"I would like to know more about my family history," said Tanushree.

"Yes, I understand. How are you going to go about it?" asked Rohini.

"I guess I should begin talking to my parents and relatives in India and just read a lot about the historical events. I'm planning to spend some time at the India Office at the British Library the coming week," she replied.

"We should take you out to an Indian restaurant tomorrow. You'll love it. It's the oldest Indian restaurant in town."

Tanushree waited for Rohini to ask her about the British Library and what she was planning to do there, but she never did.

"Rohini, have you never wondered?" she asked at last.

"About what?" her cousin said and shrugged her shoulders.

"How it must have felt for our ancestors to leave East Bengal and come to Calcutta?"

Rohini was a surgeon and even though her mind was as sharp as the knives she used for surgery, and she very often could read Tanushree's mind, this was not one of those occasions. Perhaps there was no need to ask questions about one's origin if you grew up in a place where many people are familiar with your roots. In London, there were even blue plaques to commemorate important Indians of the past who had resided there. This city was so different from Sweden, where many of her friends feared religion and few of them cared about their roots and family history. She felt people in her homeland often had a longing to belong to the group of 'rikssvenskar' – the people who spoke without dialect and erased their backgrounds thereby.

"No, I don't think I've ever wondered," said Rohini, after a long pause. Once again, Tanushree wondered to herself if she was going a bit too far in exploring her past.

That evening after coming back to her temporary room in her cousin's Harrow terraced house, she began reading an article about EEG measurements in the brains of people listening to melodies of different musical modes. Her research had taught her the anatomy and function of the brain areas, and the subject had inspired her so much she was considering a career in Music Psychology. She knew what she needed to deal with now, and that made it easier to focus on work, but as she reached the Materials and Methods section of the scientific article, she began to dose off and put her head down on the desk.

The following morning, Tanushree walked into the India Office Records at the British Library. The place was a maze. She had no idea where to begin. A librarian who wore round glasses with metal frames with a horse-tail approached her.

"How may I be at your assistance?" the man asked.

"I have come to look for material on the 1947 Indian Partition, especially about the events in Bengal," she told him.

Without asking her what her knowledge level was, he handed over the teaching material for school children. She opened her mouth, but she could not bring herself to tell him she wanted something more into-depth. Instead, she browsed through the material and realized how little she knew. She felt small and guilty for not having asked the question earlier in life. A few minutes later, the librarian came back with four articles about the psychological impact of the Partition, displacement and Holocausts. She looked at him with gratitude. He had read her mind.

"I thought you might want to explore an unknown territory." He winked at her. The smile on his face was secretive, but friendly. If she did not have a whole PhD thesis to finish within the next three weeks, she could have easily stayed at the library for years and worked on what he suggested.

An hour later, she had learned the mental consequences of losing property, something that had been trite to her until that day. Then she read about how trauma could be passed down from Holocaust survivors to their progeny. There was pin-drop silence in the library. A couple of seats were occupied by people she assumed to be researchers. She sat down at one of those desks with her articles. The next paper talked about psychological trauma in the context of caste. She highlighted important facts with her yellow pen and jotted down words in the margins. The librarian came back to her with a review about why people had kept quiet about the 1947 Partition despite millions of Indians being displaced, a million people killed and hundreds of thousands women being raped.

At lunch, she crossed the courtyard of the library, walked over to the other side of the road, and went into the Irish pub at the corner opposite to the King's Cross station. People gushed out from the station building. She thought about what she had just learned. Why did her family always try to sweep things under the rug? What bothered her more was the apathy of the common man who had witnessed the events of those years.

"Your family are refugees. You do know that, right? WE are proper Calcuttans, my uncle was born and brought up there, and my family has lived there for generations," one of the elderly men in the South Asian community had told her with a smirk when she was 17. At that point, his words had perplexed her, but his smirk had stayed in her memory. It felt like a very odd way of breaking such news to her. She knew the uncle was born and brought up in a small town in West Bengal, but it had always been very important to him and his children to point out they were from Calcutta.

She took out the articles from her locker in the basement and walked up the stairs to the top floor where the India Office was situated. Then she sat down on the same chair as in the morning and picked up the last article.

As she was clearly out for searching her Indian roots, she thought she might as well spend her third day in London hunting blue plaques in town. When she got off the overground at Hampstead Heath, it was drizzling. She took out the black umbrella from her handbag, but decided she wanted to have lunch, so she ordered a vegetarian English breakfast at a little place just across from the entrance to the station. When she was done, she felt like she was going to burst.

Half an hour later, she had her mind set on the house of one of her favourite poets, Rabindranath Tagore, who was the first non-European to have gained a Nobel Prize in 1913 for a poem collection. But to her, the short stories of her younger days was why he was important and her favourite story was one about an Afghani vendor and his friendship with a young Bengali girl, which faded with time. She had had many such friendships over the year, and it was always strange to her how people could be close friends at one time and ten years later have nothing in common. For a few minutes, she stood in front of the white terraced house next to the heath, where Rabindranath Tagore had lived the year before receiving his Nobel prize. It was only a short walk uphill from the station. Interestingly, DH Lawrence had lived just around the corner. She imagined how the great bard of Bengal had walked around in the lush neighbourhood to find inspiration. After viewing the house from outside, she went back to the overground station.

She went off at Kensington Olympia and passed by the house where independent India's first prime minister, Jawaharlal Nehru, in London. Like other important political figures of colonial India, he had studied Law in England. From there, she walked to the street in West Kensington where Mahatma Gandhi had lived as a Law student. Next to it, lay an Indian cultural institute housed partly in an old church building. She just had to go in. There were four floors worth of Indian art and culture inaugurated almost fifty years back. She envied the children who grew up with the opportunity to take part in these activities. At the reception, sat a middle-aged Indian gentleman with glasses.

"Welcome, Madame. May I be of any help?"

"I was just wondering if I could have a look around," she answered.

"Of course. Be my guest." He held out his arm.

The house was full of inspiring sounds, beautiful choreography and language teaching. She peeked into one of the rooms on the ground floor. There were a group of students practising the dance style of Odissi. They were all dressed in saris. Then she went upstairs to be met by the sound of strumming on sitar strings. In the next room, a group of mostly adult men and women sang the tans of a raga. They were similar to the variations she used to play in her younger days. This place was magic! It was like coming home to her maternal home in Calcutta, where almost each and every one practised music until old age. She was overwhelmed by all the Indianness. She reminisced about the countless home concerts she had attended in Germany. Oh, how inspiring it had been to meet Germans, Turks and Israelis who had taken Indian classical music to heart. She knew people of Indian ethnicity sometimes looked down on these musicians, saying it was not the real thing and it annoyed her. She could see it made a difference if one's ear had been trained to the music from birth or only from later in life, but then she thought about herself. In her home, listening to Indian classical music and Bengali folk music had been common practice, but she herself had chosen to practise western classical music and she would be offended, to say the least, if someone put her in a different class to those who had got western classical music with their mother's milk. She belonged to the lot who believed that exposure to any music was beneficial and could be of advantage when learning a different musical style.

Digesting the sensory impressions from the Indian cultural centre, she walked up to Kensington High Street and through Holland Park. While she stood and waited for the traffic light to turn green, a man came up to her from the side.

"Hello, princess! Look at those lovely brown eyes. They shouldn't be staring down at the ground," he said.

She was taken aback a bit at the intrusion, but at the same time, she was touched. She looked up at the man and gave him a feeble smile. He smiled back and then left her alone. She continued walking up towards North Kensington and passed by Jinnah's old home on the way. The man had been the first leader of independent Pakistan. The Muslim nation had broken out from India one fatal night in 1947, a breakup which had caused turmoil in the lives of millions of people. When she finally reached Notting Hill, she sat down to rest her legs in a small cafe in Portobello Road and ordered a cup of tea.

Her India walk that day ended off in Oxford Street in England's oldest Indian restaurant from the 1920s. The waiter came to their table with a lamb shank baked in phyllo dough. It was standing up on the plate. He put a silver-coloured sauce boat with a bone marrow sauce next to it. Tanushree had almost ceased to eat meat the past ten years, but by the recommendation of Rohini's husband, she had decided to try this dish tonight. She was a bit disappointed over the casualness of the dim dining hall, but before entering she had already paid a visit to one of the fancier rooms upstairs. There, she had been able to imagine how Nehru and one of the first female Congress presidents, Sarojini Naidu, had relished their food while discussing the Home Rule Movement back in the days. This part of the restaurant just felt like an everyday place. She poured a bit of sauce beside the lamb shank on her plate, cut off a piece of the meat and dipped it in the sauce! The bone marrow sauce was creamy and the soft piece dipped in gravy melted in her mouth.

Someone was watching her. The evening darkness was yet to fall over Regent Street, and the shops were still open. The past few days of playing with the children and having intimate conversations with her cousin had added spice to her otherwise routine life of hours and hours of violin practice and theoretical studies for her thesis. She turned up her gaze just a little bit and noted the person was walking towards her. Without seeing his face, she recognized that glance somehow. He eyed her up, and she lifted her face a little bit more to look right into his eyes and confirm her feeling. It was Joshua Salisbury! She clenched the book she was reading hard against her chest with the fingers of her right hand. He smiled. She could not. She was overjoyed to see him, but her face showed no emotions. For a couple of seconds, their faces gravitated towards each other, both with a steady gaze and expectation in their eyes. His lips said a quiet *hello* and he slowed down as if he wanted to have a conversation with her. She opened her mouth, but her heart was throbbing so hard she could not talk. She should have greeted him, but she was too caught up in the non-verbal communication. Two years had not washed away the mark of those expressive eyes. Just as the moment came to whisper a proper *hello* for her, he suddenly turned down his face and his green eyes stared hard on the pavement. It was almost as though she had frightened him. He was obviously avoiding eye contact and the friendly face suddenly turned into one of anxiety. Tanushree looked at him from the side, but unable to make him look up, she turned her face towards the impressive high white buildings at Piccadilly Circus. Joshua stared down at the ground as if the only thing he wanted was to get one thousand miles away from her. She knew the conflicting feeling very well of wanting to talk to someone but being too nervous, but she knew nothing about his reasons for feeling that way. Was he another married man looking for attention? Was she going to be another person's second choice? Someone to flirt with over dinner, only to go home to the safety of his partner afterwards? By now, she had built up a barrier between herself and the modern man.

But the day Joshua looked into her eyes from the stage after the final applause of Gershwin's Summertime two years earlier, she had momentarily stopped paying attention to her prudent side. She was in Cadogan Hall listening to his choir performing. Before the show, Rohini had briefly introduced her to her work colleague Thomas, and very fleetingly to her old classmate Joshua. They had said their hellos and exchanged glances. The moment she told him her last name something changed in his facial expression. She locked eyes with him for a moment, then she looked down.

"So, Rohini's cousin, what do you do for a living?" the rowdy Thomas had asked with his piercing voice. One could tell he was a singer.

"I'm a PhD student. I study the moods associated with different musical modes and I'm a professional violin player," she answered. Again, she felt Joshua's eyes looking back at her. Tanushree looked up instantly. His gaze lingered as if he was scrutinizing her. Thomas glanced at Joshua and put his hand on his shoulder.

"Joshua is a stellar acoustician. The two of you probably have a lot to talk about. The rest of us are just laymen who are trying our best to sing," he said jokingly.

She saw Joshua looking down at the floor with his both cheeks blushing.

"Are you a physicist, Joshua?" she asked to begin a conversation and tried her best to get eye contact again.

"I'm a pen and paper physicist, Tanushree."

"So, you're a theoretical acoustician?" She smiled towards him, impressed he had remembered the name Rohini introduced her by. He nodded with a smile and then looked away again, his cheeks crimson. She could feel his eyes resting on her while she chitchatted with the others, but they never got the chance to talk before it was time for his choir to go backstage. Tanushree knew he was a decade or so older than her, as he had gone to school with Rohini, but that did not stop her from feeling drawn to him. Sometimes, life does not give you the one thing you want more than any academic degree or any other type of recognition. For her, that thing had been companionship and so had been the case for over fifteen years that evening their eyes first met. Those first few gazes gave her a sense of connection to him. She was obviously impressed by the fact that he practised music like herself, but there was something behind those glances that intrigued her. The way he looked at her when she told them her surname…Why did he do that? That evening two years ago, after coming home, she found a note with Joshua's email address in her coat pocket, which she availed as soon as she got back to Berlin. Through the month-long correspondence which followed, she had learned why he enjoyed singing, what kind of music he listened to, which books he read, which films he watched and the museums he visited. She knew which were his favourite parts of London and some of his opinions on education, healthcare, ethics, environment and immigration…but she never dared to ask why he gave her that glance when she mentioned her name. One day his daily emails had stopped, but from his long glance this evening, it seemed he still remembered her after two years of no contact.

"Wait, Joshua!" she turned around and shouted, and then walked to where he had stopped.

"Umm…Are you in a hurry?" she asked. She tucked a few strands of hair behind her ear.

Her voice trembled. She regretted deeply that at first, she had just passed him by like that without a greeting. At the moment Tanushree did not know what to say, even though she had wished their paths would cross again for the longest time.

"No, not at all. I'm so sorry, Tanu, I didn't mean to…"

"Oh, don't worry. I'm just happy to see you!"

She touched his arm and saw his face burst out in a smile.

"Should we grab a coffee?" he asked with a smile.

It was as if her gesture had given him courage.

"I would love to," she replied.

Chapter 4

The next Sunday when Isiah knocked on the door to the Roy Chowdhury residence in Tollygunge, Debu's sister opened and peeked out to see who was there.

"Good morning, Debapriya! I thought you would still be asleep when I got here," said Isiah and smiled at her. She smiled back at him as she opened the door a bit wider.

"I'm not a sleepyhead at all. You shouldn't believe everything my brother says," she replied.

She wore a new saree today. It was a saree in silk, like the first one he had seen her wearing, but it was light pink with golden leaf pattern embroideries this time. Her feet were bare, but he noticed she wore anklets and light nail polish on her toenails.

"Mr Cohen, are your eyes so unused to seeing traditional Bengali women that you need to scrutinise them every time you come across them?"

Isiah was a bit surprised by the straightforwardness of the girl who had been timid in his mind since he had first met her only a week ago. He felt his ears turning warm, and the colour of his face had probably become crimson. He was so abashed he dared not look back at her for a good few moments, but when he finally did, he noticed a mischievous smile on her lips.

"Please take a seat at the table. I'll get you some tea," she said.

He sat down and tried his best to steer his gaze away from her. From the living room, they heard the tick-tock from the grandfather clock. Sparrows chirped outside the kitchen window and she began to speak to him. Her lustrous lips made it difficult for him to look away.

"Dada told me you were born and brought up in Calcutta, but I take it you don't speak Bengali at home," she said.

He could smell the bread being toasted on the frying pan in the kitchen as she appeared in the dining room with a plate of two slices of toasted bread in

35

one hand, and the butter dish in the other. She put both of them down on the table in front of him. Her body was so close now that he could feel the warmth from it. He was spellbound by the sweet rose scent.

"No, we speak English at home and Hebrew when we go to the synagogue. I have tried to learn as much Bengali as I could. It just makes it easier to integrate with society," he answered.

While she went back to the kitchen, he picked up the butter knife and spread butter on his toasts. Then he used the spoon to take out lemon curd from the glass bottle and put it on his bread.

"That's very impressive. Tell me about life in Calcutta, Mr Cohen. I only just arrived. Are all the women dressed in frocks and wear make-up? Are they all smart and confident?" she asked from inside the kitchen. While he took a sip of the milk tea, the lemon curd and butter melted in his mouth.

"Please call me Isiah, Debapriya. No, Bengali women usually begin wearing sarees when they approach their late teens, I would say. But my sister still wears frocks, and so do most Jewish women and Anglo Indians," he replied.

"Are you married, Isiah?" Debapriya asked.

Isiah smiled at her sudden innocent question. Then he blushed. He stared down at the first page of the Statesman on the far end of the table, unable to make out a single word. He had never been asked so many personal questions by a young woman outside his family before, but he quite enjoyed it.

"No, Debapriya, I'm not. Debu is the first in line to get married among our friends."

Just as they were speaking about him, Debu came running down the stairs.

"Has my bookish sister found a kindred spirit in my newly found friend?" he asked in a jovial tone.

Isiah thought it was funny how Debu referred to his sister as bookish, as if that was the only attribute which could be used to describe her. She had announced interest in so many topics the past half an hour, he was quite certain she was far from only being the bookworm her brother had first described her as.

"Do you mind me asking where your name comes from?" Isiah and Debapriya had fallen behind his classmates on their walk along the river, but neither of them showed any sign of wanting to catch up with their friends and sibling.

"Isiah is the Hebrew name of one of our most important prophets," he replied politely. "What about yours, Debapriya?"

"My name means God's favourite in Sanskrit," she replied.

The meaning of her name made Isiah think Debapriya's parents must be pious Hindus. What were the chances they would ever allow a Jewish man like him to ask for her hand?

"What's the matter? Why did your face suddenly become so serious?" Debapriya asked with concern.

"Oh, it's nothing. Let's catch up with the others," he retorted.

The evening dusk gave the arched marble monument at Prinsep Ghat a bluish tone. The two of them walked along the dirt coloured water of the river Hooghly, which emanates from the holy river Ganges. Many people had come to Strand Road for their evening walk that day. The calmness of the water and the light breeze made Isiah draw a few breaths to slow down his racing heart. From the group of friends ahead of them, he suddenly sensed someone's eyes on him. It was Jyotish Ganguly who observed his interaction with Debapriya with disdain. Isiah had noticed at college that Jyotish only talked to women when he was spoken to, and he showed difficulty in keeping steady eye contact with the women he did speak to. Isiah decided to stop.

"Would you like a cup of tea, Debapriya?" he asked.

"I would love to," she said.

Isiah took out a few coins from his black silk suit trousers, and handed them to the chaiwallah who sat next to Judges' Ghat. They heard fishermen shouting out the kilo prices of the newly caught fish. The little straw baskets, which lay on the last step by the shore were brim-full. On the water, there were still some fishermen in rowing boats, even though the sun had begun to set.

"Have you been to Howrah? It's on the other side of the river." He pointed in the direction of the opposite river bank with his hand.

Without thinking, his slender fingers entwined themselves with Debapriya's and led her down the stairs to the bank of the Hooghly river. Sometimes, she felt just as much as a sister to him as Hannah, but she certainly made him feel something else than just brotherly love…an emotion that was very new to the bookish young man. They sat down on the steps and their fingers lost contact again. He watched her look out over the brownish water in her own dreamy way. Her light brown eyes squinted, but a smile began to appear slowly on her light-complexioned face with the distinct sharp nose in the middle.

"Debu tells me you are an avid reader. He always refers to you as the more bookish and less boisterous one in the family. Is this true?" Isiah asked.

"Yes, recently I have been reading Crime and Punishment by Dostoyevsky. I was fascinated by how it made me question the legitimacy of taking another person's life. Completely played with my morals," she said.

"Yes, he's a powerful author. I had a similar sensation when I read the book recently, but then again I was a couple of years older than you at the time," said Isiah. She struck him as a mature mind in a child's body.

"What do you do yourself in your free time, Isiah?"

"I play the piano and I like to go on strolls in the city…and I quite enjoy reading too."

At the moment, he said that their eyes locked.

"Remind me to show you some of my favourite Bengali works. It's a perfect way of deepening one's knowledge of the language," she said in a precocious manner.

For some time, silence reigned between them.

"We forgot about the others!" Isiah startled at Debapriya's sudden exclamation.

"And they forgot about us," he reminded her quietly.

"You're absolutely right. They did forget about us. We should just sit here until the sun sets in the horizon. We're more than capable of finding our way back, aren't we?" she asked.

He nodded towards her with a smile.

Isiah watched Debapriya from the dining room as she stood with her back against him in the kitchen and poured the hot water from the saucepan into the tea kettle. She wore a deep-necked red blouse with puffed sleeves and a yellow cotton sari with red embroideries this Sunday. He enjoyed seeing her dressed in new saris every weekend. She was so elegant, albeit a child. The sun that shone in through the little window with green painted grills in the Roy Chowdhurys' Tollygunge family home made her black curly hair shine. He leaned against the wooden frame of the door to the kitchen as he observed her. The kitchen filled with a scent of freshly made Darjeeling tea. No one else was in the dining room. He tried to be extra early on Sunday mornings just to have a few moments with her on his own. It was a few minutes past eight in the morning. There was pin-drop silence, something he would seldom experience on weekend mornings in his own part of town.

"What brings you here so early today, Isiah?" she asked, with her back still turned against him.

Isiah kept silent, even though he had known the answer since that day two weeks ago, when Debendranath's little sister had come down the stairs with her beautiful face beaming at him. He longed to let his fingers stroke her cheek, but he knew she was off-limits. A crow put in its beak through the green window grills. It had probably noticed the shining metal vessels in the kitchen. Debapriya tore off a piece of bread and put it on the window sill. The bird picked it up with its beak and flew off, and then it was just the two of them again.

"You're awfully quiet," she said after a while.

"Ehm…" He cleared his voice and lifted his head from the door frame to change his posture. He stood, looked towards the floor and folded his light blue shirt cuffs to find an excuse not to speak. Then he said in a taut voice, "I could leave if you would like me to…"

"That was certainly not what I meant," Debapriya replied in a resolute tone.

She turned around with a good-natured smile on her dark pink lips and looked into his eyes, which made it clear to him she enjoyed his company, and did not want him to leave at all. He looked into her coal-rimmed light brown eyes. Her face was just as doll-like as the first day he had laid his eyes on her, but something had changed. The talkative girl he had met at his friend's place only a week ago, had become shy. Had she noticed his infatuation with her? Was it making her uncomfortable? They locked eyes for a moment. Slowly, she walked up to him with a cup of tea in her hand. He could hear the dragging of her bare feet on the floor and the tinkling of her anklets.

"Here you go," she said putting the porcelain cup forward. When their faces approached each other she smiled again, but it was a shy smile this time. Her cheeks blushed and she turned away her face.

"I should probably go and wake Dada up," she said quietly referring to Debu while they still stood face to face with their eyes locked with each other. As she brushed past him softly, his eyes followed her movement and he could smell the faint smell of her rose perfume.

"Thank you for the tea," Isiah uttered in a softly modulated voice at the moment their bodies touched.

"My pleasure," she replied, looking up at him with another one of her recent mysterious smiles from the side.

Next Sunday, in the middle of November, Abdul did not join them for their weekly study session. On top of it, Debapriya had been lying ill in her bed that morning. Instead, Isiah found himself accompanied by Jyotish alone on the walk from the house to the tram stop when they had finished for the day. There was a long awkward silence as none of them spoke. Unlike the moments of silence shared with Abdul, this long quietness made Isiah try to reach for words and table topics for conversation. Finally, Jyotish was the one to break the silence. He cut straight to the chase.

"What do you think of Debu's sister?" he asked.

Isiah felt his face beginning to burn and inside his chest his heart throbbed. For a few moments, he was unable to utter any words.

"I think she's a very amiable young lady," he heard himself say at last.

"She certainly doesn't have any problems talking to young eligible men," Jyotish said and crossed his arms.

It was like someone was putting a weight on his diaphragm, because certainly, his lungs no longer expanded when he tried to inhale.

"You do know they belong to the moneyed elite of Bengal, don't you? The girls from those families are shameless. They think they own the world," Jyotish said to him. His eyes were narrow and he looked fierce.

Isiah had not pondered too much over the financial status of the Roy Chowdhury family.

"That's not the impression I have of her at all. She seems very down-to-earth with a sincere interest in literature," Isiah tried his best to convince his classmate.

"Are you sure that's not only what she's making you believe?" Jyotish insisted.

Isiah's blood was boiling in his veins. He wanted to teach Jyotish a lesson for being so judgemental, but as the sober gentleman he was, he abandoned that idea and pretended to listen to his classmate's words.

"You do know that when they finally marry, they only go with their own sort, don't you?"

Jyotish's venomous words made a permanent scar in Isiah's heart and yet he continued walking side by side with the man, pretending as if nothing he had said moved him. Why should it?

Chapter 5

As Joshua and Tanushree walked down Regent Street, both of them were silent. It was unusually rainy and Tanushree's face felt cold from the water drops which had assembled on her face and were dripping down from her nose on the bare skin of the neck. They crossed the high street and walked into a dim coffee shop and restaurant combined on the other side. They stopped on either side of a table placed right next to the window. The overcast clouds made the outside look dark, and the staff had not yet lit up the gloomy place. Tanushree and Joshua both pulled out their chairs to sit down, and she hung her black leather Fiorelli purse on the backrest of her chair. Apart from the two of them, the cafe and restaurant were empty of customers.

"So, what brings you to London, Tanu? Last time we met, you lived in Berlin as far as I remember," he said.

She thought he would probably never want to see her again if she told him the truth of her mental condition.

"I still live in Berlin...officially..." she cleared her voice.

"But?" he insisted. She knew her creased brow and hesitation had already given her away, so she gathered courage by pretending to read the menu for a moment.

"I had a bit of a burnout...I became obsessed with work," she said looking up at him.

She was so focused on observing his reaction, she did not even notice the waiter had come to their table. Joshua smiled towards her and glanced towards the man who wore a deep red vest with a white shirt underneath and black trousers. He first filled Tanushree's cup with hot tea from the pot and added milk to it, and then handed Joshua his cappuccino. After the waiter had gone, Joshua finally opened his mouth.

"I'm sorry to hear that. So, you're having some time off work then?" He was more laid-back about her burnout than she had given him a reason to be.

41

She wondered if she should maybe just tell him the whole truth, that it was actually much more than just a burnout, but she kept it to herself.

"Yes, sort of. But, actually, I'm here to search for my roots. I've been spending time at the British Library," she said.

Tanushree did not feel like elaborating too much on her sentence. She was afraid to sound sentimental, but his eyes widened and he once again fixed his gaze at her.

"Is there an underlying reason for searching your roots?" he asked diplomatically.

When he began posing follow-up questions, she relaxed a little bit. He was sincerely interested in knowing. When she told her friends at home about her recent interest, they seldom raised any questions. In fact, whenever she ranted on about any of her quirky interests, there was seldom a response, and it had always made her feel awkward. Lately, she had solved it by keeping people in the dark about her peculiar extra-curricular activities.

"Well, I had dreams about dead relatives and family friends in the 1947 Partition, World War II and the Naxalite movement. I felt there were questions I needed to deal with," she decided to share her experience with him little by little.

"That's very sad of course, but quite interesting, if I may say so. I've read some articles on how trauma can be inherited. I don't think there are too many follow-up investigations done on victims of the Indian Partition, but there certainly are on the Holocaust and its survivors."

She wondered why he spoke about trauma when she had only referred to the nightmares as dreams. At this minute, she was not quite prepared to tell him that she, in fact, had hallucinated. What if he thought she was a drug addict? But the moment she had digested what he actually just said to her, her lips parted slightly.

"Yes!" she exclaimed. "How do you know this?" She beamed with her whole face at him and before she had given him the chance to speak, she continued.

"I was handed articles on such victims at the library, but I don't know whether the events are compatible. I mean the Holocaust had millions of victims and most people were killed by direct commands from the government. The Partition led to the demise of fewer people, and at the same time the perpetrator was the common man."

She tried to take the conversation to a more intellectual level in order to not dwell on what she had been through herself, but only because he had stimulated her, and she had longed for someone to go to the bottom of this with for months and months.

"That's a worthwhile reflection, but I sometimes wonder if they are so different after all. Some people say that the British government actually instigated the conflict between Muslims and Hindus in Bengal to weaken the opposition against the imperial regime," he said thoughtfully with his gaze slightly turned to the table.

His knowledge fascinated her. For some time, she just sat quietly and digested what he had just said. Then she nodded and smiled again.

"I thought you were a Physicist, Joshua Salisbury." She fixed her eyes on him.

"Modern Indian history is my obsession, Tanushree Roy Chowdhury," He said and looked back at her with that fade enigmatic smile. He had remembered her whole name. Then they both burst out in laughter.

"That's very impressive!" she said.

"Well, thank you very much!" he replied in a playful tone with a broad grin on his face. She could not decide whether his smile was of the type of those one would give a child, or if there was something else than only kindness behind it. After all, this was the man who had left a note with his email address in her coat pocket two years ago!

The next morning the rain had stopped and Tanushree and Joshua met in Harrow on the Hill. When they finally sat down to talk in the little cafe on top of the hill, her nervousness had subsided, and by the sounds of it, so had his. The sun had begun to set in the pink horizon.

"14 times in 12 years?" Joshua exclaimed. Then he put down his cappuccino cup on the table, leaned back on his backrest and chuckled.

"My goodness! Why on earth?" he asked.

"I guess I was on the search for something I couldn't find in Sweden," she answered.

"You really are a vagabond," he teased her. His lips had a broad smile on them just like the evening before, and she could see the dimple in the right corner of his mouth she had noticed that evening two years ago. Apart from a few grey hairs, he had not changed much since Cadogan Hall.

"Yes, I am. When I was little, I used to listen to a song in Bengali called 'Ami ek jajabar', which means just that, I am a vagabond. When I was 21 that was the journey I embarked on." She gave a nervous laughter, but Joshua's face seemed unmoved.

"Did you find what you were looking for on your journey?" he asked.

"Well, I came to the realisation that the grass is not always greener on the other side. The trips taught me all kinds of things about society, history, aesthetics, languages and geography that I would never have thought about if I had stayed at home. I made friends from all over. So, yes, I did find something, but maybe not what I set out to find," she replied thoughtfully.

"So what was it you set out to find?" he insisted.

The light finally came on in the coffee shop, and it was about time because outside it was almost pitch dark by now.

"I think I wanted to be part of a context, a bigger community. It's not like I've been isolated all my life. Occasionally, I was part of resident groups and research communities, but every time I moved I had to start over…and when I was younger in Sweden I shied away from the people I wanted to get to know the most," she replied.

"Is inclusion not a mutual effort, both from the outsider as well as the group in question?" He looked at her intently, but she was out of words, because he had uttered what she herself had concluded just a few days back. When she kept quiet, he took the opportunity to continue digging.

"So, does this mean you never felt at home in Sweden?" He had asked one of those forbidden questions. Luckily, the waiter approached their table again, and with a big smile on his dark pink lips, he asked,

"Is everything alright?" She almost felt a bit relieved to have him there and sighed quietly.

They both nodded at him and Tanushree swallowed.

"Well, when I was younger I considered Sweden heaven on earth, especially compared to Calcutta," she said.

When she pronounced the name of the metropolis, she saw a spark in his eye and a faint enigmatic smile on his lip. Then she remembered how their eyes locked when she had pronounced her surname that evening two years ago. There was something he had not shared with her yet. She was sure of it. He cleared his voice.

"And when you got older?" he insisted again.

"I began wondering how it must be to grow up around family since I myself grew up far from extended family, cousins, aunts, uncles and grandparents. In Sweden, people knew nothing about my roots and my family was elsewhere, " she replied, paused and took a sip of her tea. Then she cut another piece of the apple crumble with her fork and put it into her mouth. The custard had just about the right sweetness, and she could still smell the butter from the dough.

"And was there prejudice?" he asked bluntly.

He looked up from his coffee and caught her eye again.

"Well, there were moments of mistrust. Lately, I have indeed begun to wonder if life had been different had my skin colour not spoken of a different ethnic origin. Or how it would be to grow up in a country where Indians are a significant minority like the US or the UK."

"And were there no other Indian children?" he asked. It was clear he wanted to get to the bottom of whatever he was trying to dig out.

"There were, but I always felt like the odd one out."

When she did not elaborate on that, he finally changed the topic. It was not that she had anything against his inquisitiveness, but he had asked questions she had not yet defined the right answers to, and it made her feel doubtful. She was not used to expressing opinions without thinking them over at least ten times before.

"How often did you meet your grandparents…in Calcutta?" Joshua asked.

"About once a year, but I never met my paternal grandfather and my other grandparents passed away when I was very young. My parents had me at old age," she replied. He nodded as if she had acknowledged something he had suspected.

"And the grandfather you never met, do you know what he was like?"

She was quite enjoying his interrogation, mostly because the questions were so timely.

"No, Joshua, my knowledge about him is very limited, but I know he was a lawyer and studied at Presidency College in Calcutta at the beginning of the last century. He was also an ardent Congress party follower."

He stared down at the table and nodded to himself again.

"Like my grandfather," she thought she heard him say to himself quietly, but she was not sure if she had misheard. Then he looked up again and their eyes locked. Before Tanushree had the opportunity to ask, he said, "Why did you settle in Berlin? Do you feel at home there?"

"I longed for a stable physical network, and there were so many everyday activities I felt I wanted to do like taking singing classes and giving violin classes. I just wanted to stay in one place," she replied, sighed and looked down on her black ballerinas. In fact, she had learnt to adapt to new environments over and over again, exploring the surroundings and accepting differences, questioning and re-questioning her initial hypotheses, the values she grew up with and the conflicts in her teenage head. She was just longing for stability and felt she was able to integrate her dreams, life experiences and present life differently now. At the same time, she was exhausted. She spent years on the road with her belongings in a suitcase. The tough emotional trip every time she moved, wore her out.

"You cannot imagine how hard it can be to say goodbye to people all the time. In the end, you just stop making bonds to avoid the emotional journey," she said after a while.

She was surprised at how easily their conversation flowed after what she had heard about him from Rohini. He had a very deep side and was insightful and curious, even though they had lived different lives. Tanushree was waiting in silence for his next remark, and enjoyed his sparse speech and qualified questions because she was tired of her own temporarily brooding mood and constant complaints. It felt like his efforts pushed her in a direction she had been wanting to go for a long time. When the silence and her glance made his face turn red and stare down hard at his coffee, she smiled towards him. He could interrogate her, but comfortable silence and glances made him blush. Joshua's long fingers curled around the white cup with a thin brown line on the brim. As he looked down, he had a smile on his pink lips with the same deep dimple that was there that evening their paths crossed. He just avoided eye contact with her.

"Actually, I can imagine the emotional trips of continuously saying goodbye to people, Tanu. I have had my share of journeys too."

She blushed because she had assumed something about him that was not true and his face burst out in a smile, as he tilted his head back.

"I suppose I haven't told you everything about myself yet, but my journeys were between phases in life rather than geographical locations." He looked down at his cup again, while he spoke with her in a mellow voice. She could see a glimpse of the enigmatic smile on his lips.

After a moment's silence, he opened his mouth.

"Well, you would be able to find that kind of balance in London, Tanu."

His eyes squinted, but he must have noticed she was out of words, because he did not expect her to retort.

"I'm sure Berlin is different, though. It seems so alternative and relaxed and has such a rich unique history. I've thought about living there many times in life, but I've never had the opportunity. London can be really uptight sometimes." When he said that, her eyes fixed on his green Ralph Lauren sweater, while she tried to figure out if he expected an invitation, but remained silent.

"What are you up to tomorrow, Tanu?" Joshua looked at her and there was that expectation in his eye again.

The moment she stepped into Rohini's terraced house in Harrow that evening, she felt guilty. Perhaps, seeing her cousin reminded her of what she had not disclosed to her old classmate whom she had just talked to for almost three hours. She had told him she was on the search for her family history, but she had trivialised the flashes she had about dead relatives and family friends in India by calling them dreams. The reason she had avoided the topic was that she did not want him to think she was a total nut case, but the moment he had revealed that Indian modern history was his obsession, something changed and she just wanted to open up to him now. She needed someone to confide in and exploring with, without having to explain every single detail all the time, but she knew she had to be honest.

"What's wrong, Tanu? You look pale," said Rohini as she let her in.

"Oh, it's nothing. I just need some rest," she said.

She took off the black cashmere coat and hung her brown flowery woollen shawl on the same hook. Then she walked up the carpeted stairs slowly, and into her temporary room. Tanushree pushed the power button of the white Hewlett Packard laptop and while she waited for the computer to start, she pulled the duvet over her knees and positioned the laptop on top. Then she looked out through the double-glazed window towards the residential street and the goosebumps on her arms and legs. The constant rain and spending the whole day outside this day in late June had lowered her body temperature a notch. She then glanced towards the digital alarm clock on the bedside table and noted it was already 8:30 p.m. Once the laptop had started, she opened her Gmail and searched for Joshua's name. A list of eight emails from 2015 came up in the search results and she copied the email address and pasted it into a new template. Her fingers began to type.

Dear Joshua,

There was something I didn't tell you that I really want you to know. When I got ill a couple of months back, I began having nightmares and hallucinations about dead relatives and family friends. It wasn't only dreams, I was actually having illusions because of too little sleep and too much stress lately. I saw pictures of a half-bombed Calcutta in WWII. Then I began to see explicit images about the Indian Partition in 1947 in my head. There were dead corpses lying everywhere in Dacca town, a city I had not even visited. Finally, I had illusions about the Japanese bombings in Rangoon. I don't want you to think that I'm a complete lunatic or an addict, the reasons behind are those I mentioned. I wanted to confide in you because I felt relieved today when you told me about your interest in Indian history. I know very little myself. My family never wanted me to dwell on the past, but I've realised now that it's time for me to find some answers…and I feel I want to discuss this with someone who knows a bit more of Indian history and can pose the right questions.

See you tomorrow,

Tanu

After a while, she fell asleep in her bed. She only woke up when Rohini called her from downstairs and she realised it was time to call her parents.

"I saw Rabindranath's and Nehru's houses yesterday. I've also visited the British Library and I've learnt so much about the Partition," Tanushree said cheerfully on the phone.

"Why are you running around all Indian heritage sites? Shouldn't you be resting?" Menakshi Roy Chowdhury replied on the phone in her usual strict tone. Tanushree who was quite excited about what she had done the past few days, became quiet.

"Yes, Mother."

"Don't spend all your money on nonsense!" her mother reminded her.

Rohini turned around from the dining table and gave her a sympathetic glance.

Was this the only thing her mother had to say after Tanushree had shared her stories of visits to all kinds of exciting historical sites. She thought about how it would be if she introduced Joshua to her parents. They would show no interest in his academic pursuits. Probably, they would bore him with their many life anecdotes. Even her once so music-loving mother had become bitter with age, and seldom discussed the topic with anyone, let alone rehearsed. Her father, Alokesh, was only interested in politics and the history of India. Would Joshua even understand their Bengali accent? Her parents were children of the language revolution, not English medium school alumni as their elder siblings. Maybe the psychologist was right after all! Maybe they were too different for a well-functioning family. But the next moment she realised that the only reason she roamed around the historical sites like a madwoman as her mother put it, was her father's ranting about those historical personae…and the only reason she pursued music as a career, was that Menakshi Roy Chowdhury sat her down every week from an early age to sing scales. On top of it, every time she did not manage to hit the note on the violin for the first ten years of her active musical life, her mother patiently corrected her. Then she reminded herself that life had not been fair to her parents, so she should be kind.

"I'm not spending all my money, Mother. I'm trying to deepen my knowledge of Indian history," Tanushree replied calmly after a few moments' silence. The former History and singing teacher became quiet on the other end.

"Fair enough. OK, whatever you do, be very careful," said Menakshi.

"OK, Mother. Good night, now."

"Good night, dear!"

What could have ended in an argument, had been a polite conversation form the beginning to the end, only because she had managed to figure out where a piece of the puzzle would sit. She heard the click from the receiver being hung up on the other end. After finishing the call, she sat down at the dinner table with Rohini's family, a bit more balanced than she would have been, had she not thought carefully.

"Why don't you tell us what you have discovered about old India in the past days," Rohini said. Tanushree gave her a grateful smile.

"Were you brought up in a religious home, Tanu?"

It was only when Joshua uttered those words that she began to question why she had brought him to the Gurdwara in Holland Park.

"No, I've never visited a Hindu temple in Sweden. My parents are socialists," she replied.

"Oh," was the only thing he said in response.

As he raised his brow, she became unsure of whether she should have mentioned the last part.

"Are your parents religious?" she asked to make up for the blooper and tucked her hair behind the ear. They walked up the carpeted stairs to the large prayer hall. In front, was a screen projecting a video of an elderly Sikh gentleman in a blue turban, playing the harmonium and chanting religious songs.

"No, I wouldn't say so, but they do go to church and synagogue for the festivities," he replied.

"Like Christmas and Easter you mean?" she asked.

"Well, my mother is Jewish and my father Anglican, so we observe so many holidays that I've lost count," he smiled.

"So, which religion do you belong to?" Tanushree asked him.

"I like to think of myself as a mixture, but I only go to the synagogue for Pesach, Yom Kippur and Channukah," he replied.

"And to church?"

"I try to go to church every Sunday," he said quietly. "It makes me calm down." She swallowed, but his remark reminded her of a quote by Mahatma Gandhi, which had first caught her full attention in the Kolkata metro the last time she visited the city. While she searched her cell phone pictures, they sat quietly and absorbed the music. She showed him the screenshot of the little whiteboard with deep blue writing. It said, 'The Allah of Islam is the same as the God of Christians and the Ishwar to Hindus'. After a while of listening to the music, he looked at her.

"Having been brought up in a socialist family, you seem to ponder a lot on religion," he whispered in her ear. She smiled and brought him down to the dining space.

When Rohini's husband, Gyandeep, brought them there last year, she had helped the members of the congregation to make chapatis. It was like a factory where the part-takers were all echelons of a wheel. One person made the dough, another made little balls out of it, while a third person rolled them out and the fourth person fried them. There were frequent loud jokes between the parishioners and each new person who entered the hall was greeted warmly by their fellows. She seldom felt so included in Indian congregations in Sweden. Why this was the case she knew very well, but was not ready to deal with at that moment. Instead, all she could bring herself to say was:

"I think growing up, Muslims were the only religious group I could identify with."

"That's interesting," he said. "But you're Hindu, aren't you?"

"Yes, by tradition. Are you very religious, Joshua?" she retorted.

"Well, quite a few years ago now, I decided to devote my life to God as much as I could. I live in celibacy, Tanu."

What? What about all the long glances and reddened cheeks? Had she misjudged again? She only hoped he had not caught her jaw drop when he announced his pact with God.

After a few minutes, when the initial shock had subdued, Joshua woke her from her thoughts.

"Do you believe in God?" he asked.

"I have my doubts," she replied.

"Why?" he asked.

"I need evidence."

At the moment she uttered those words, she regretted again, feeling like it would drive a wedge between them. Joshua just nodded his head, as if he had heard that argument a hundred times before.

"Have you lived in celibacy all your life?"

"Only the past twelve years," he answered.

"What made you decide for that?" she asked.

"I wanted to dedicate my life to God, and not become distracted by other feelings," he said.

His voice had become quiet, and he avoided looking into her eyes as if there was something he tried to hide. It was at that moment Tanushree realised there was something else behind his religiosity, but she spared him the interrogation. Instead, she began to convince herself, he would never be hers despite the signs she had seen the past two days. He was just one of those men who could not control the signals they send out. A part of her was angry, but she was going to neglect all his signals from now on.

On the train back home, she felt empty. At the back of her head, she heard the voice of her childhood friends telling her how bad she was at reading body language, and how it explained why she had never been in a relationship.

"You are just imagining!"

This was the reply every time she mentioned to them that she had exchanged glances with someone she had a romantic interest in. How could they judge without being present?

"I simply send off the wrong signals when I become interested. I cannot look into their eyes anymore, let alone speak," she wanted to retort every time her friends came with that comment. But she refrained from it, only because she did not want to come across as over-confident. She thought of the handful of dates she had been on in life, and how she had backed off every time someone had attempted to hug her goodbye. For a brief moment, she almost felt relieved about Joshua's celibacy and how she would never have to worry about physical performance. It was a relief because performance pressure just made her anxious.

Chapter 6

Isiah, Debu and Abdul walked towards the entrance of the Tipu Sultan mosque in Dhuromtallah Street. It was Friday afternoon and the sun shone directly on Isiah's face, so he took out a handkerchief from his pant pocket and dabbed it on his forehead. They walked in through the main entrance and took off their chappals by the gate. Around them, were men wearing topi caps and colourful salwar kameez. Isiah glanced down at Abdul's orange raw silk attire, while his feet burnt on the stone ground, where the sun had been shining for hours. For the occasion, he had taken on a kippa, so the sun rays could not reach the thick wavy dark-brown hair.

A few minutes after sitting down in the prayer hall, he heard the imam saying 'Allah hu Akbar'. The voice was low and melodious. Isiah quite enjoyed hearing the chanting. In the hall were hundreds of men sitting on mats on the floor bending down over their legs and putting their heads against the thin straw material placed on the stone flooring. He had never been to a mosque and became quite thrilled when Abdul offered to take him to the Tipu Sultan mosque where he went every Friday for prayers. By the look of Debu's inquisitive eyes, he could judge that he was just as curious as himself. The only person who had chosen to stay behind was Jyotish.

After the prayers, the imam, who had a white goatee, came up to Abdul.

"Hello, my son. How are you?"

"I'm fine, thank you, Uncle. I brought my classmates Debendranath Roy Chowdhury and Isiah Cohen today," Abdul said to the imam.

The elderly bearded man with the topi cap greeted them both, and then he turned back to Abdul.

"So nice to see you are showing your friends our traditions."

At first, Isiah thought they would become accused of trespassing, but quite on the contrary, the priest seemed delighted to have them there. After seeing the reaction, he decided to himself the next religious mission would be to bring his classmates to the Maghen David synagogue.

"Hearing the hymns was a bliss to my ears, Abdul. It makes me want to study Arabic. Thank you for bringing us here."

From his words, it was apparent Debu had had a very similar experience to Isiah's.

That evening, they took the electric tramcar southwards, and finally walked the last stretch to Park Circus Maidan, where Abdul lived with his sisters and parents. At the family dining table, the three young men were served Mughal delicacies. His mother went a first-round around the table to serve them mutton biryani and raita. When they had emptied their plates, she made another round to serve chicken rezallah and naan. On top of it, they had gazar ka halwa for dessert.

On the living room walls hung miniatures from the Mughal period, resembling those in the Roy Chowdhury residence. In a dark frame in the section of the room where the dining table was placed, hung an Arabic scripture, which Isiah could only assume was of religious nature. The middle-aged woman came by the table from time to time, to attend to the young men who sat and relished their dinner, but his younger sisters seemed to be hiding in their rooms.

"Isn't my wife a lovely cook?" the well-dressed senior, Mr Huq said upon passing by Abdul's father was in the jute business, just like Isiah's, and the family had enough money to own their own five-room flat in Park Circus. In those days, the area was mixed, albeit largely a residential area for the Muslim upper-middle class. But there were also churches, burial grounds for the British and just a short walk from the Huq residence was the Jewish girls' school in Park Street. From their balcony, one could view the local maidan.

Isiah made his way back to Marquis Street by foot that evening. Park Street was lit up and decorated as Christmas was drawing near. Chowringhee was as busy as usual. On passing Grand, he saw a dressed-up family probably on their way to dine at the hotel. At the time he had reached home, the food had finally made its way towards his colon.

Just when they were about to adjourn for the day, Isiah heard the sound of footsteps and tinkling anklets coming down the stairs. He knew who it was and yet he leaned to the side to catch the first glance of her.

"Isiah, good thing you're still here. You have to see my collection of stories by Tagore. I know you'll enjoy it," Debapriya exclaimed while climbing down the last steps.

She took a firm grip around his wrist and pulled him up from the chair at the dining table. Abdul looked a bit surprised as she barged into the dining room, but there was nothing malicious in his gaze. Before leaving the table, however, Isiah also caught a glance of Jyotish, who observed them with disapproval quickly and then turned away his face. There was something furtive about the man every time Debapriya was in the picture. Debu, on the other hand, seemed largely unmoved. Isiah concluded that it must be commonplace in their family to take strangers by the wrist and lead them away. She took him through the living room and up the stairs, and it was only when they reached the landing that she loosened her grip. Isiah's palms were warm, almost a bit sweaty.

"This is the library where our parents keep their books. They usually pass them on to us children, but in the village house in East Bengal we have a much larger collection," she explained to him.

"Why do you have books in so many foreign languages?" Isiah burst out and leaned forward towards the shelves to study the books more carefully.

"My father always had a knack for languages. He was self-didactic, and always believed learning many languages opens up your mind to different types of thinking and ideas," Debapriya said.

"How many languages do you speak yourself?" Isiah asked curiously, while he glanced at her over his shoulder.

"Only Bengali, English and a little bit of Sanskrit," she answered.

"How about yourself?"

"English, Hebrew and a little bit of Bengali," he replied to her question.

"Maybe we should exchange linguistic skills? I could introduce you to the literary works of Bengal, while you teach me some Hebrew. What do you say?" she suggested.

Isiah nodded, feeling quite excited about more chances of spending time with her one on one. The next moment it dawned on him, he had read nothing apart from the Tanakh in Hebrew. His cheeks became a bit warm and he looked down with a troubled gaze, but luckily she was too caught up in her Tagore books to notice.

"Have you read the Kabuliwallah, Isiah?" he asked.

"I have heard of it, but no I haven't read it yet."

"Let's read it together then! I absolutely adored it," she said.

Debapriya began reading the story aloud word by word. When she read, her voice became louder and more authoritative, but there was also a theatrical expression in it. Her reading skills made it easy for Isiah to just sink in, even though he understood far from every word. A few moments later, he began to focus on the details and felt he did not understand a single word any more. Was his Bengali really that poor? Debapriya looked up at him and raised her eyebrows.

"Do you have any questions?" she asked and raised her eyebrow.

Isiah muffled a chuckle. She looked and sounded like a precocious teacher. When he did not respond, she continued speaking.

"The problem with Bengali is that the written language 'prakrit' is far from the spoken one," she explained to him.

While walking up the stairs to his family's flat, Isiah could hear the sound of a creaky female voice piercing the air. The sound of the voice was a familiar one. Upon knocking on the green painted wooden door, he heard her feet brush against the mosaic floor, and when the door finally opened he looked right into his grandmother's wide affectionate eyes. Her face was beaming and she stretched out her arms to give him a big embrace. He smiled, hugged her, putting his cheek towards her shoulder.

"Come in, boy. We have plenty of things to talk about," his grandmother announced to him enthusiastically. As much as he loved her, the moment he heard her voice uttering those words, he knew what had brought her to his parents' flat that evening. For a moment, he thought of discretely vanishing into his room, but he was too fond of her to do anything like that.

"I brought pastries from Nahoum's," she exclaimed in her happy voice and pointed towards a parcel, which lay on the table beside her.

The elderly, Mrs Cohen, lived in Sudder Street, just around the corner from Hogg Market, where the famous confectionery had opened only three years earlier. Isiah sat down on the chair next to her in the living room. She poured him hot tea from the kettle, and his mother brought him a white porcelain plate with a chocolate rum ball from the kitchen.

"I just visited Mrs Meyer, her grand-daughter stays with her now. The young girl grew up in Bombay, but has come to Calcutta to take care of her grandmother. Such a beautiful young girl. You just have to meet her, Isiah." she said and patted his shoulder with her pale wrinkled hand.

He had known it from the moment he stepped into the living room! His grandmother always went on about the importance of marrying a good Jewish girl. For the past months, she had come to their home almost every Sunday to suggest young suitable girls from her social circle to her 18-year-old grandson.

"I don't feel it's time to get married just yet, Grandmother. What kind of woman do you think would like to marry a penniless student?" he asked her.

"You're far from penniless, my son. Think about all the wealth you will inherit from your father's jute and furniture business," she reminded him and put her hand on his arm again.

Then she became quiet. Her wide light brown eyes observed his face for a moment and her squinting eyes made him uncomfortable.

"You look fresh, Isiah. Your skin is shining as if it had been invigorated, and your lips have a secretive smile on them. Don't think you can hide it from me! Tell me, who is the young woman in your life?" she asked him.

For a moment his heart stopped, and then it began throbbing so hard he was afraid it would jump out of his ribcage. While he kept silent, he felt the eyes of his mother and Hannah suddenly glancing in his direction. The younger Mrs Cohen's jaw dropped.

"She better be Jewish. You know our community is very small in Calcutta, and we should do our best to keep up the numbers and carry our traditions to the future generations," his grandmother said.

"No Grandmother, there is no one," he lied. In fact, all his head was thinking about was Debapriya, but he could hardly tell his family he was in love with a Hindu girl. It would cause an uproar. To avoid the scrutinizing glances of his family members he turned down his face, but could not help wringing his hands and after a few seconds, his whole body cringed where he sat.

"I must go and wash up, Grandmother."

After a moment's silence, which seemed like if it was never-ending, Isiah had finally excused himself and left his family members behind in the living room as he walked out of the uncomfortable situation his grandmother's words had caused. He went straight to the bathroom. When he looked at himself in the mirror, he noticed his burning face had the complexion of a cherry. To cool it down, he splashed water on it. Then he walked into his room, sat by his desk, and gazed out the window until his pulse had gone back to normal. He lay down on the bed where he dozed off. He was exhausted from all the intense emotions he had felt during the past hours. It was only when he heard a knock on the door that he woke up, and he only knew one person who knocked that gently and that was Hannah.

"Come in," he said and sat up on his bed.

The door handle was pushed down and in she came, with her two braids tied up in buns on either side of her head.

"So, is it true?" she asked.

"What?" Isiah tried to play the card of ignorance.

"That you have a young woman in your life?" Her voice became shrill and sounded impatient.

For a moment, he thought to himself whether he should be honest or simply keep the truth to himself. He walked up and closed the door behind her and she came to sit beside him on the bed.

"Debu has a sister, Hannah, and her name is Debapriya. She is the same age as you and you should meet her." He had exposed enough facts for her to join the dots.

"Is she the apple of your eye and the reason why you blushed when Grandmother asked you that question?" she asked.

"Yes, I think that might possibly be true," he said thoughtfully.

He fidgeted again, where he sat on the bed. This was not a topic he had ever spoken about with her sister.

"How are you going to tell our parents you are in love with a Hindu girl?" she said. His face became serious and he looked into her eyes steadily.

"I have no intention of telling them, Hannah…and neither should you!" he said in a strict voice.

"Are you only trifling with her?"

"Hannah!" He was beginning to lose patience.

"OK," she said obediently.

"Do you promise?"

"Your secret is safe with me. My lips are sealed," said Hannah and smiled at him.

"But you must introduce her to me. When can I see her?" she asked, stood up and looked down at him where he sat on the bed gazing out the window.

"Let me give it a thought. I'll arrange something," he assured her.

Isiah knew his parents would never accept Debapriya, but maybe things would get easier if he had Hannah on his side.

"I feel a bit ill, Hannah. Could you please tell Mother and Father I will not be joining for dinner today?"

Chapter 7

As Joshua and Tanushree parted that Monday evening she brought him to the Gurdwara, he squeezed her hand and left a book in it for her to read before walking down Kensington High Street. His stride was relaxed, but his face turned to the ground. He was very different from the quiet man she had met two years earlier, not to mention the initially anxious man in Harrow on the Hill! After strolling down a few yards, he turned around and his lips mimed 'goodbye' with a smile. Without thinking about what he had just shared with her, she blew him a kiss, and he smiled shyly without showing any sign of disapproval. She stepped on the last train to Harrow that evening, and she felt hopeful they would meet again. The book he had given her had a brown cover with a man wearing a chequered dhoti and a half sleeve shirt standing in the decorated hallway of the marble palace in Calcutta. He handed over the book without a word of explanation, but paper-clipped to it was a note reading 'I thought you would like to look at this'. She opened the book and began turning the pages as she stood there on the platform waiting for her train to come. Almost every page had little notes scribbled on it in an almost illegible handwriting. She could see he had studied the text with great care, but she wondered why. Suddenly, she remembered the remark about his grandfather she thought she had misheard. After coming home to Rohini, she lay down on her temporary bed and began scrutinising every single word he had written down in the book. On one page, it said 'This was his residential neighbourhood' with the same almost unintelligible handwriting. He had apparently researched on behalf of a male person who had lived in Calcutta. It must have been the grandfather he mentioned! While she flipped through the book to the last page, she saw pictures of buildings and monuments she knew like the back of her hand. As a child, she spent most summer vacations in the city, and she used to love discovering its hidden gems. Colonial architecture could be so beautiful sometimes, but it was difficult to notice the beauty through a blemished and worn out surface. The dust and sound pollution had bothered her, and coming home to the serenity of Sweden after the summer, was always a relief. But as she became older, she realised there was no other place she felt so connected to due to the familial ties she never had with the country she was born in. At the last page of the Calcutta book, she found a poem.

Perfection is spending your summers rehearsing every day until your fingertips begin getting numb.

Perfection is when the last thing you look at before going to sleep is the list of words for tomorrow's French class test, only to make it sink in deeply.

Perfection is when you spend a whole week crying over an error on a Physics exam and when you are judging yourself so hard that others start believing your judgement.

Perfection is what makes me not want to look up when you pass by in the street, even though I can feel your gaze following my every movement as I come walking towards you.

She was not sure Joshua meant for her to read this. Suddenly, she was reminded of Rohini's words about his upper-secondary-school days. She had described him as someone who was always immersed in his own thoughts and had pointed out that he had tons of anti-social sides. Apparently, he had been quite serious about his musical training, and she recognised many of the emotions in the piece and especially noted the last sentence. She had sensed the insecurity from him that evening in Harrow on the Hill, and she often felt that type of insecurity herself, so it was not hard to recognise. He was scared of being judged by others, which is common in social anxiety. But what intrigued her more was why he had handed her a book about Calcutta full of notes scribbled in it. What was he trying to say to her? Someone knocked on the door and she sat up hastily on the bed.

"How was the rendezvous with your soulmate, Tanu?" Rohini asked in a loud voice where she stood at her doorstep. Her cousin had caught her leaving the house in the evening to meet Joshua, so she had needed to explain, but now she could feel her face slowly blushing.

"Shhhh, Rohini, the whole house will hear, but if you have to know, I had a really lovely time."

"I want to hear about all the juicy details," Rohini said and winked at her.

Tanushree smiled and told her a bit about her day with Joshua.

"You deserve to be with a man who makes you happy and in the meantime continue doing all those things that fulfil you – those things that make you who you are. You're one of the sweetest people I know," Rohini said. Tanushree looked at her with affection, but could not bring herself to talk about Joshua's celibacy.

In the middle of their conversation, her cell phone rang.

"I just wanted to know if you got home alright, Tanu, and thank you for spending your evening with me! I had a really nice time today." His voice sounded deeper on the phone, maybe his vocal cords were just too tired to produce higher tones.

"I really enjoyed our evening too, Joshua, and thank you for the book. Did you want to tell me anything special?"

"No, I just thought you would like to see it. Calcutta is very close to my heart, even though I've never been there," he said.

"Is there a reason for that?" she asked.

"I will tell you someday, I promise." This man surely knew how to make her puzzled.

"Well, I will show you the city someday, I promise," she retorted.

That night she was so excited she could not fall asleep. So, in the middle of the night, she pushed the power button of her laptop, waited until it started, and then spent the whole night finishing up the first draft of the Discussion section of her PhD thesis. It was soon time to hand it into the examination board.

On Wednesday evening, she was invited to his apartment, and she knew after the disclosure about his celibacy he had no romantic motive. Joshua lived in a three-room basement flat in West Kensington his parents had bought him when he began college.

"Why don't you sit down, Tanu? I'll get you some tea," he said after she entered the flat.

He took out two large turquoise mugs from the kitchen cupboard with laughing Buddhas painted on them. After pouring in water, he brought out the milk container from the fridge and poured some into a little porcelain cup he put on the wooden table. She helped him bringing the cups to the round table placed to the side of the windows in the living room. After they had drunk their cups of tea, Tanushree asked to see the apartment. Joshua led her to the study first, and his work desk was full of scrap paper with all sorts of mathematical expressions. One of the walls in the room was lined with dark wooden bookshelves. Then he led her to the bedroom, which was a stylish chamber with a mahogany double bed-frame, two candles on either side of the bed, and black velvet tapestry on the back wall. She asked if she could see his books, so they went back into his study and she scanned the wooden cases.

"Le Zahir Paulo Coelho. Die Verwandlung Franz Kafka. A Picture of Dorian Gray Oscar Wilde. Something Indian which even I can't read. You speak so many languages, Joshua! Is this how you spend your free time?" she asked and looked at him with wide sparkling eyes.

"I'm still a learner of most of them. It's only possible for me to read the books with the help of a dictionary," he said humbly.

Her eyes spotted a framed black-and-white picture on Joshua's desk she had not noticed before. The moment it came into her sight, she was horror struck. After a moment's freeze, her trembling fingers picked it up. The motive was an elegant young man in a dark suit with hair parted perfectly in the middle, a sharp nose and light brown eyes. He was sitting on an ornate black wooden chair and it seemed to be a studio portrait. She stared at the picture for a long time. There was something familiar about the man, which made her shiver.

"Is this your grandfather, Josh?"

She put down the framed picture on the desk again.

"Yes, it is," he replied.

At the very moment he replied to her question, she knew where she had seen that man before. Then everything began making sense to her, his reaction when she had first told him her surname, his curiosity about her grandfather, and the Calcutta book.

"When and where was this picture taken?" she could hear the agitation in her voice.

"In a studio in Calcutta, a couple of years before he moved to England. I believe the picture was taken at some point in the twenties," he replied and then became silent.

"You never told me your family lived in Calcutta," she said.

"You never asked. Calcutta was a city he loved dearly. He lost his memory towards the end of his life. One of his last sentences on his death bed was 'See you in Ezra Street, Joshua.' I always wondered what that meant. He must have mistaken me for someone else." She gasped for air, because she knew exactly what was in Ezra Street.

"Isiah Cohen was your grandfather? You knew all along, didn't you? That he knew my grandfather?" Her voice sounded agitated.

"I didn't know, Tanu, but I guessed by his age and when you mentioned that your grandfather was a solicitor in Calcutta and studied at Presidency College. I knew somewhere at the back of my mind he was a distant relative of Rohini's. I remembered the name of grandfather Isiah's partner was Roy Chowdhury. Debendranath, was it?"

"Yes, it was," she answered in astonishment.

She could not hide her excitement, but his eyes teared up when he began to speak about Isiah.

"He had the great luck to live until he was 97 and his mind was sharp until dementia got the better of him. He never stopped talking about his life in Calcutta, and yet he never went back to visit at old age. That was something I never got my head around," said Joshua.

"What else do you know about him?" Tanushree asked.

"As a young man, he used to be active in the freedom struggle and riots in Calcutta. He could talk about his early youth and his hometown relentlessly. He mentioned the names of some people over and over again, especially the dearest one of his old classmates and partner Debendranath Roy Chowdhury. It was as if he wanted me to wonder about that man and find his footsteps. I knew I would not stop wondering until I met him, and unfortunately, now that will never happen…but I was lucky enough to meet you."

He went to look out through the window in his own dreamy way, but she knew he was shedding tears, and she was close to being petrified. His reaction made her think he had been very close to Isiah. She had never seen him become emotional before, but more importantly, she had never guessed Joshua Salisbury would be a close relation to her grandfather's best friend.

"You never talked about him." Her voice was feeble. The picture had made her speechless. She did not know what to say any more. With his back against her, he began telling her the story about his great uncle, and she stood there still slightly petrified.

"He stayed with us in Hampstead for many years after his wife Esther, my grandmother, passed away from breast cancer. My grandfather took care of me while my mother continued working."

He turned his face towards Tanushree, and she felt she finally knew who he was now, so she could tell him her true history and doubts too, without worrying about their differences.

"I never met my grandfather, Joshua, but I know he worked as a solicitor in Calcutta and was posted as a governmental legal advisor of some kind in the state of Bihar and East Bengal before the independence in 1947. He passed away with lung cancer before I was born, so I was never lucky enough to meet him. I hear he spent his last years of life in apathy and became a chain smoker. Obviously, the situation changed after the partition of British India, but I do not know much of the details. A part of his family fled from their estates in East Bengal only to come and live in a small-town house they had built in the suburbs of Calcutta."

She paused for a moment.

"Ezra Street in Calcutta is where their law practice is situated, Joshua," she said after a while.

"Oh." He turned around and stood, looking at her with his lips slightly parted for a while, as if he was trying to digest what she had just told him.

"Grandfather Isiah showed me Debendranath's letters when I was little, Tanu. They were light green aerogrammes smelling of damp air. That's how I imagine the smell of Calcutta, as he often said it reminded him of his home town. How did you recognize the picture of him, Tanu?"

"I have an album full of pictures of my grandfather and his friends. I must have looked through it a thousand times only to get a feel for what kind of person he was. He had carefully noted the names of all his friends behind every picture and Isiah Cohen's name appeared often," she replied.

"I've always wanted to go to Calcutta, but I've never been lucky enough to make it there," he told her.

"Maybe we could trace their footsteps together? Will you come with me to Calcutta one day?" she asked at the spur of the moment. He still stood there teary-eyed. Then she walked up and hugged him and her lips touched his cheek for the first time, because she had fought those emotions often in life. "And will you show me the letters?" she whispered.

On Thursday evening, Tanushree and Joshua were invited to his parents' home in Hampstead. It had been a very spontaneous decision on their part, after hearing Joshua's story the previous day. This, on one hand, made her feel intimidated as she was scared to become scrutinised. And yet, she knew she would never be more than a friend to him because of his sacred pact with God. On the other hand, she could feel that he very much wanted her to meet them. In the evening, after they figured out the connection between her own grandfather and his, he had talked a lot about them and how he was certain they would like to meet her. It seemed like there was an important purpose, but she did not have the faintest clue of what it was.

It was one of those perfect days. Runner's high in the morning, fried sea bream for lunch and Tate Modern in the afternoon. It just felt good, and mainly because of his steady company every evening, which helped her figure herself out. Her legs could go on running forever, she felt stronger when she thought about him. The air was a bit windy now, but they had decided she should take the Northern Line to Hampstead and they would meet and walk from there across the heath. At seven o'clock, she reached Hampstead and saw his radiating face the first thing she did when she came out from the lift. They decided to go for a short walk on the high street and get some tea before they headed for his parents' place. She had Earl Grey as she often did, and he had a cup of cappuccino. They were quieter than usual, but it was a comfortable silence. He let his spoon play with the heart patterned foam. It was as if they had talked so much that they had not given themselves the time to discover each other in non-verbal ways, despite so much becoming clearer only over a couple of days.

A moment after they rang the doorbell to the terraced house, a middle-aged man with hazel eyes in a dark red blazer and black trousers opened the door. There was a friendly welcoming smile on his face as he took her hand and shook it firmly.

"Nice to meet you, Tanushree." Steven Salisbury kissed his son welcome.

"Where is Mum?" asked Joshua.

"Judith is taking care of the stuffed chicken in the kitchen. She'll be here soon," said his father.

"Why don't you two come and sit down in the living room."

They were led to a dark coffee table with heaps of albums and photographs on it. Judith came in after a while, with a platter of stuffed chicken from the kitchen. Tanushree could see she was overjoyed to see her and so was she. Joshua's mother took her hand and she gave her a warm hug and a kiss on the cheek.

"Hello, Judith, it's very nice to meet you," she said.

"It's nice to meet you too, Tanushree. We've heard so much about your adventures with Joshua the past days that we thought it was time for a gathering."

She put down the platter on the dining table.

"You must be wondering why all these pictures and sheets are on the table. Well, the reason is I want to show you something. You see, I heard from Joshua that your family is from Calcutta and that your grandfathers were both solicitors. I guessed a long time ago from your relationship to Rohini that you must be the grandchild of Debendranath Roy Chowdhury. These are the pictures my father brought with him from Calcutta. First, let us have dinner, and we can talk about these things later on."

She was more curious than ever and took a breath of expectation. Tanushree knew there was something there to teach her about her own history. Joshua had been so insistent on her seeing his parents today. They all sat down at the dining table and Judith served fried potatoes, stuffed chicken and gravy together with tomato and corn salad.

"So, how was your journey to London? Did you come by flight?" Steven tried to open a conversation with her and she replied politely. They also talked about her research studies, how she met Joshua the first time in Cadogan Hall and what she thought about life in Berlin. The dinner was full of interesting conversations, but none that led to what she was apparently there for.

"Let us adjourn to the living room. Do you take milk with your tea, Tanushree? We have Darjeeling," said Judith.

"Yes, milk but no sugar, please," she replied.

She was so curious now she could hardly wait.

"So, Tanushree, do you recognize this picture?" Judith showed her the picture of a palatial building and she recognized it immediately. It was the house on the painting in her parents' living room, only a bit more ornate than the depiction of it. She guessed it had been difficult for the artist to copy all the intricacies.

"If I remember correctly, this was the house my family left behind them in East Bengal. I think the town was called Vikrampur," she said to Judith.

"You see, Tanushree, this photograph was taken by my father on his only trip to East Bengal forty-two years before the Partition of India. He owned one of those old Kodak cameras, which he brought along when he attended Debendranath's and your grandmother Chandramukhi's wedding. My father left for England soon after the wedding,, because he thought he would find better prospects here. They were worried about what was going to happen to India after the British left. I heard from Joshua you know the name of Isiah Cohen. When he told me about you, we both remembered a bundle of letters we had once found in my father's study with your grandfather's name on them. So, your paternal grandfather, Debendranath Roy Chowdhury, and Joshua's maternal grandfather, Isiah Cohen, were very close friends." Judith paused for a while, looking a bit worried she had exhausted her guest.

"I wanted to share these letters and diaries with you. There's a wealth of information here, but you have to read them into detail," said Judith. "I also have pictures of Debendranath." Tanushree continued looking through the documents.

"These are my father's diaries," said Judith and handed them to her. Tanushree picked up one of the exercise books and flipped through the pages. The paper had turned yellow and the edges slightly brown. It smelled like it had been kept in a closet for years and years. She wondered what those pages had to disclose about the life of her grandfather.

"Why don't you bring these home with you?" asked Joshua's mother.

At the same time Tanushree heard Judith's words, she felt scared of what was to come. Why did it feel like she held back information from her, which she wanted her to discover by herself? Suddenly, all three of the Salisburys looked at her with pity. Then she thought about the disillusioned gaze on her grandfather's photo again, and had to bite her lip and look down at the floor. A lump had formed in her throat.

"I'm sorry, I have to go. Thank you so much for inviting me for dinner." The lump did not go away. She bit her lower lip hard, grabbed her handbag and barged out into the night, right before the tears began to fill her eyes.

On the train back to Berlin, she was relaxed, even though in her head she could not stop thinking about how hers and Joshua's faces had gravitated towards each other the first day, and how much she had appreciated how he had questioned her beliefs and pushed her really hard. Last evening just became too much, but she still felt bad for barging out the way she did. She dozed off as the train entered the darkness of the tunnel and when she woke up they had already passed Calais and were well on their way to Paris. Her head was throbbing after all those thoughts about Joshua. She used to joke and tell her friends she would probably not meet anyone before she was in her eighties. In front of them, she always laughed about her pathetic situation of 33 years of single-hood, and they laughed with her.

That Saturday morning, she came home to her room in Lottumstrasse and was finally on her own again. She knew she was not allowed to have those feelings for a man she hardly knew, but she could not bear the thought of never seeing Joshua again. It scared her because something in her right brain hemisphere was convinced they were meant to be, either platonically or romantically. She had not even told Rohini she had met his parents, let alone barged out from their house in the middle of the late evening. The first time she had mentioned Joshua, her cousin had warned her of his awkwardness, but Tanushree did not understand what she meant and wished to not become more influenced by her opinions about him. Even the sweetest people could be wrong sometimes, and she was certain this was one of those cases, probably due to something that had happened in school a long time ago.

This first Saturday morning in Berlin, she stumbled in through the front door of her flat in Prenzlauer Berg. She had pushed herself so hard to run, she felt giddy and her mouth filled with a metallic taste. Then she looked at her reflection in the mirror, as she washed her sweat covered face. She was red as a cherry and her hands were trembling. After coming out from the shower, she hurried to change into the new turquoise knee-length dress she had bought from Monsoon in the summer sales. The 45-minute run had made her exhausted, and it was only 10 am, so she could not go back to sleep now. Her second last day off of the week had to be used to the fullest.

With her backpack on her back, Tanushree began to walk towards the Kollwitz Kiez along the street which was lined with chestnut trees. The sun was scorching and her walk was brisk. She felt the sweat on her face, took out the handkerchief and dabbed it on her forehead and the rest of the face. Good thing she seldom wore make-up; it would have been smeared by the sweat. After walking past restaurants, organic food shops, and a few cafes, she finally reached the farmers' market. The street was busy with people. The stalls, which were lined up along the square, sold everything from bread spreads and cheese to pastry, but she was there to get vegetables and fruits as per custom on Saturdays.

"Ich hatte gern zwei Zucchinis und vier Apfelsinen, bitte," she asked for two courgettes and four oranges. The friendly vendor handed her a brown paper bag containing what she had asked for. After paying the three euros it cost, she continued to the neighbouring stall. There she picked up another small brown paper bag, and began filling it with purple-coloured figs. She loved how the availability of fruits and vegetables changed with the season because it made her feel she always had access to fresh produce. Her backpack still had room, so she decided to get a rye baguette from one of the bread stalls. As often on Saturdays after buying groceries, she went to a shop north of Pappelallee. Her eyes scanned every little table as she walked through the grocery shop, and she decided on vegetarian gnocchi dish for the evening. After doing her groceries, she sat down to have her Saturday breakfast tea at the nearby cafe Anna Blume. Today, she chose a piece of Schokolade Sahne Kuchen to go with her tea. It was one of her favourite cakes, and she justified indulging herself by saying it was the weekend, and after all, she had just run 45 minutes.

After munching on the cake and sipping her tea, she jumped on the U-Bahn from Eberswalder Strasse and took out the earplugs and the cell phone to listen to Anoushka Shankar. She loved listening to the sitar, sometimes even more than the violin. As a child, her mother had her practising different scales and variations every weekend that she referred to as 'paltas', but they sang them in Bilawal and Bhairav which are the equivalents of the major and minor modes in western music. She was used to the names of the tones in the Indian version of the DO RE MI, the SA RE GA MA PA DHA NI SA. She did not have many issues remembering the order of the tones of the paltas, but her voice had not become used to the less harmonic modes like Asavari and Marwa, and she sometimes sang out of tune. The day she began learning western music, she had stopped learning Indian music. Western music elated her, but it felt so wrong that she should call herself a musician, and still know nothing about her own music. This bothered her so much that four years earlier when she first arrived in Berlin, she enrolled for Indian singing classes to learn more about her own cultural heritage. In Sweden, there had been no opportunity to learn Indian music as she grew up. So, late in life, she had taken up Indian classical music again. She owed it to her mother, not only because she spent so much energy training her, but also because she herself had worked so hard, yet had never had the chance to become recognised as she had moved to a society where she and her music were alien. Fifty years earlier when she arrived in Sweden, people would stare at her in her colourful sarees. As a result, she began wearing pants and shirts. Then there was the problem of pronouncing her name, which had disturbed her so much she had changed the spelling. After that, there were the university degrees that never got accepted. She had to go back to becoming a lower secondary school student in her new country, only to learn the foreign language and the social system, and later began university studies anew in a completely foreign language close to the age of forty. As if that was not enough, her Indian driving license had not been accepted. Her driving examiner had made her drive down Chowringhee Road, one of the main thoroughfares in Calcutta, the morning she had her first driving test. She had been so confident at 18, but now her body trembled of nervousness whenever she went for her lessons. She tried to catch up with everything at the same time as she was rearing a child. In the mornings she woke up and practised her music because it was her responsibility to keep it up even though no one was there to appreciate it. She had graduated first in vocal music from one of the top music academies in Calcutta, and had gone on to do diploma studies and a teaching degree in vocal music from the performing arts university in Calcutta. Singing had been the love of her life, maybe more than her daytime job as a higher secondary teacher of Philosophy and History. Then, there were the judgemental comments from the other Indians she and her husband had befriended in Sweden. She was tired of the gossip and missed discussing politics and rehearsing with her siblings. After years of constantly battling and trying to get back to the kind of life she had left behind, she was drained. One day she could not get out of bed, and she called her parents to say how much she missed them. They told her to come home, and as she put down the receiver she cried. No one was at home to hear her, so there was no need to be brave anymore, because she knew she was trapped in her new home country. Naxalites had already visited her in-laws in search for her husband, whose best friend had been murdered. She walked into the kitchen and took a large chunk of the chocolate cake which was kept in the fridge from the day before. Her previously slender body had become chubby, but she did not care anymore. As Tanushree thought about what her mother had confided in her, she became sad, but more determined she could not give up her musical journey. She had to become proficient enough with the Indian classical modes to be able to improvise and translate to western music, so that people understood the uniqueness of each style. To her, they were like two different languages that completed each other, like how she had grown up with Swedish and Bengali side by side. The train stopped at Senefelderplatz and she went off as planned.

Chapter 8

As the pujaris chopped off the head of the goat, Isiah had to look away. When he turned back his face towards the floor where the animal stood, it was covered in dripping fresh red blood. So, this was how it was done – the sacrifice of animals to the Hindu Gods.

Where he stood close to the deity in the Kalighat temple, he concluded the act had been just as barbaric as he had imagined it. Debapriya looked at his face from the side. Around the statuette of Goddess Kali, it was crammed with people. Many of them, her included, had stood there unmoved at the moment the axe fell.

"Are you used to this?" he asked her carefully.

"Yes, when we were younger, my grandparents used to organise a public Kali Puja at home, and the sacrifice was part of the rituals," she replied.

He did not say much, because he wanted to show respect to her religion, but his face had already given him away.

"You thought it was cruel, didn't you?" Debapriya asked looking back at him. He wished she had not asked him that question, because it reminded him once again about their differences in religion, but he nodded his head. The next moment, she walked up to the statuette of Mother Kali, kneeled down and bent over putting her palms against each other like a wedge between the light stone floor and her head. Then she stood and accepted the offered food, the prasad, handed to her by the priest.

On Saturday when he knocked on the door of the Tollygunge house, it was much to the surprise of Debapriya's brothers. Debu did not raise a brow, he seldom did, but his younger brother Narendranath was speechless for a few seconds upon opening the door. Then he looked at Debapriya, who wore one of her elegant silk sarees, and he nodded to himself as if he had come to a realisation. At the moment he looked back at him again, Isiah felt his face burning. Debapriya lowered her gaze and squeezed past her brother in the doorway. No questions were asked, only a fade "See you in the evening" was uttered by her.

He was enthralled by the actors on the stage, even though his knowledge of the Mahabharata was limited. She had introduced him to Girish Chandra Ghosh, while he had always wanted to visit the Star Theatre. But when he was lost, Debapriya whispered in his ear to explain. When he felt her warm breath wafting out of her mouth a few times, all he could think about was how glossy and soft her lips were. He felt something ungodly in his body and longed to touch her, but he told himself to take self-control. He cleared his voice, and when the light came on, she looked at his face.

"What is the matter, Isiah? Did you not like the play?" she asked and frowned.

"Yes, I did," he answered.

She raised her brow a little bit more, and in her face, he could see a trace of disappointment, but then she began to speak about the parts she had liked and those which were not to her liking.

"I absolutely loved the scene where…"

He could not utter a single word as she ranted on. Instead, all he did was to stare at her angel-like face and inhale her heavenly rose scent. They had walked all the way down Cornwallis Street, and he had forced his eyes to behave a handful of times. He took her hand and led her to College Park, where they sat down on a bench. It was already 7 pm and dusk had fallen. His face still burned, and she suddenly stopped talking. Their eyes locked and he touched her cheek with his fingers. At that moment, Isiah noticed her face was just as warm as his. At first, his eyes fixed on her lips, but suddenly, he had no idea how to go about. He had never been this close to a woman before. He took her face in his slender hands and stared into her eyes again, upon which he pressed his lips against her cheek.

Isiah had never been to a more crowded place before. Albert Hall was full of young loud elated men, and in every corner of the room, stood a group of people who had political discussions on their own terms. Debu had brought him to meet his party comrades for the first time.

"How can the British Government divide the province of Bengal when a majority of us have opposed it?" a middle-aged man with a voluminous voice shouted rhetorically from a stage in the middle of the hall.

"Well said," responded a few men in the audience loudly.

The sound of the murmur subsided, and in a few seconds, the powerful orator managed to bring the audience to pin-drop silence.

"I think they are trying to create tension between Muslims and Hindus to distract us from our goal," said Debendranath in a loud voice and clasped his hand behind his body.

"This is most certainly a possible reason, young man," retorted the speaker on the stage.

Debu never ceased to impress him. He was always very vocal in class, but oh, how Isiah admired his guts to speak his mind in front of some of the most influential leaders of the city. As the middle-aged gentleman addressed his classmate, everyone's eyes were on him. But he did not seem bothered by it, almost as if he was used to this type of attention.

"Many of us have our roots in East Bengal. Do we want Dacca to lose its prominent role? After all, the city has a much older history than Calcutta, and speaks of a time when the Muslims ruled our country. At the same time, there are remnants from the Buddhist dynasties. Becoming detached from the eastern parts of our province, we will lose access to some of our most valuable cultural heritage," said the speaker, addressing the whole audience of men on the floor.

Isiah observed Debu from the side, who looked spellbound by those words. He thought about how happy he had become when he told him he was going to come to Vikrampur for his wedding, and how proud he always seemed when he spoke about his East Bengali heritage.

"I agree it is important to remember how Hindus and Muslims lived in harmony before the British came. We must not forget how the Muslim population has been wronged by our imperial lords to get into power. There has recently been a book published on the topic, if you would like to study the matter further," an elderly man with a blue topi cap announced to the audience, who spoke like he was well prepared for opposition.

Isiah was probably the only Jewish man in the congregation, but he felt like he was part of a group for a change, a group that would change the future of British India. He knew the words that were uttered by those men were rooted in strong nationalistic emotions. By the looks of their faces, he could tell they would do their utmost to bring their words into action.

"Tell me where you see yourself 20 years from now, Isiah. What are your aspirations in life?" Debu asked and crossed his legs. They sat at a road-side tea stall in College Street. It was dark outside, and the air was crisp, but they had both felt a need to discuss after the political meeting.

"I would like to study Law," he retorted diligently.

Debu gave him a fond smile and nodded.

"So do I. Is there any particular reason you would like to study Law, my friend?" Debu asked.

"I think it could provide me tools to change individual lives, tools which are equal to all citizens, independent of their socioeconomic, religious or ethnic background," Isiah answered, put his hand under the chin and elbow on the table between them.

"Why do you think social equality is so important to you?" Debu asked in a curious, but philosophical tone, also put his elbow on the table next to his clay teacup.

"Well, I think it's due to that I grew up in a religious minority in Calcutta, and I always wanted to be like the Bengali children," said Isiah without a moment's thought.

"It's funny how we haven't discussed this before, despite the topic being so close to both of our hearts. I grew up in a Bengali family, and I also wanted to be like everyone else like you. I don't appreciate it when people point out to me that I was born with a silver spoon in my mouth. Even if you have all the money in the world, this is seldom the case," said Debu.

"What do you mean?" asked Isiah tilting his head and staring into his classmate's eyes.

"Well, I did not grow up with a lack of money, but despite this, my father would beat me with a cane every time I didn't come home with the highest marks in all subjects on my school report. He would say I was a disgrace to the Roy Chowdhury family. I still remember the red traces the cane left on my back," answered Debu and looked into the air.

Debendranath's words came as a surprise to Isiah. His family had seemed so harmonic when he went to visit them in Tollygunge each Sunday. The dandy-like Bengali gentleman on the picture, certainly seemed like he was of good pedigree.

"I'm sorry to hear that," said Isiah and put his hand on Debu's arm.

"Well, luckily it's in the past now. My grandmother caught him in the act of beating me one day when I was 14, and threatened to throw him out of the house if it ever happened again. Were your parents strict about your schooling, Isiah?" Debu asked.

"Yes, they were, but my parents never beat me. They did, however, question my every decision, so much that it made me feel I was always doing something wrong," he answered, sighed and looked down at his cup.

"There's the root to the self-critical you," Debendranath said under his breath.

Isiah heard the subtle comment and stared at him with wonder. So, Debu had understood he was self-critical? This seldom happened to him with anyone, apart from Hannah.

"What made you think that?"

"Oh please! You always think twice before uttering your words. I can tell that anything that leaves your mouth has been thought through a million times."

"Oh, I didn't think it was that evident."

"Sadly, life is more than logic and correct analyses, Isiah. It's also about bringing forward your opinions and standing up for yourself. Otherwise, people will rule you over."

He nodded in agreement. Those words spoken to Isiah more than he let his friend believe. He had made those conclusions too, but standing up for himself was not one of his strong sides. As a result, people would make judgements that were not true.

"It seems like Jyotish and Abdul are late today. Let's listen to some music," said Debendranath.

He walked into the sitting room and turned on a gramophone. From the loudspeaker, Isiah was surprised to hear the songs of a woman, probably one who earned her living by entertaining men.

On next Monday, during the last lecture of the day at Presidency College, which was Political Science, they had been introduced to Karl Marx. The rumour had it their new lecturer was a communist. After finishing, they went out from the hall and walked down the stairs eager to leave the establishment. To their surprise, Debapriya stood outside the high gates waiting for her brother and his friends to come out. It was late November, the rain poured down from the sky, and she was drenched.

"Why have you come here in the pouring rain, young lady? You'll catch a cold!"

It was not often that Debu scolded his younger sister, but this was one of those rare occasions. She did not reply, but instead, her eyes looked for Isiah in the crowd and locked when she finally caught sight of him. He had longed for her, and she had made an effort to come and see him this time.

"I see," Debu said and looked at Isiah with a smile.

"Will you take me to the Imperial Museum, Isiah?" she begged.

"Of course I will, my dear," he replied.

They began walking down College Street, and halfway to the museum the rain finally stopped, but Isiah's coat was already wet.

"We'll both catch a cold," he said with a chuckle.

"At least, we will have spent time with each other," she retorted and raised her brows with a smile.

They went into the inner court. The museum was a beautiful white-washed building from 1814 with arched verandas, like many other buildings from this era.

"This reminds me of home, Isiah," Debapriya said where she stood in the middle of the courtyard and looked around her at the arched verandas. For a moment he tried to picture what their village house must look like.

When they saw the mummy in the Egyptian exhibition, her eyes sparkled.

"I wonder what this mummy was like when it was alive," she said.

"Maybe it spooks about at night," he teased her and imitated a ghost raising his cupped hands in the air. She laughed, and was equally enthused when she saw the stuffed animals. For a moment, he felt grateful to be with an inquisitive woman with a multitude of interests. He would never trade her for someone whose only aim in life was to become a home-maker and only cared about her appearance.

"Isiah, look at that goat. It has eight legs," she exclaimed and pointed with her finger.

He smiled at her sudden exclamation and when no one could see, he took her hair lock and tucked it behind her ear.

"Promise you'll never change," he whispered in her ear.

Chapter 9

The last Sunday before she went back to work, Tanushree treated herself to a brunch at Jules Verne. The restaurant was a quaint little French place with dark red walls and old posters hung on them, in the formerly British sector of Charlottenburg. She always thought of this part of town like Prenzlauer Berg of the West, and was very fond of the architecture of the neighbourhood, and also of the myriads of restaurants and cafes. However, they all seemed a bit more traditional than those in her own part of town. After finishing her food, she stayed on a little while to read about a recent study from England on the effects on the mood of different ragas. She enjoyed reading articles in the hum of voices. The background noise made her focus better. When she was about to finish the Discussion section, a young couple sat down at the table next to her. She noticed the smile on the man's face, and then she packed her bag and asked for the check.

After leaving the brunch place, she walked down the trafficked Kantstrasse towards the station at Savignyplatz. Just around the corner from it, was an independent cinema she used to visit from time to time. She paid for her ticket at the counter and walked into hall three. The halls were much smaller than in the commercial cinemas. The film she watched was about a girl who had an immunological disorder, which made it impossible for her to be outside the house and have physical contact with others. As a consequence, she had never been allowed to have a relationship. Tanushree felt the tears running down her cheeks at the thought. The film had struck a chord in her, but she knew there was another reason she cried. She cried because she never stayed in one place long enough to get to know people. The tears rolled down her face because she gave strangers the impression, she was an introvert. She was ashamed of being attracted to someone who had made a pact with God. On one hand, he had given her some kind of romantic confidence and on the other hand, he began to slowly break it down to crumbles when he told her about his celibacy. Why did she long for someone whom she could not get? The heart certainly had its mysterious ways. She was alone, and had been alone well over two days, feeling empty. That morning she had just wanted to go back to bed and cry in despair. She could not put her finger on what it was, but something had made her feel very connected to Joshua. It was a feeling she seldom had about anyone. She remembered the last time a man had moved her in that way – many years had passed! She had asked him out on a date and gone out on her first date at the age of twenty-four. They had visited the Victoria and Albert Museum and talked about immigration politics for seven hours, but the next day she received an email saying he did not see their relationship going anywhere. She had gone into a depression and lost confidence in herself. For many years she buried herself in work and extra-curricular activities pretending to be free as a bird gave her ultimate happiness. She had managed to fool most of her friends and family.

She thought about the first time she had felt this lonely. She was at the cinema in Odeon Rue Saint Germaine in Paris. At the age of twenty, she had cried through the whole film just like today, not because it was sad, but because sitting in a movie theatre alone reminded her of how she lacked romantic companionship and had never been in a relationship. Since then, she had purposely done all kinds of things solo, which were traditionally regarded as couples' activities. After moving to Berlin, she had spent every evening alone, working at her favourite cafe. On weekends she would go to restaurants and have dinner alone, and once in a while, she went to the cinema or the theatre. Almost all the journeys she made were on her own and since she had noticed how fulfilling it could be to live the life of a spinster, she had begun enjoying herself. Now, her inner voice told herself to cheer up! How could she allow herself to shed tears when this had been her everyday bread for as long as she could remember? She wiped her tears with the back of her hands, sat up with her back straight and decided she would take on those trainers from time to time and be on a monoamine kick, so she could prevent these emotional outbursts. Reminding herself of that, she continued watching the movie, burying her emotions in denial once more.

When she got off the S-Bahn at Alexanderplatz that evening and was running down the escalator to take the U2 to Senefelder Platz, she knew she had to excuse herself for her behaviour at Steven and Judith Salisbury's place. The moment she entered her apartment, her fingers began to type on her laptop.

Dear Joshua, Judith and Steven,

I am truly sorry for running out like that on Thursday evening. I really appreciated spending time with you and thank you for the delicious dinner. I hope we'll be able to meet again under better conditions.

Sincerely,

Tanu

She exhaled as she clicked the send icon, switched off the light, and looked forward to discussing her final draft with her supervisor in the morning.

On Saturday morning the week after she came back to Berlin, Tanushree woke up by the ringing of the intercom. When she glanced at the alarm clock before rising from bed, it showed 8:25 a.m. To be more precise, she used to sleep on a red sofa-bed, which served dual purposes, in the high ceilinged living room with white painted walls. In the room, there were two copies of paintings on the walls. One was on the wall opposite to the sofa-bed and depicted a young female violinist from the Philippines. The other copy, which was on the short wall by the door, was a sketch of the Calcutta High Court. While she wondered to herself who was calling at this early hour, she rubbed her eyes to get rid of the sleep sand, which had gathered overnight. She was exhausted after a week of making final corrections to her thesis and felt like sleeping in, but in a few moments, she was up and answered the phone by the white wooden entrance door in the hallway.

"Hello," her husky voice answered.

"Hello Tanu," a cheerful familiar voice retorted.

For a moment, she was out of words, but after the initial surprise had subdued, she pressed the yellowish plastic key button, until she heard the sound of the front door to the apartment building closing. Hastily, she went into the bathroom, washed her face and cleared her voice to awaken her fatigued vocal cords. She heard the sound of the doorbell and went out into the hallway again, and pressed the gilded metallic handle gently to open the heavy entrance door to the flat, which was almost as high as the ceiling. She was met by a well-shaved middle-aged male face full of expectations.

"Good morning, Ms Roy Chowdhury!"

"Professor Salisbury, to what do I owe this honour?"

His face burst out in a contagious smile, which caused her own lips to smile too.

"I figured I wanted to explore the past with the woman who always leaves me in awe."

His choice of words made her take a deep breath, but the next moment she reminded herself of his pact with God, which meant he would never be hers.

"Do you mean our common history?" she cleared her throat.

"Yes. I brought all the letters and pictures with me. We should read them together. I've never read Isiah's diary Tanu, I couldn't."

"I cannot begin to tell you how grateful I am that you came all the way to Berlin for my sake, but do you really have the time?" she asked, still standing in the doorway.

"I figured I might as well spend my coming months in Berlin while writing my Theoretical Acoustics textbook."

"Where are you staying?" she asked.

"I moved into a little flat not too far from the main train station — Hauptbahnhof, yesterday evening. It's in Invalidenstrasse," he replied.

Her heart again acted disobediently and skipped a bit at the excitement of having him near her for the next few months.

"Oh, that's a lovely plan. Please come in and sit down."

She put her arms around him in her eagerness not even considering they never hugged, and then gestured for him to come in. Moving away from the door, she gave him a way to enter her humble abode. She walked into the kitchen to turn on the water boiler. In a cup, she put a Darjeeling Hampstead Teabag and drowned it in hot water. She brought the cup to the living room and put it down on the table in front of Joshua.

"Why have you never read your grandfather's diaries?" she asked, standing up in front of him.

"I felt I wasn't prepared emotionally," he answered quietly while sipping on his hot tea.

She did not push him to elaborate, even though his remark made her realise he had a close relationship to Isiah. It still felt unbelievable that his grandfather was her own grandfather's close friend. Instead, she jumped into the shower and left him in the living room to sip his tea alone. While she was in there, she decided she should show him her own beloved places in Berlin. After all, he was a stranger and she had lived there for almost four years now.

From her front door in Lottumstrasse, they walked northwards along Schonhauser Allee and onto Kollwitzstrasse. She adored how the chestnut trees lined that street. In autumn all the leaves would turn yellow. Their walk took them past the playground, which was appropriately positioned in the part of Berlin with the highest density of families with children. Before entering one of her favourite coffee shops, she took a detour.

"Have you seen a book tree before, Joshua?"

On the western side of the cafe, stood the tree which had built-in shelves with plastic flaps in its trunk. There, people could exchange the books they had read for books other people had left in the trunk of the book tree.

"It is just one of Berlin's quirks," she said.

"I love the idea, and it seems like it works too," he responded, opened one of the flaps and took out 'Zorba'.

She took him around to the entrance on the other side, and after staring at the cakes for some time, she went up to the counter.

"Ich hatte gern ein Stuck Schoko-sahne Kuchen und einen schwartzer Tee mit Milch, bitte," she said to the woman behind the counter.

Joshua observed her while she spoke and smiled at her to show he was impressed by her German. She felt how her cheeks turned hot. It was going to take a good few days to make her physiological responses obey the logic of her frontal cortex, which knew he would never have a romantic interest in her. The next moment, the waiter looked up at him to have his order.

"May I have a piece of the strawberry cake, and a cup of cappuccino, please?" he asked.

They sat down by the window next to the book tree. It was still quite early and few people had made their ways to the cafe, but in the far corner sat an elderly couple sharing a breakfast plate, accompanied by a boy and a girl who seemed to be their grandchildren.

"Do you come here often?" Joshua asked.

"Yes, I usually sit and work here in the evenings," she replied.

"It's very cosy. I like your taste," he said and looked down at his plate.

He looked up at the wall painting of a young girl by the entrance, but avoided Tanushree's eyes. Even though he had made the effort to come all the way to Berlin to spend time with her and had made it clear he had no romantic interest, there was still a bit of shyness in him and it suited her well.

"The name of the cafe comes from a poem," she said to begin a new topic. At once, he took up his phone and began searching for it, just like she had done years earlier.

"Oh, there's an English translation – Eve Blossom. It begins with oh thou, beloved of my twenty-seven senses, I love thine!"

His voice was expressive.

"Please read the whole poem to me," she begged.

While he read, the waiter came to their table and left the check. Tanushree handed him a 20 euro note while still listening to Joshua's poetic voice.

"I really enjoyed that. You have a knack for poetry reading," she said to him.

As they left the cafe, her legs just wanted to walk in one direction. It was perhaps not the prettiest of places, but it was one of those places which had commemorated one of the constructions that made Berlin the city it was. For better or for worse! They walked towards Bernauer Allee and in a convenient silence.

"Have you been to Berlin before?" she asked.

"No Tanu, I haven't, but I'm quite excited about the coming months. No doubt I have to focus on writing, but I hope I'll have enough time to discover the city," he said.

"I like your way of thinking! So much has happened since I moved here, but there are still little gems I want to show you," she said with a smile.

They had reached the wall painting in Bernauer Strasse, which showed a soldier by the Berlin Wall. A part of the structure was still there.

"Imagine partitioning a country with a physical wall and forcing people to separate from their families and close friends!" she said.

"Yes, it's still unfathomable to me…" he said quietly.

She did not know why her feet had brought them there the first thing they did, but for a good few minutes, they stood staring at the remnants of the structure, which had divided the once so flamboyant and liberal city into two.

That first Saturday evening Joshua was in Berlin, he and Tanushree sat down to have tea at the Tajikistani tea house in Oranienburger Strasse in the centre of the old East Berlin. She had been introduced to the place by her colleague the first year she lived in the city. The moment they sat down on their cushions at the low table on the floor, a young female waiter with hair as red as carrots and magenta coloured lipstick walked up to them. The bright green coloured walls of the tea salon were decorated with equally brightly coloured paintings and a couple of carved ceiling-high wooden pillars stood on the floor in a straight axis through the middle of the room. On the floor under the sitting cushions lay red Persian carpets.

"What would you like to have?" the waitress asked.

"A pot of tea and two plates of vegetarian pireauges, please," Tanushree answered.

While the waitress made her way back to the cashier, Joshua took out one of his grandfather's diaries from his black computer bag. She remembered what it looked like from the day she had visited his parents.

"What would you say about beginning the journey?" Joshua asked Tanushree with a fade smile on his lips. She swallowed and took a deep breath, but she knew if she did not accept this time, she would never be able to cross the threshold, and she would probably keep on asking the same questions all her life.

"Yes, let's do it," she swallowed and said resolutely.

He handed her the book and she opened the first yellow page of the diary clad in green silk as if made of a Banarasi saree. She remembered the moist smell of the paper from the evening in Hampstead. Then she cleared her voice.

Thine eyes have bewitched me. Oh, those treacherous squinting amber stones! How I long for them to look at me every Sunday when my queen looks out from her pedestal on top of the stairs. And that girlish voice, which is both abiding and demanding at the same time. How I adore it every time it pronounces my name, knowing that I will soon be in her embrace. And those scarlet cheeks, which are just like newly picked apples from the highlands, ready for the common man to take a bite of. Oh, how thou enthral me, my queen! And oh, how I love touching your bare skin with my fingertips and feeling your rose scent wafting through the air and slowly intoxicating my senses. If today were our last tete-a-tete, I would sacrifice every bit of myself to lie in your arms once more. Oh, my queen! Oh, my God-given gift.

Tanushree cleared the momentarily expressive voice again, which had read the poem aloud at the candlelit table in the Teestube in Mitte. For the two very pragmatic people sitting face to face to hear the heartfelt poem of a young love-struck man, had been uncomfortable. She knew he felt the same way as her because he had fidgeted in his seat while listening to it a couple of times. When she looked at his face, she noticed the blushed tone of his cheeks and his eyes looking down at the floor. Why was he avoiding eye contact again? None of them spoke. There was an awkward pin drop silence. Then the waitress came back to their table.

"Could we have another pot of tea, please?" Tanushree asked. She knew Joshua had rather left the place to get out of the situation, but she felt a need to talk.

"I know Debapriya was my great aunt, but I had no idea Isiah was in love with her."

He took another sip of his tea and remained silent, but by the look of the eyes, he was moved.

"Why did you go into celibacy, Joshua?"

Since he had remained silent, she had taken the chance to ask. She knew it was none of her business, but the more she thought about it and the more time she spent with him, the less sense it made.

"To devote myself to God," he answered in a quiet husky voice while staring down at the low brown wooden table.

For a minute she thought she should just let it go, but she was not in that sort of mood after reading his grandfather's declaration of love to her own great aunt.

"Have you ever been in love?" she asked insistently. He avoided eye contact, but his cheeks were clearly reddening.

"Maybe," he said evasively. For a moment she caught sight of his moist eyes again. She told herself she should not push, but she knew the signs of a burn far too well.

"Who was she?" she asked after a long silence with as much as compassion in her voice as she could.

"A classmate in secondary school...I was only 17."

"Was the love unrequited?"

"No, I think she had emotions for me. We never talked about it, but I'm quite certain."

"How could you tell?" Tanushree asked.

"Well, there were long affectionate gazes and she always teased me, but she encouraged me too, and she stood up for me when I couldn't defend myself."

She wondered to herself why he had needed to defend himself so often?

"She sounds really wonderful," Tanushree replied.

"She was. The best thing about her was that I never had to explain how I felt to her. She just knew."

He took another sip of his tea and looked down.

"And what happened?"

"I don't know. I never dared to tell her what I felt. She tried to get closer in all the ways possible, but I just got nervous and went inside my cocoon. When we did our A levels, she began dating another one of our classmates."

Tanushree touched his hand without thinking, but he did not pull back.

"How did it make you feel?"

"I pretended I didn't care. At that time in life, school work and musical rehearsals took up most of my time," Joshua answered.

"Let me guess. The only thing that mattered was to ace the exams," Tanushree said.

"Yes."

"But why celibacy?"

"I couldn't take the emotional rollercoaster another time, Tanu. I met a few women in my twenties, but all I thought about was her."

His voice broke. She knew she had rubbed it in, but in some way, he seemed to be relieved to talk openly to her, even though it was clear he had plenty of unfinished business.

"Thank you for letting me in, Joshua. The more we meet, the luckier I feel to be able to spend so much time with you. You're a wonderful person. I just want you to know that."

Chapter 10

A middle-aged woman wearing a cotton saree came into the room, where Jyotish, Isiah, Debu and Abdul sat on the floor. She wore the end piece of her saree over her head like a veil and put her palms together to greet the young men in the traditional way. Then she served them tea and biscuits in silence. This Saturday they had been invited to Jyotish's childhood home, and the middle-aged lady with a rather dark skin complexion and dry dark pink lips was his mother. When Debu asked her to join them, she just encouraged him to eat what he had been served by saying "Khao, baba, khao" in her quiet voice, and then she disappeared into the kitchen again. On a hard bed in one corner of the hall room, sat Jyotish's father on a dark wooden low structure, reading a Bengali newspaper. In his mouth, he had a pipe, and Isiah watched the smoke puffs coming out from it. He also observed the man who must have been in his mid-fifties, and seemed to have little interest in making conversation with the guests. The floor was grey cement with cracks in a few places, and it was where they sat, on a brown jute mat.

Jyotish was the third sibling out of seven, and the first family member to attend university. His older sister had never been to school, and his older brother had begun working as a clerk in the company where his father worked, from the age of fifteen.

This Saturday like all weekends, Jyotish's mother and sister had just finished milking their Shiva linga. It was a weekly puja they carried out to pray for the male members of the family. The older sister came in to serve the young men rice and red lentil daal. The rice was para boiled and had the smell of soil, which Isiah could not handle, but ate politely.

"Will you join us?"

Debu made a second attempt to ask one of Jyotish's family members to sit down, but the young girl who had also covered her head just smiled and disappeared into the kitchen. Jyotish never raised an eyebrow at his mother and sister not joining them for lunch, and so Isiah concluded this must be common practice in their home. When he saw the withdrawal of Jyotish's sister, Isiah once again was reminded of his classmate's ill-tempered words about Debapriya and how it had disgusted him. But seeing his family in action made things a bit clearer to him. He began understanding why Debapriya had struck Jyotish as too straightforward.

"How long have you lived here in North Calcutta?" Debu asked while the other men ate in silence.

"Our family is from Midnapur, son," Jyotish's father looked up from his paper and replied.

"Why did you move to Calcutta?" Debu insisted as the curious young man often did.

"We were ousted from her homes from the zamindar who rented the property to us. There was no other way than to look for work in the city," the man replied.

"I'm sorry to hear that," Debu replied.

Then again followed a long silence. At the end of the meal, the older sister of Jyotish came with metal mugs filled with water.

"You will never be allowed to leave this house without me again," a male voice growled from the opposite building in Marquis Street.

Isiah turned around from his place on the mosaic floor in his own bedroom in Marquis Street. Through the green grills of his window, he spotted the couple in the opposite flat. The husband's fierce bloodshot eyes were wide open and he held his wife's clasped hands in a firm grip. Debendranath, who was visiting this afternoon came running into the room only to be met by his friend's anguished face. As Isiah turned his face towards Debu's, he heard the echoing sound of his neighbour's strong hand slapping his young wife's tense cheek.

"Let me go," the woman howled in Bengali.

"Now, that's fully unacceptable! How can you sit there and just watch your neighbour being abused by her husband?" Debu exclaimed and turned towards Isiah.

Isiah, who was already petrified turned around dumbstruck only to see the shocked expression on Debendranath's face.

"I don't know if we should intervene," he said in his own contemplative fashion.

The moment Isiah uttered those words, he felt like a horrible human being and he knew he would be judged.

"Do you think it's acceptable that a man slaps his wife?" Debu asked and crossed his arms.

"No, that's not what I meant."

Before he had the time to explain, Debu was already on his way down the stairs. Isiah looked down from the window and saw his classmate banging on the neighbours' door. The husband, a Parsi man by the name of Mr Yazadi opened it. His cheeks were flushed from the recent domestic events, but he spoke with a deceptively calm voice.

"Hello, who are you looking for, if I may ask?" Mr Yazadi's brow was creased, which gave the face a puzzled expression.

"I am looking for your wife Mr…" Debu replied.

"My name is Mr Yazadi and my wife is not at home." When the man opened his mouth, Isiah saw Debu stepping back with a disgusted look on his face.

"Damn liar! I just saw you slap your wife from the window. I would like to see if she's alright. If you don't bring her here, I shall search your house in person," Debu threatened the man.

"You have no right to trespass. Whatever goes on between these four walls is none of your business. Who are you anyway?" Mr Yazadi asked.

Isiah saw the man's eyes turning as fierce as when he had laid hands on his own wife. For a moment, he feared he would beat Debu up.

"Mrs Yazadi," Debendranath shouted at the top of his voice. "You are safe now, we saw what happened. Please come down. We will not let your husband go near you. You can come with us to our house."

For the first time, Debu looked like he had his heart in his mouth. Why was she not coming down? After a short moment, the young slender woman in a bright cotton saree, who had walked down the stairs bare-feet wearing anklets similarly to Debapriya, showed herself at the door behind her husband who was guarding the entrance with both his arms. Her eyes showed traces of tears, and her limbs were trembling. On her cheek, there was a red mark from her husband's palm. When Isiah saw her at the doorstep, he exhaled.

"You are not allowed to leave this house," her husband shouted at her. He stood in her way and stretched out his two arms to either side of the door, so she would not be able to pass by. But Debu took hold of one of his arms and forced it to let go. The young wife cried loudly, but seemed to be hesitant about what to do, just like Isiah had imagined.

"You have no right to tell my wife what to do," Mr Yazadi insisted.

"Come, you are safe with us," Debu said calmly this time, and looked the young Mrs Yazadi in the eye. Slowly, she put one foot forward, but it was not like she showed desperation in her attempt to leave the house.

Debu brought her to the oval brown table in the dining room of the Cohen family and let her rest for some time, while Hannah brought her a cup of tea. When Debendranath looked at Isiah with an angry eye, his friend was abashed. He was embarrassed not to have taken a stronger stand against the abusive Mr Yazadi, but he kept it a secret that he had seen the woman being abused by her husband a dozen times before, feeling the same inner conflict as he had today. Debendranath came into his bedroom and closed the door behind him.

"What do you mean we should not intervene? Do you not have any sense of empathy? Should we just stand by and watch women getting abused?" Isiah was taken aback by Debu's tone. He was not a man of conflicts, but he certainly did not want his friend to think of him as someone who did not care. He definitely did not want him to convey that image to Debapriya, who waited in the living room.

"That was not what I meant," he said quietly.

"What did you mean? Please tell," Debu said adamantly.

Isiah flinched. "Ehm, I did not know if it was right to meddle into other people's affairs, but you are right, I should have done something before...I suppose I've been a petty man all these months."

The moment Isiah uttered those words, Debu's eye twinkled and he began to look at his friend with pity. Then he sighed.

"Yes, you should have done something, Isiah. Never be a bystander! Just follow your heart and you will have no regrets," Debu told him in a much less confrontational tone than just a minute ago.

Those words spoken to Isiah, and he was relieved to know his friend understood him and did not regard him as indifferent. It was the first time anyone had encouraged him to stand up for himself, and although it was only a few words, they would never leave his memory.

Before the two of them had the chance to reconcile properly, Debapriya opened the door and paced into the room.

"Stop blaming him, Dada. It's not his fault. Not everyone is as overconfident about themselves as you," Debapriya said resolutely.

"What did you just say?" Debu asked in an upset tone.

"You heard me. There are so many consequences to consider, but you just barged in there as if nothing else mattered," Debapriya retorted.

"And what are those consequences, if I may ask?" Debu provoked his younger sister.

"Just think about what society will think if she separates from her husband," she said in an insightful manner.

"Is that more important than her well-being?" He continued provoking her.

Debu glared at his younger sister and she turned down her glance towards the floor.

"And the promise she has made to another," Debu said under his breath, but Isiah stood close enough to hear it. He was perplexed by the last sentence. It seemed like the siblings were arguing about something that was beyond him.

"No, it's not." Her voice broke.

Abdul, who sat on the sofa in the living room, lifted his face from the Statesman and now all three of them stared at Debapriya. Isiah saw her eyes slowly filling with tears as she looked straight into his face, then turned to Abdul, and finally back to her older brother. But as she brushed past Isiah, she avoided making eye contact with him. Instead, she walked outside slowly with her face turned towards the three of them, stretched her arm to grab the banister, and turned for the stairs. Her bare feet ran as if they were fleeing a predator. Isiah wondered whether to follow her or not. Then Debu's face turned towards him and his eyes were full of pity. Something was going on and without having the faintest clue of what it was, he knew by now it entailed him.

"I should probably just let her…"

Before Isiah could finish his sentence, Debu interrupted.

"No, Isiah!"

He flinched from the sudden exclamation.

"One cannot run away from life forever. Go down to my sister and demand to know what evil truth she has kept from you."

Isiah was as still as a statue, but his heart was throbbing violently. Something was wrong and he had been kept in the dark. He looked at Abdul whose eyes spoke of fear, but Jyotish who had come in from the dining room to see what was going on, looked as if he was hiding a smirk behind the sports section of the newspaper, just as if he had won a bet.

"Go down, Isiah. I beg of you," Debu repeated.

With his feet dragging, he made his way down the stairs from his family's flat in Marquis Street. He knew from the beginning that girl would be the death of him, and now all that remained was to face up to reality.

Isiah stood behind Debapriya, who had stopped at the collapsible gate with her face buried in her hands. She removed her hands and their eyes met and she cried loudly and shrieked as if she had lost a close relation. He put his hand on her shoulder and stroked it while he tried to touch her face, but she backed off.

"I've wronged you, Isiah. I'm so terribly sorry."

She continued crying and he tried his best to understand her words between the sobs.

"I don't understand…"

He handed her the light blue newly washed handkerchief of linen from his chest pocket and stroked her slender fingers. She wiped away her tears, but the kohl left dark marks under her eyes. Then she took a deep breath while Isiah prepared for the worst. She walked up a flight of stairs and they sat down beside each other. Then she knelt down on the floor in front of him and put her arms on his lap. For a long time, they just stared at each other.

"I am betrothed, Isiah."

Her words suffocated him slowly. By now he was absolutely certain his heart had stopped, for he no longer felt it thumping in his chest cavity.

"His name is Sathananda Dasgupta and he returned from England two days ago. We have been betrothed since I was 12, but we all thought he would never come back for me."

Isiah stood up and backed towards the entrance door to his home, shaking his head and looking at her in disapproval. He despised her. That was the only emotion he could feel at that moment.

"Please say something, Isiah."

But he did not. Instead, he opened the gate and walked out in the foreign land of infidelity.

"Wait, Isiah!" he heard Debu shouting from upstairs, but he had no wish to listen to another pledge by the brother of the woman who had bewitched him.

Isiah bit his lower lip so hard that he could feel the metallic taste of blood, but continued browsing the pages of the book, perhaps a bit more in a frenzy than before. He sat in the Roy Chowdhury dining room as per custom on Sunday mornings. The lump in his throat would not subside now, he knew it. So, he stood.

"Please tell Debu I've gone out for a walk," he said to Debapriya with the little voice he had left.

"But your tea, Isiah…"

He could not turn around to face her once more that morning. Instead, he walked up to the door resolutely, opened it and stepped outside in the morning sun. After closing the door behind him, he leaned against it for some time and wiped the tears that had begun rolling down his cheeks. Then he began walking through the streets of the strange land. Even though four days had passed since she had made her announcement, there was no mention about it this morning, and he had no wish to be anywhere near her. The area was much less populated than Marquis Street in central Calcutta where his family lived. Tollygunge was the lush serene oasis, where the British came to relax or play golf. Every now and then he wiped his cheeks with the back of his hands. The tears kept falling, out of control, and the lump in his throat showed no sign of going away. How could she just give up on them like that? Why was he not worth fighting for?

He turned right at the little alley that led to the golf course, which was built as one of the first outside the British Isles in the beginning of the 19th century. A week earlier was when he first sensed something had changed. On that Sunday he noticed she had stopped given him affectionate glances. In fact, she had avoided him the whole morning. That evening, his little sister Hannah had knocked on his bedroom door and caught him with his contorted face full of tears. For the first time in his life that evening, he had shared his romantic adventure openly with another person.

"Why do you always have to take on impossible missions?" she had asked.

Her innocent words had made him laugh and when she left the room after giving him a steady hug, he had felt grateful to have such a loving and understanding sister. But the next morning, the agony came back and had paid him a visit every morning since then until that fatal Wednesday evening when he had learnt the truth. To dampen his inner voice, which seemed to care about nothing else but Debapriya, he had begun playing the piano in the mornings. Sometimes it worked and sometimes it did not.

Chapter 11

As they walked up Langhansstrasse the following Saturday, Tanushree heard the uncomfortable, but familiar sound of white power music. She had walked along this street in Weissensee several times before and this particular stretch along the tram line was lined with simple concrete buildings in different shades of yellow.

"This is one of the more racial neighbourhoods of Berlin if you are to trust the election polls," she explained as calmly as she could to Joshua, but his eyes widened and his lips parted as he inhaled quickly.

"I would be afraid to walk here, Tanu."

"You get used to it," she said trying her best to sound indifferent.

"At least it's not hidden racism," she continued in a quieter voice.

For a moment he stared at her from the side. She realised he had not taken to heart her attempt to calm him.

"I think you're capable of much more damage when you've crossed the limit of announcing your views in public," he retorted resolutely. She wondered to herself why the question was so close to his heart. After all, he was a middle-aged Caucasian man who grew up in one of the most multicultural cities in the world. She was far from that.

When they finally reached the Weissensee lake, Tanushree took out the red quilt from her rucksack and spread it out on the grass next to the water. Then she reached for their towels and finally put the bag on the quilt.

"Come on, I'll race you to the fountain," she shouted and hurried to take off the knee-length black dress she wore on top of her swimwear. Dressed in the dark purple bikini, she plunged into the water and began to take breaststrokes, but Joshua soon overtook her crawling.

"I've been waiting for ages," he said with a grin on his face when she finally reached the centre point of the lake where the fountain stood, all out of breath. He stood with his chest pushed out and gave her a cheeky smile. She smiled back and nodded her head at him. They continued swimming a few laps around the lake and he slowed down to breaststrokes to be able to swim next to her.

"I need something to drink," she wheezed when they had finished their third lap. They went back to where she had spread out the quilt. When she changed with the towel around her body and her back against him, she felt his eyes staring at her from behind. But after last weekend she had taught herself to neglect his signals. They just confused her and he had a pact with God. Instead of overthinking his behaviour, she sat down on the quilt and took out the cheese and bread from the rucksack. She poured two glasses of brownish Apfelschorle with gas for the two of them.

"That was a lot of fun. I rarely go out and swim," Joshua said in a cheerful voice biting into his slice of bread. Something had changed last Sunday night after he had opened up about his love life. He had become less serious, and he did not back off every time their bodies happened to touch. It was like she had taken off a weight from his shoulders. After finishing their snack, they walked around the circumference of the lake to the artificial beach on the other side, and sat down by a table under a parasol in one of the bars.

"I would like to have two cups of tea, please," Tanushree said to the bartender in German.

"I don't understand what you're saying," said the young man with a hair so blonde that it seemed to have bleached in the summer sun. There was something fierce in his voice and his eyes squinted at her. She repeated what she said, only in a quieter voice.

"Oh, tea, yes of course. All Indians like their tea, don't they? Perhaps it's time to go back to the plantations at home?"

"For your information, her home is in Sweden, not in India," Joshua said to the bartender in a threatening voice. His cheeks looked flushed and his jaw clenched. He shook his head at the bartender. Tanushree had never seen him angry.

"Let's leave, Tanu. They don't deserve you as their customer."

The two of them left the bar in silence. Tanushree was deep in thoughts. She had been a bit more affected by the bartender's attitude than she cared to admit, despite several previous encounters with that type of attitude in life. Joshua walked beside her in silence until she opened her mouth again.

"Come, I'll show you the Vietnamese market," she said. She forced her lips to smile when they reached the stop at Indira Gandhi Strasse and they got on the tram.

"No, I haven't…at least it hasn't been required," Tanushree replied to Joshua's question.

He looked at her in surprise where he sat behind his wooden kitchen table in Invalidenstrasse. The cold air came in through the sides of the kitchen window behind Joshua and caused goosebumps to form on Tanushree's arms. It was an old building with only double-glazed windows and not enough insulation for cold evenings.

"How come you've never met anyone? You're 32!" he exclaimed,

"And amazingly beautiful!" he added under his breath.

But she heard him and she was dumbstruck just long enough for him to notice she had overheard what he said. Their eyes locked for a moment, then she looked away pretending like nothing had happened.

"If I knew the answer to that I would be married and have children by now," she said in a joking tone.

"Have you been OK with it all along?" he asked.

"With what?"

"Never having a male companion by your side?"

"It wasn't OK when I was younger, I used to feel so awkward. But I've learned to come to terms with it."

He looked down at the light oak wood floor under their feet for a little while.

"Did the boys in your school make you feel awkward about yourself when you were younger?" She did not know where his question came from, but suddenly she thought about Rohini's first description of him that evening after the concert in Cadogan Hall. She had thought he was an odd-ball. There must be a reason he had brought up that question even if the topic was off-limits. She had brushed those thoughts off her shoulders her whole life and always forced her lips to smile whenever she knew it had affected her. She sat quietly pondering if she should mention all those times her classmates had frowned at her or how she was never invited to parties in higher secondary school. He looked at her from the side as he always did when he studied her, and nodded as if he already knew the answer to his question.

"I think I just belonged to a rare breed, Joshua."

She thought about the first time an immigrant living in Sweden had made comments on her skin colour. She had been disillusioned. After all, she always defended immigrants in school discussions because she knew how much they had to struggle. At the same time, she had understood she was just as exotic to ethnic Poles, Arabs, Persians and ex-Yugoslavians as she was to ethnic Swedes. Finally, the revelation that people were equally ignorant and prejudiced no matter where they had their roots, had made sense to her. He put his hand on her shoulder, but she was unable to talk. Then she heard him walk into the bathroom while she remained sitting on the foot end of his IKEA bed. His apartment always became a bit chilly after the sun had set. She rubbed her palms against her bare legs as she heard the water from the shower pouring down in the bathtub. She swiped across her right eyelid with her finger to prevent a tear from falling. She did the same thing to her left eyelid, but she could not do away with the lump in her throat. Her muscles became tenser and tenser. It was a necessary reaction in order to hold back an outburst. All kinds of negative events she had been reminded of when he had asked that question went through her head. Why had no one fought for her? Was she really that insignificant? Sometimes she even wondered if her mission in life would be accomplished when she was done with her musical journey. Maybe there was no point of living on if she was not even worth the love of a man. At last, she let out the tears she had been struggling to keep back since Joshua had asked the question. The white and red flowery dress barely covered her thighs and her legs were full of goosebumps. As she sat there the tears found their way down to the thin cloth of the short sleeveless dress. They gushed out now, but she muffled her cry. She put the side of her head on Joshua's pillow and let the tears run down her face and wet the pillowcase. A second later she heard another muffled cry from her mouth and tears fell uncontrollably. After a while, she fell asleep and only woke up when she heard the click of the bathroom door opening and the odour of fresh mint poured into the living room. Before she had opened her eyes, he was already sitting beside her on the bed stroking her face with his fingers. She knew he had seen her tears, but she had no energy left to pretend any more. He put one of his arms around her waist and the fingers of the other hand stroked her cheeks and wiped away the tears. He leaned down and put his forehead against hers so their nose touched. He rubbed his nose against hers and kissed her cheek. His fresh after-shave smelled heavenly.

"I think you're incredibly beautiful Tanu," he said, out loud this time.

"What about your celibacy," she asked seriously worried whether this was just a spur of the moment act on his part. He put his index finger to his mouth.

"Shhhh…Why were you crying, Tanu?" She felt his fresh breath in her face and opened her eyes. He leaned over her and she put her arms around him with her face buried in his neck like a child who needs to be carried. The smell of his aftershave was crisp. He pulled her up from the bed.

"Come, it's time for us to have dessert!"

He took out a big bowl with chocolate mousse from the refrigerator and put it on the kitchen table. Then he opened one of the kitchen drawers and took out two spoons. He handed her one of the spoons and kept the other one to himself.

"Dig in!"

She was surprised how the careful and tidy Joshua had invited her to eat from the same bowl as himself, an act which would inevitably lead to an exchange of bacterial flora. He saw her eyes lingering at the bowl and then at the two spoons.

"Let's forget about the rules tonight. OK?"

He smiled at her. She was puzzled.

"Umm…OK."

When she dipped her spoon in the chocolate it became absolutely silent and after a while, he eyed her up like that day at Harrow on the Hill a month earlier. They sat gazing at each other and her heart began to throb. Then he came over to her side of the table and put his arms around her waist.

"Will you sleep in my bed tonight?" he asked.

Her heart skipped a beat.

"I expect nothing but having you by my side throughout the night and wake up to the loveliest face I know in the morning."

His blue eyes looked like light sapphires in the light of the tea candles. His face had reddened and she could feel the heat from it against her skin. Yet neither of them made any attempt of kissing the other. Instead, he took her hand and led her to the bed. He laid her down on her back and landed next to her with his arm still around her waist. Tears kept falling down her cheeks, but she no longer knew if they were happy or sad. Her fingers reached for his face. She wanted to press her lips against his and explore other parts of his body, but she did not know if it was allowed in celibacy land. She knew he would not breach his contract with God. Instead, they lay there cuddling within the premises of what was allowed in Joshua Salisbury's world, the introvert physicist who had made a promise to God at 30, but whose loins in this awkward moment revealed to her what he really longed for.

She woke up beside him in the morning as per the pact they had made the previous evening, but she was scared her heart would break because she knew now what he felt for her even though their lips had never touched. In the heat of the moment when his fingers had caressed her face in the dark, and she could feel the heat from his face, he had whispered the three forbidden words into her ears. She had been speechless, but her lips had kissed his cheek and told him she never wanted them to be apart again.

"Good morning, beautiful."

Joshua leaned over and kissed her on the cheek as she lay in bed beside him. She wished she could stay in his arms forever not having to deal with his sacred bond or going back to her own island of solitude again. Secretly, she wondered what his expectations were, but it did not feel like a good time to talk about it.

"Why were you crying yesterday, Tanu?"

By his act the previous night she knew he had figured out the reason, but he wanted to hear her say it.

"I've never been in a relationship, Joshua. I've lived through disappointments over and over again and I've questioned myself, but was it due to racial prejudice I never met anyone? I honestly don't know, and I've always tried to be optimistic about other people."

Her voice broke. She hated how she could never discuss this topic without getting emotional.

"I love being with you, Tanu. Two years ago I used to live for your weekly emails. I'm sorry I stopped replying."

She wanted to know why he stopped writing, but at the same time, she wondered what he was trying to tell her now. Was it going to be the two of them? Then she looked into his eyes and kept her gaze steady. Her face felt warm and he had reddened just like the previous evening.

"So, is this pact with God negotiable?" she asked with a smile on her lips.

"May I have some alone time with Him to figure it out?" he replied.

Tanushree put the tip of her index finger against the snooze icon on the cell phone screen. It was only 5 a.m. but she made sure she had enough time to thoroughly look through the 30 000 words plus summary chapter of her PhD thesis like she had done on a daily basis over the past four days. While she lay there thinking about the work ahead, she forced her body to sit up in her bed, and she yawned with the right palm covering her mouth. Her lips felt dry against the skin of her hand, and when she licked them, there was a slightly metallic taste. It was probably a result of the past months of neglecting her body and health. She walked into the bathroom and splashed water on her face.

When she came out to the kitchen, she made herself a large cup of coffee, as per custom the past four days, and turned on the white Hewlett Packard laptop. In fact, it was not so white any more, it had both tea and curcumin stains. Since she was discharged from the hospital, she had made it a habit of drinking turmeric milk in the evenings to fall asleep easily. She began to read what she had written from the top, and here and there in the text, she entered missing words or letters, but at least the structure was fine now.

By lunchtime, she had finished correcting the summary chapter, after sitting glued to the computer screen for the previous seven hours. She decided to go down to the Vietnamese place just around the corner. So, she walked down the stairs slowly, closed the green wooden entrance door behind her, and went to the part of Schonhauser Allee, which was closest to the Rosa-Luxemburg-Platz U-Bahn station. She stepped into the restaurant and sat down by the table next to the window in the far corner, which she always opted for whenever it was vacant, so she could watch the people passing by outside. The young waiter in a short-sleeved black shirt with matching black smart pants came to her table.

"Was darf es sein?" he asked politely.

She pointed at the name of a rice noodle soup with shrimps. He nodded, jotted down what she had ordered on his pad, and took the menu card with him back to the kitchen. Her mind felt at peace, as she could finally sit down for a while, knowing she only had to click on the *send* icon. She was exhausted from work stress and emotional roller coasters, but from this evening she was going to begin her new dietary regime! She dared not think of how much weight she had gained during the past few months.

The waiter put down a large bowl on her table. The soup was steaming hot, and the smell of Thai basil and shrimp paste was mouth-watering. She took up the wooden chopsticks, picked up some rice noodles and brought them into her mouth. As delicious as it was, this was going to be her last carbohydrate-rich meal until she defended her thesis in October.

Children gushed out through the gates of the primary school in Torstrasse. The few trees in the street had begun to bloom and it was one of the last days of term. On this Friday afternoon, Tanushree and Joshua walked in the direction of Friedrichstrasse on the opposite pavement to the school in order to look for a book.

"Look at all those lucky children. Not a worry in the world," Tanushree said.

"Why do you think that?" Joshua retorted.

"Why? Do you think they all carry around the weight of the world on their shoulders?" she said.

"No, but I think children can be very different from each other. Some are more aware of themselves and the world around them than others," he said.

"Is that how it was for you?" she asked.

A lorry drove past them in the street and she moved closer to Joshua to hear what he was saying.

"Well, I wasn't the most sociable child, if that's what you're asking. Throughout the first year in primary school I sat on a wooden bench and watched my classmates play every time we had recess…and I rarely spoke up in class," he said.

Tanushree wondered to herself what kind of upbringing could make a child so self-conscious.

"And when you were at home, did you have friends to play with?" she asked.

"When I came home from school, Isiah taught me how to play the piano. He was one of my few friends in those days," Joshua said with his head bowed.

"So he lived with you?"

"Yes, he moved in with us when I was six. That was the year my grandmother and his sister Hannah passed away," he replied.

"Wasn't he quite old then?" she asked.

"He was 93, but he was an active man. He went for an hour-long walk in Hampstead Heath every single day, and when he came home, he spent hours and hours at the piano." Joshua's lips had an affectionate smile on them.

"What did you talk to him about?" Tanushree asked.

"He used to tell me anecdotes about his youth in Calcutta and mentioned your grandfather over and over again. That's why his name is etched on my brain."

"Do you remember any of his anecdotes?" Tanushree asked.

"Oh yes, many of them. When I first began school he told me about his own first days at Loreto house in Calcutta. He used to take me to school every day and he told me I was just like him, because he too had been aloof in social contexts as a young child. He seldom spoke to his peers and the older boys at school scared him," Joshua said while reminiscing.

"That's such a nice thing to share with a child who is having a similar experience," Tanushree said.

"Yes, he made me feel like I wasn't the odd one out, but in fact, I was a bit odd." Joshua chuckled.

"What did your parents say to you?"

"My parents were workaholics, and the few times they actually talked to my school teachers, the only thing they said to me back at home was to shape up. My mother was so scared I would get a neuropsychiatric diagnosis of some sort."

Tanushree could see now why Isiah had played such a major part in his life.

"Do you miss him, Joshua?"

"I felt very lonely when he passed away. I had no one to confide in any longer. With my parents, things went in through one ear and out through the other."

Tanushree nodded her head because she knew those emotions far too well.

They stopped in front of Kulturkaufhaus Dussmann in Friedrichstrasse, and she held open the door to him.

"There is a book about India written by VS Naipaul I recommend you to read if you want to get oriented in Indian history," Joshua said to Tanushree and pinched his nose while they got on the escalator.

They went up to the third floor and Tanushree picked up the book he talked about, in German. It was going to be her tool for ameliorating her German vocabulary and learn about her Indian roots. That early afternoon, she had finally submitted her thesis to the examination committee, so it was all in their hands now, and she could spend her days delving into her newly found field of interest. After paying for the book at the downstairs counter, they walked down to Unter den Linden, where they went into the city library. The building was still being refurbished, and it had been, ever since she moved to Berlin. Tanushree led Joshua to one of the quiet reading rooms. He sat down opposite to her behind his laptop and began to type, whereas she read the first few pages of the book she had just procured with an online dictionary to her help. From time to time, she glanced over at him. He stared at the screen so focused, as if he had shielded off the surrounding world. At times, he scribbled down formulas and keywords on a sheet of paper next to the Mac. She felt exhausted and not at all concentrated on what she had come to do. The adrenaline which had pumped in her blood the past few weeks had finally gone down. She walked up to him around to the other side of the table.

"I need to go home and take a nap," she whispered in his ear. She crossed her arms and held them close to her chest while glancing over at his screen. The cold room and wearing a dress with no sleeves caused the naked skin on her arms to become full of goosebumps, and she shivered.

"OK, I think I'll hang around for some time. See you tomorrow evening," he said and looked at her briefly. She was not even sure he had overheard her words.

"See you tomorrow evening." Then their eyes finally locked, and both smiled.

She wandered down the parade street, and felt a hot flush going through her body, but her face was cold and she longed for her bed.

Once in her apartment, she set the alarm for 3 p.m. When it rang, she was still as exhausted, but then she realised she had not had lunch. Her blood sugar level must have dipped. She cut a piece of rye bread and had it with cheese spread. After drinking a glass of water, she went down to do the groceries at Kaiser's. For a good few minutes, she just wandered around at the supermarket. It was hard to make decisions because she was still in a daze. Then she walked back to the entrance, picked up a shopping basket and bought groceries according to the list in her pocket. She looked forward to the home concert next week with Joshua and her closest friends in Berlin. Besides, they had a reason to celebrate.

Chapter 12

As Isiah's fingers travelled over the piano keys on Friday evening in the family's living room in Marquis street, he heard a knock on the door. He made his way to the door with dragging footsteps, which gave away his emotional fatigue, and wondered to himself who might be at the door at this late hour. They had already finished their Shabat dinner, so it was not an invited guest. By the sound of the hard knocks, it could also not be his grandmother. As he unlatched and opened the door, he saw Debu's concerned face in the dark of the stairwell.

"I'm sorry Isiah, I didn't know."

Debu clutched his friend's arm. A few hours had already passed since the last time they had met at the college. The past week Isiah had said few words to his friends.

"You didn't know about what?" asked Isiah while he crossed his arms and stared into his eyes.

He knew very well what Debendranath was alluding to, but pretended as if nothing had happened. It made the pain go away, at least for the moment.

"I didn't know about your feelings for my sister until very recently."

"Ehm…" Isiah bowed his head slightly hearing his shaky voice. Before he had said anything, Debu took the liberty to continue speaking.

"And we honestly didn't know that Sathananda would turn up at our doorstep one day after all these years he has been away in England," Debu said quickly, sounding a bit upset.

Isiah stared down hard at Debu's well-polished black shoes where he stood by the door. He wore the same facial expression he had more than a week earlier when Debapriya told him her honest opinion about their relationship. His father, who sat on the chair at the sofa table with the Statesman newspaper on the dark wooden table in front of him, leaned down to make eye contact with Isiah. The young heartbroken man finally looked up.

"Isiah, are you not going to ask your friend to come in?" said his father.

He opened the door slowly, but again crossed his arms on his chest. He had tried to put this behind him. Debu greeted Mr Cohen politely as he came into the living room and took off his shoes.

"What brought you here today?" he asked carefully and continued staring down at the floor as he walked ahead to lead Debu into his own bedroom.

"My sister looked so guilty when she explained to me you had gone out for a walk last week when we met at our house, I had to interrogate her. I'm sorry to have been so blind. My younger brother suggested to me once there was something going on between the two of you, but I just brushed it off," said Debu.

"It's alright. I suppose it wasn't meant to be," Isiah said, still speaking with a frail voice, but making eye contact with Debu this time. "There were too many hurdles in the way."

"Isiah, it can still be fixed. She told me she had feared our parents would not approve of the two of you. But she never dared to confront them." Debu leaned forward to make eye contact with Isiah again. He spoke faster than he usually did. It was clear he had come to see Isiah in a very upset state.

"She probably thought I wasn't worth it. The lecturer seems like a sophisticated man," Isiah replied.

Debu had the same compassion in his chestnut brown eyes as five days before when Isiah had come back to his own family home after the walk. He creased his dhoti and tucked it in so the cloth would hug his waist tighter.

"She's a wimp. I don't think you should beat yourself up if this is really the case. You need someone with a backbone, not a child who cannot stand up for herself. Like Chandramukhi! I've begun to notice my future wife has quite a character despite her young age."

The words made Isiah burst out in a smile, but he refrained from asking any personal questions.

It was only 5 a.m. but Isiah sat down by the piano in the family's living room. Almost seven hours had passed since his heart to heart talk with the older brother of the woman who had broken his heart. His fingers moved over the white keys. He felt like only playing in C major today, but he allowed his fingers to play a nocturne from Opus 55 by Chopin. His childhood piano teacher had been a young Parisian nurse who had come to Calcutta with her husband for work. She had taught him all pieces she knew by Frederic Chopin, and he had taken a liking to the melancholy of many of them. This was a mellow piece, so there was no risk of waking up the rest of the family. It suited his mood. While his fingers moved freely, he thought about what Jyotish had told him. Girls from zamindar families only married their own kind. It turned out he was right. How could he have been so foolish to believe in the impossible? But the next moment he thought about the visit to Jyotish's home and how his father had told them about the local zamindar who had ousted them from their home. At 8 am Hannah stepped into the living room.

"What is the matter, Isiah?" she exclaimed.

His younger sister had cut right to the chase. He knew he could not fool her, but he was in no shape of talking about his troubles.

"Let's go out and buy some sweets for our parents, shall we? It's Shabbat after all," he turned around and said to her.

She did not object. As soon as they walked out in the fresh air, he felt better. It was like he had left his troubled mind inside by the piano. Whenever Debapriya's face appeared in his head, he forced it away. Instead, he looked up at the impressive architecture, which surrounded them. She had no right to snatch his happiness away from him. His lifestyle in Calcutta had been carefree from birth and he had never before felt yearning for a woman who was out of his reach. The moment he laid eyes on her, he had made a vow to himself she was not going to change him, but yet she had managed to do him irreparable damage.

Hannah knocked on the door to the house in Bagbazar they often visited on weekends. Inside, lived an elderly confectioner who made *rossogollas* with his son and sold them to the masses. The Cohen siblings loved the sponge-like dairy-based sweet ball boiled in sugar water. As soon as they stepped outside the house, both siblings dipped their fingers in the clay pot and took out a *rossogolla* each. The spongy texture and the sweet syrup felt godly to Isiah's taste buds where he stood in the middle of north Calcutta.

"This is my granddaughter Nelly," Mrs Meyer said with pride after the sermon that Saturday afternoon. Isiah looked at the fair-complexioned girl, who wore a stylish mint-coloured velvet hat with a brosche on the part of the brim, which covered her forehead. The young girl stretched out her hand towards him. Her handshake was soft, and her thin lips smiled feebly.

"Isiah is studying for his BA degree at the Presidency College in town," his grandmother's friend told the oldest daughter of her only son. They stood in the

Maghen David synagogue. The rabbi had stood on the bimah and recited from the Torah rolls only twenty minutes earlier, but then he returned them to their case, and today's session had finished. It was December 8, and only two weeks left before Channukah, but this festive season he was going to spend with his friends to celebrate the wedding of Debu.

"How do you find Calcutta?" Isiah asked Nelly in order to begin a polite conversation.

"I haven't been around too much," she replied.

"But you live on Chowringhee. Surely, you must have had some kind of impression," he insisted.

"Well, the streets are certainly busier than Bombay," she replied after a moment's thought.

"So, what brought you to Calcutta, if I may ask?" Isiah asked.

"My parents thought it was time for Grandmother to have some company where she lives. After all, it has been many years since Grandfather passed away, and she's quite elderly now. So, they sent me to live with her."

There was a forced smile on her lips, and Isiah wondered if she had been reluctant to come to the city, but he decided not to push the issue further.

"I'm so glad the two of you have found something to talk about," the elderly, Mrs Yasmine Cohen, said to the two youngsters. It was not entirely true they had found something to talk about, but Isiah played along.

"Why don't you and your grandmother come for lunch at my place?" Yasmine Cohen exclaimed.

Nelly looked down with doubt in her eyes, but Isiah's grandmother, who was usually quite good at feeling people, made no note of it. The past half-a-year she had tried every week to get her grandchild to meet at suitable Jewish girl, so this was probably a kind of victory to her, Isiah thought to himself.

At Yasmine Cohen's table that afternoon, Isiah was seated beside Nelly. The whole situation felt a bit trite to him, but though unwilling, he did not oppose. He spread out the white textile napkin over his lap, and observed his young female neighbour doing likewise. It was just the two elderly ladies, Mrs Meyer and Mrs Cohen, and their two grandchildren, Isiah and Nelly. He knew Yasmine had really wanted him to find a Jewish partner, so he gave it his best. Mrs Cohen served them a goat stew and fried vegetables. The four of them had been given a glass of red wine each.

"Cheers," said Yasmine and lifted her glass from the dinner table.

"Dried apricots, walnuts and figs," Isiah heard a vendor shouting from the open window in the living room.

"They make such noise, these vendors!" said Yasmine and went up to close the window.

"What kind of books do you read?" asked Isiah and turned to Nelly.

"I'm not much of a reader," she answered. A bit frustrated that she never tried to keep up the conversation, he sighed, but gave it another attempt.

"So, what did you do in your leisure time in Bombay?"

"My parents and their friends often threw parties. There was always something to do on the weekends." Her voice had a longing in it, and for the first time, her face burst out in a smile.

"Oh, that sounds nice," he answered and spent the rest of the dinner in silence, while hearing Mrs Meyer and Yasmine discussing the successful lives of both their sons.

As Isiah practised the pieces fervently which he had been taught several years before by his music tutor Madame Beaulieu, his veins filled with an ungodly sentiment. His fingers pressed one key after another, while his mind imagined how Debapriya in a few months' time be sitting in front of the fire on the white marble floor in the Vikrampur home side by side with Sathananda. He knew his own absence would upset her, but that was exactly what his mind wanted. When he walked back from the living room to his bedroom after rehearsal that evening, he was met by Hannah who stood leaning against his door with her arms crossed. In her right hand was the ornate red and white invitation card to Debapriya's engagement.

"Isiah!" she exclaimed in a strict tone. She wore a navy-blue lace dress and her stocking clad legs were crossed as she looked at him with squinting eyes.

"Why did you not go for Debapriya's engagement party?" she said.

"It's none of your business. Could you please let me enter my room now?" Isiah said in an agitated tone.

"How could you? I thought you loved her. The invitation was for our whole family and you kept it to yourself."

"Yes, but she doesn't love me," he answered coldly. When he sat down by his desk, he sighed with exasperation and looked down.

"Who told you that? She definitely holds you in high regard. I can tell by the way she talks to you," Hannah answered.

"Why should I spectate while she joins another man in holy matrimony?" Isiah said provocatively and turned around and stared his sister in the eye.

"Get over yourself, Isiah. Stop being such a child. She chose another man to pay obedience to her parents, but you certainly did not make any attempt of convincing her to stay with you. She's not the only one at fault," Hannah yelled at him.

"She made it very clear we had no future," he said and pressed his lips together.

"No romantic future doesn't mean she doesn't like you as a friend. You are being very immature. Admit you did this to hurt her," his sister exclaimed.

She felt a kind of connection and empathy for Debapriya he did not understand. He was impressed by his little sister's analytical skill, but he had no intention of giving in to her. Instead, he forced his way past her to go back to the piano, and slammed the door behind him.

"You're being extremely immature," he heard Hannah's still girlish voice shouting from the hallway.

When she was gone, he went back to his bedroom. He lay down on the bed and when he woke up it was already 6 a.m. Sunday morning. What was he going to do with his day? Ever since the Roy Chowdhury's had come back from their vacation, he, Debu, Jyotish and Abdul spent their Sundays at their house and studied together as before. The siblings had their own cook, who usually prepared mutton, *chickpea daal* and *aubergine bhajis* on Sundays. Some days they even had biryani. The deserts were always brought by one of the three classmates. Isiah's bodily inertia made him stay in bed. Even though he could hear the happy chirping of sparrows, he felt no motivation to wake up. He was drained of all energy. Maybe he should not have spent four hours playing the piano every evening the past several days, but it helped him to bury his emotions. He had found it difficult to digest how Debapriya had whisked him off in favour of someone who had not given her any attention for years and years. That morning was the first of many the coming fortnight his body would refrain from leaving his bed.

Earlier that Sunday evening, Isiah threw a stone into the Hooghly River and carefully stepped down the stairs at Judges' Ghat. The rain had left a sheet of water on the ground. The last time he was there, he took Debapriya's soft fingers into his own hand and led her down. For a moment, her fingers had lingered in his grip as if they belonged there. Just like that day, he now sat down on the stairs with a clay cup filled with tea in his hand. The sun had begun to set and the fishermen had come back from their last trip for the day. His eyes filled with tears now, and one by one they rolled down his cheeks. The negative thoughts came back. He tried to picture what Sathananda must look like. He wondered what Debapriya's betrothed had which he himself lacked, apart from being a zamindar's son.

"Are you alright, my son?" an elderly Bengali gentleman asked from the base of the stairs. The man stood there with his cane to support him in one hand and looked out on the water just like Isiah. But he had turned around towards him suddenly and Isiah looked up.

"I'm fine, Uncle. Thank you for asking," he answered in his well-mannered fashion.

He forced a smile. From the look on the old man's sceptical face, it seemed like he was not convinced. But instead of asking more questions, the old man offered his silent company by remaining at the landing and looking out on the river branch, which emanated from the holy Ganges.

For a moment, Isiah thought about the words of Debu and Hannah. They both seemed to think he should have given another try. Was it true? Had he just given up on Debapriya in his fear of conflict? It was pitch dark now. He put his palms on his knees for support and stood up.

Chapter 13

I must admit the Roy Chowdhury siblings have spellbound me. I have never felt this welcome to a Hindu family before. For the first time in life, I feel part of society in a different way than I have before. I often mention Debapriya, but her brother, my dear classmate Debendranath is no lesser a person than her. In a short time, I have gathered that he has a keen interest in gender issues and socioeconomic equality just like myself. The other day, he brought me to one of his political party meetings. No matter what Jyotish says about the Bengali moneyed elite, Debu's words and passion have struck a chord in my heart. This is mainly because his interest lies in matters, I have pondered on for most of my life. Another reason I appreciate him is that he seems to see each new individual in a different light. He never judged me for not being active and forthright like himself. He seems to look through my doubts, and encourages me when I need it, but refuses to express it in words. I hope life will provide me with ample opportunities for us to get to know each other, and maybe one day even fight for our common causes together.

"It's the first time I've ever had an in-depth account of him," Tanushree said when Joshua finished reading the excerpt from Isiah's diary. Her lips quivered and she stared into space. It was Saturday morning. A day had passed since they last met, and they again sat at the table next to the book tree at Cafe Anna Blume.

"Isiah held him in high regard. Your grandfather seems to have been a beloved man with strong principles," said Joshua.

How lucky she was to have found him to show her the window to her past. The next moment, Joshua tried to catch her eye, and after a while, he put his hand on her arm.

"Tanu, the dreams and illusions you had when you were poorly, were not far from the truth."

He looked at her like someone who was about to give some bad news, and her heart began to throb. It was like she had suspected. He knew more than he had given her reason to believe.

"Can we take one step at a time, Joshua?"

"Of course!" he answered.

He touched her hand again, although hesitating a bit this time. He gazed at her as if to see how she had taken his last sentence.

"My grandfather kept diaries all his life and your grandfather is often mentioned. I know, because I have browsed through the pages, even though I have never read them word by word. Debendranath's life was not a bed of roses, Tanu. I just want to prepare you for what is to come."

Later that morning as Tanushree closed the bathroom door in her flat behind her carefully, she heard the welcoming sound of a well-tuned violin from the living room where she used to rehearse. The piece sounded familiar; it was the Gigue from Bach's second Partita, which she had been practising the evening before and left on the note stand. She sat down at the kitchen table and listened. Joshua was a skilled violinist; he played the quavers with ease, evenly and at a high pace.

After a while, it became quiet. He had noticed she sat at the kitchen table and was hurrying to pack up the instrument. Half a minute later, she ambushed him.

"That sounded great. You're a very good violinist," she said.

"Sorry for using your sheets, I just hadn't played that gigue for a very long time," he replied.

She could feel her cheeks changing colour as he addressed her, and she had to lower her gaze so that he would not notice her reaction. He had come in the early morning because she had invited him for lunch at her place. Only a few days had passed since they last met and spent the night in his bed together. All kinds of thoughts had revolved in her head the past days, but luckily her thesis had distracted her. It was true that the way he looked at her sometimes with his beautiful expressive eyes swept her off her feet especially after that night, but his subtle acts of boldness made him special. She had seen evidence of his boldness quite a few times by now. The fact that he had been daring enough to go in and play the violin pieces she had left on the stand in the living room intrigued her. He could go from the extreme of being quiet and withdrawn to being really sociable and bold at times. His stare was enough to keep up the short-term attraction, but his gestures made her want to tread on a life full of adventures with him, and yet she was not allowed to.

"How long have you been playing the violin?" she asked. "I thought you were a pianist." Then she thought about the poem in the Calcutta book. Was it the violin that had made his fingertips go numb?

"It's a long and complicated story, but I started playing when I was five," he replied shortly with the hands in his pockets.

"A long and complicated story?" she asked.

"Yes, I had better tell you some other day. Go on and rehearse now! That's an order!" He smiled and winked at her. She loved his moment of mischief.

When she came into the kitchen after rehearsal, she found him waiting at the dining table for her. He had taken the liberty to prepare lunch for the two of them. It was grilled trout with rosemary served with aioli and boiled potatoes. "Tell me about your long and complicated story with the violin," she begged while watching Joshua pouring the white Merlot in her glass.

"Well, I used to spend hours and hours rehearsing every day when I was younger, both the piano and the violin. Grandfather Isiah passed down his passion for music to me as well as his piano, and I was accepted to the Royal College of Music in London."

"I didn't know you had studied music," Tanushree said.

"I guess I haven't revealed all of my dark secrets to you yet." He smiled.

"So, how was it studying at the Royal College of Music?" Tanushree asked.

"I really enjoyed it. Everyone loved what they did and the teachers were very inspiring."

"Wasn't it competitive?" she asked.

"Yes, people think it is an elitist school, and in many ways it is. There was definitely jealousy, but most of them were not at all as competitive as you would think," Joshua replied.

"Why do you think that was the case at such a prestigious institution?" She took a sip of her rosemary water.

"I think they just didn't have time for it! They were people who had been practising hard since they were children and never learnt how to make somebody else's misfortune their own happiness. We were young, we had high expectations, the frustration and the stress had not left their traces yet. There were days when I practised for ten hours and I really had a passion for it."

"And then you became a theoretical physicist? What happened?" Her questions were almost as direct as he had been a few days earlier, she noticed.

"It was a tough life for me, both with respect to theoretical studies and practising music and then there was the time you had to invest in it... You probably know better than me what classical musicianship can be like. It's easy to drown. I started feeling that there was so much I had missed in life! Things that other people did at my age...I felt the work I was putting down would never be appreciated if I didn't make it to the top, and if neither I nor my audience would appreciate it enough, what was the point of continuing? Besides I work in the field of acoustics, so I'm not completely off."

He finished his story abruptly, smiled and stood, as though he worried he had intimidated her by opening up too much. His story spoke to her. She recognized all those emotions.

"So, you gave up playing the violin because of self-doubt?" she asked.

"So it seems, self-doubt got the upper hand. I finished my BMus with a first, but I just knew at the end of it that I wasn't cut out to be a musician. I actually haven't performed since my graduation concert at music college."

A part of her got upset on his behalf. How could he give up? Did he not have any teachers who could mentor him? She at first avoided asking those questions only not to stir up emotions in him, but she could not hold back.

"How was your musicianship looked upon in your family and friend circle?" she asked thoughtfully.

He ran his fingers through his hair, became silent and looked down at the table again.

"People weren't exactly too pleased by my choice of profession," he replied after a while.

"What did they say?" she asked.

"My parents thought I didn't care about my finances. My former classmates often told me I was a slacker and a bohemian."

"When in fact you were highly disciplined and very skilled at what you did," Tanushree finished his sentence. She knew because she had experienced it herself.

"How about performing with me next weekend?" Tanushree challenged him. His cheeks turned red, his eyes looked worried and he cleared his voice.

"It's really just a small piece. Rohini has already told me what an amazing pianist you are," she said.

"Umm…" His doubt made him look down at the floor.

"Come on, it will be fun! You just need to accompany me. I'll walk you through the piece this afternoon." She said cheerfully and touched his shoulder.

The day finally came! It was the day of Joshua's first performance since music college, which Tanushree hoped would break his vicious circle of low confidence and refraining from playing. She dressed up in a half-sleeved black silk dress, and a turquoise pashmina shawl. She wore a pearl necklace and little white silver earrings. For the occasion, she had even put on foundation, powdered her cheeks with rouge and used the dark red lipstick Rohini had given her for Christmas. Light blue eye shadow accentuated her eyes and she rimmed them with kohl. She felt different as she rarely wore make-up. But then she looked herself in the mirror. She was surprised by what she saw, but pleased by the effect.

At quarter to eight in the evening, someone knocked on her door. It was Joshua.

"Are you ready?" she asked with a smile upon opening the door.

"Yes Madame, I am. You look absolutely stunning," he said and inhaled. His chest was slightly pushed out. She liked when he showed confidence. It made her dare opening up to him too.

By his tone and the way he looked at her, she could tell he was sincere.

"Thank you, Professor Salisbury!" She smiled.

They took their positions in Tanushree's living room, where the audience of seventeen people was waiting for them to open the evening. He at the piano and she by the silver note stand next to it, with the violin and bow in her hands. As they began to play, her bow had its own life. It kept control throughout the piece. She could hardly feel her right-hand moving. Her face felt warm partly because of the make-up, and partly because of the intensity of the piece. She had not felt such a verve for a long time. From time to time, Tanuhsree smiled towards Joshua. He looked unusually calm and focused. Recalling his life story, she could not help but feel proud of him. Half-way through the gigue, right before the quavers, he smiled back at her from behind the piano. He looked happy. After they finished playing the gigue by Bach, there was applause from the audience who were mostly old flatmates and colleagues. They both stood up and bowed. She finished the soiree with four pieces, Fyra Akvareller, by the Swedish composer Tor Aulin.

"Tanu, I feel tired. Would you mind if I went back to my place?" She wondered if it was all the people around him that made Joshua exhausted. Or was it Akash's judging eyes? He was Mr Perfect according to her parents, the son of their friends from Calcutta, and she knew he had a crush on her and their parents had even tried to persuade the two to marry a few months ago, but Tanushree hadn't been interested. She had sensed his eyes looking at both of them from the audience. To her surprise, he had shown up at the recital, making the long journey from Leipzig. Although she had told Joshua about Akash, she did not want him to feel scrutinised by the man who was considered the ultimate marriage material by her parents. She wanted to ask if Joshua enjoyed the recital, but from his facial expression when they played, she took it he had. She let all questions go unanswered, and instead gave him a peck on the cheek and let him walk out alone in the night.

"Good night, Joshua. You were great today!"

He gave a feeble smile and then went out. When the front door closed behind him, she sighed. She leaned her back against the door, clasped her right wrist with her left hand and just stood there for a moment looking down at the floor. Oh, how she wished, he would take her words to heart!

She went back to the living room again and saw Akash talking to her lab colleague, Elodie. So, she engaged in a conversation with one of the new residents that lived in the flat she had stayed in two years ago in Charlottenburg. From time to time, she could feel Akash's gaze on her, but she avoided him. She knew it was not a very smooth move, considering that he would soon be miles away, and they probably needed to talk after all the efforts their parents had put down.

It was 1 a.m. already. The wine she had been drinking was making her drowsy. She wanted to be alone with Akash and tell him about Joshua, but the last guests were just about to leave. "I'm going back to my hotel, Tanushree." He hugged her firmly and held onto her a little bit longer than usual. There was more than friendliness in the hug, and with all the unresolved issues around Joshua, it made her very uneasy.

"Good night. You were amazing today, Tanushree," Akash said.

For a moment, she wished they could talk, but he showed no sign of wanting to do that. He had closed that chapter for the evening, even though his body said otherwise. She could feel it from his way of addressing her. She just wanted to be honest to him. She wanted to say Joshua was different and she wanted to have his understanding and part as friends. At the same time, a part of her felt relieved. He stepped back, turned and went for the stairs. Back in her room, she could not hold back her tears anymore. In fact, she was quite relieved Akash claimed to have moved on from their parents' ridiculous proposal, but the whole episode had made her exhausted and she knew she still had to confront her parents about it, and disappoint them again. She slid down with her back against the window and sat down on the window sill, but then turned and looked down. She could still see him walking down Lottumstrasse talking to Elodie. He had brought the plastic whiskey glass with him and smoked a cigar. Akash did not look as cheerful as the past few times she had seen him at his parents' place. She even caught him looking up towards her window as if he felt she was hiding behind the curtain. There was something in his eyes. A feeling of uncertainty, she had felt the whole evening, and who would blame him after noticing the chemistry between her and Joshua.

When she woke up and looked at the alarm clock the morning after the recital, it was already ten. Instead of taking breakfast, she walked down Torstrasse and went to call on Joshua's entrance door intercom. She wanted to tell him she was going to be an hour late for their rendezvous at Hauptbahnhof and invite him for breakfast, but no one opened the door. Somehow, he had managed to get up earlier than her, and had already left the flat. Tired of waiting by his door, she made her way back to her own kitchen to prepare breakfast for the two of them. She began mixing a pancake batter. When she opened the door to the refrigerator, an envelope fell down from the top rack. In it was a small piece of paper with something scribbled on it in black ink. She stooped down to pick up the note from the floor.

Tanushree, I can see you have found someone to make you happy. I have accepted your decision. We should not let this get between us. Come and visit me in Leipzig if you can. Please don't be mad, I'm not good with goodbyes.
Akash

This was highly unexpected! So, this was why Akash had not stayed to talk yesterday. Whatever did he mean by *I have accepted your decision?* It was as if he owned her. She shook her head and poured some batter in the frying pan. After she had fried all the pancakes, she waited two hours for Joshua to call, but there was not a single trace of him.

117

Two hours turned into two days, and then followed more days. Every day, she called Joshua at breakfast, lunch and dinner, but no one picked up. On Thursday, she went to his apartment building again, but to no avail. The time passed slowly after the evening of the recital when Akash and Joshua had both left. Neither of them had said a proper goodbye in person, but at least one of them had the courtesy to write her a note. She emailed Joshua on the Friday six days after the recital, but again, there was no immediate response. She found herself spending most of her time on her own, struggling to find the energy to wake up in the morning. The Monday after writing the email, she forced herself to go out running as she had vowed, but the air was slightly cold, and it was becoming harder to breathe fast for each day that passed. So, running was not a good way to find energy in the prevailing weather conditions. It was late September now. She was alone. She had been alone well over a week, feeling empty, and there were mornings when she just wanted to go back to bed and cry in despair. She could not put her finger on what it was, but something had made her feel very connected to Joshua. It was a feeling she seldom had about anyone. In fact, the last time a man had moved her in that way was nine years ago. She had asked him out on a date and went on her first date at the age of twenty-four! They had visited the Victoria and Albert Museum, and talked about immigration politics and the nature-nurture debate for seven hours. But the next day, she received an email saying he did not see their relationship going anywhere. After waiting so many years for a romantic liaison, it was just a bit too much for her. She had gone into a depression and lost confidence in herself. For many years, she buried herself in work and extra-curricular activities pretending to be free as a bird gave her ultimate happiness.

She had dinner with Elodie on the Wednesday one and a half weeks after the recital. Her colleague said an uplifting thing or two, but it was not the same without Joshua. On Saturday morning, two weeks after the recital, the tears she had held back for so long began to run down her face. She cried because for the first time in life she let down her defences and allowed someone to acknowledge that she was not worth fighting for. Why did she long for someone who was doing her harm? The heart certainly had its mysterious ways. She cried again because she never stayed in one place long enough to get to know people, and she cried because she gave strangers the impression that she was an introvert. She wiped away the tears, and the next morning at the breakfast table, she cried because of the shame of having fallen in love with someone she had not got to know well enough. Berlin had become her enemy; day by day, she realised how much she did not want to stay there.

As she sat there at the table, she began imagining what her future would be like. She would not always be alone. During the days, she would be surrounded by her colleagues, and once in a while she would meet acquaintances for drinks, go out for a pub quiz or spend more evenings dancing away the pain, but she would have no one in Berlin to explore her family history with. She wanted to remain a brave young woman, put on those trainers and go out running in the morning. After coming home, she would be on a monoamine kick and feel good about herself. She felt an immense connection to Joshua, and just because he had left without a trace, still a part of her felt bad about what had happened with Akash.

On Monday evening, she sat down and gave the first version of her PowerPoint presentation a final touch. After all, there were only four days left now for her first rehearsal of the defence of her thesis. But she allowed herself to check her emails again. She checked several times, and was hoping Joshua would reply, but there was nothing in her inbox. She tried to call his phone and the answering machine picked up. How can someone so wonderful just cut off all contact like that? She would give the world to know what was going on in his head that evening of the recital. She sensed something was the matter. A part of her became very worried while she sat there behind her laptop, and she called Rohini.

"He hasn't picked up the phone or responded to my emails for two weeks!"

"Maybe it's time for you to call his parents, Tanu. There is something you don't know about him."

Chapter 14

They could see land from the steamer on the Padma River now. It was mid-December and on the water lay a thin mist. Two men were standing on the shore with a cow carriage. It was Isiah Cohen's first time on the other side of the river, even though many of his classmates originated from East Bengal. The first trip was going to be in the city of Dacca. They were supposed to stay in the townhouse of the Roy Chowdhury family until the engagement of Debendranath and Chandramukhi, and later move on to the family estates in Vikrampur. In Dacca, four palanquin carriers took them to an old part of the city from the Nawab Dynasty. The house had a large inner court and arched verandas. As Debendranath's three classmates entered the court, trays of sweets were escorted in by servants. On a stage in the inner court sat their friend on his chair ready to get engaged to his soon to be much-beloved wife, Chandramukhi Basu Roy, who sat next to him.

The court was full of visitors; the women were clad in silk saris and glittery jewellery. Some of the men wore ornamented turban-like headgear. Laughter and loud speech could be heard everywhere. Isiah, who had never been invited to a Hindu wedding before, looked around him in bewilderment. The sound of the blowing in the conge pierced the whole inner court they stood in. Debendranath took up a Sandesh as carefully as he could from the packet and fed Chandramukhi with the sweet. He observed his future bride with what seemed to Isiah as fondness and admiration. It was funny how a few days of acquaintance could turn into attachment.

Debapriya and her fiancé stood in a corner of the court next to the stage, overlooking the ceremony. At times, she looked away dreamily. In an otherwise boisterous family, she had always seemed out of place to Isiah. He had set eyes on her before during the past hour, but not dared to walk up and speak to her. What would he say? How would he explain the feeling that made him stay back at home for her engagement? He imagined what their conversation would be like, had they been strangers.

"This must be quite an event for you, hosting your brother's engagement," he would say.

"Yes, Mr Cohen, he is the first one of us to get married. Always plenty of preparations to make around these kinds of events. I have to admit I am quite exhausted, being in large crowds does that to me," he imagined her reply.

He would smile at her and explain to her he could very well relate to the exhaustion of social gatherings, he was a bit of a loner himself.

"What do you do when you are not busy preparing for weddings, Debapriya?"

"Well, I'm often busy with my studies and singing. I have been home-schooled. But I am moving to Calcutta to attend Bethune College soon."

"Well, then our paths will cross again. I take it you will be staying with your brother."

"Yes, Mr Cohen."

Isiah would smile a bit at the thought of having her near him in Calcutta, and she would lead Isiah out to the little garden on the backside of the house. They would sit down on a bench.

"I usually hide out here when the crowd becomes too rowdy," she would confide in him. Then their hands would touch by chance.

His daydream was suddenly interrupted by the penetrating sound of someone blowing in the conge. At the same time, from the other corner of the hall, he sensed someone's eyes on him. It was another gaze of disdain from Jyotish Ganguly, who had caught him staring at Debapriya. He had thought so much about her that he had little attention to spare her betrothed, who looked like a dandy straight from a theatre play.

On a chair in the corner of the hall room in the Dacca townhouse, sat the friend Debu wanted to introduce Isiah to.

"Harun is my oldest friend."

He was a quiet withdrawn young man, who did not make many attempts to mingle with the rest of the crowd.

"His father was a farmer of the village and his mother took care of me when I was a little boy. Harun used to come with her to work and we played every day," Debu smiled and the skin around his eyes crinkled.

When they approached Harun, Debu switched to Bengali, but Isiah could still follow the conversation and replied back in a staggered accented Bengali.

"This is my classmate Isiah," Debu put his hand on Isiah's shoulder.

The young withdrawn man put his two palms together to greet Isiah in the traditional way, and he did likewise. Harun wore a topi cap with holes on the top between the blue embroideries. His dress was not as fancy as the others Isiah noted. The greyish-silver *salwaar kameez* looked rather dull in comparison to the glamour in the hall. Debu brought a chair for Isiah to sit on.

"Why don't the two of you get acquainted with each other?" Debu said.

"Are you still living in Vikrampur, Harun?" asked Isiah.

"Yes, I have taken over my father's farm. I live there with my mother and wife."

"Did you attend Mr Roy Chowdhury's school when you were younger?" Isiah asked curiously.

"Yes, I was lucky to study there for a few years in my younger days, but then duty called, and I had to help my family to afford their daily bread," Harun replied.

"I'm sorry to hear that," Isiah responded.

"No, that's alright. I consider myself quite lucky to have something to make my living from, and I at least had a few years of schooling. That's more than most people can boast about where I come from," he explained.

The moment he heard his East Bengali accent, it dawned on Isiah that in his universe it was such a natural thing for men to educate themselves and gain a university degree that he had never looked at the world the way Harun did.

"I know Calcuttans view the world in a different way, but we villagers in East Bengal are actually quite content with our simple lives," Harun mused.

It was as if he had read his narrow-minded thoughts. Isiah's ears turned red and he studied his feet for a moment.

"I would be happy to welcome you to our humble abode, Isiah. Why don't you and your friends come over for breakfast when we reach Vikrampur?"

The first morning in Vikrampur when the four of them had arrived at the front door of Harun's family and Debu knocked, an elderly woman clad in a white saree answered.

"Oh, my darling boy. Look at how you've grown," she exclaimed.

Debu bent down to touch her feet, and she took him in her arms. The house was simple indeed. The straw roof framed the clay house like a fringe. Inside there were only two rooms. The larger one was where they were to have their breakfast, and the smaller one only had two beds in it. Outside, on a string hung newly washed clothes. The elderly woman put out banana leaves on the floor, where she asked the young men to sit down. She and her young daughter-in-law did not join them for their meal. Instead, they were busy preparing food on an open fire outside the house. Isiah could smell the appetising odour of deep-fried bread, luchi, and his mouth watered. From a small stable outside the house, they heard the sound of cattle.

"This is our little princess mooing. She provides the whole family with milk every day. We also have hens. I'll show you after breakfast," said Harun.

When they had finished eating, Harun came in with a mug full of water. He poured it on Isiah's hands while he rubbed his palms and fingers against each other. Once more, he was impressed by the open-mindedness of Debu. Who would have known his closest childhood friend would be a Muslim peasant, whose mother had been a servant of the Roy Chowdhurys'?

On the way home, Isiah walked next to Debu.

"I can see why you enjoy your life here," Isiah said.

"Yes, I'm free of all my worries here," said Debu.

"Are you not worried about married life?" Isiah asked.

"Of course I am, but don't tell anyone," Debu whispered.

They both smiled.

"My father has promised to help us with our finances until I finish my legal studies, but there is so much more to married life than money," he continued with his eyes wide opened.

"I hear she has been quite pampered by her parents," said Isiah.

"Yes, it's true, dear friend. Her father owns a cinema hall and numerous businesses. On top of it, she's the oldest child in the family," Debu replied.

Then he cleared his voice and looked down with a creased brow. He looked behind as if he did not want anyone to hear him.

"She has grown very particular about her appearance due to her upbringing. When her family travels to Calcutta, they always stay at expensive hotels," said Debu in a quiet tone so that only Isiah could hear.

Debendranath turned the key of the brass colour padlock. He disentangled the chains and pulled open the heavy gates for his three friends to enter. Inside was a statuette of a blue-skinned Krishna with a golden flute standing next to his beloved Radha. This was one of the temples owned by the Roy Chowdhury family in Vikrampur. Although Jyotish Ganguly was the only one who shared his faith, the others were well-versed with Hindu mythology through classical music and theatre. Debendranath himself had read the Quran, the Bible and the Upanishads.

The three men went back to the pink gravel road. In those days, few roads were paved in the rural areas. They sat down on the marble stairs leading to the pond. A male servant wearing a turban came with terracotta mugs filled with tea on a dark wooden tray. Isiah sipped on the hot Darjeeling tea. Every morning, the family got milk from one of the peasants in the village. He could feel the freshness of the thick creamy cow milk.

"It's quite a beautiful place you have here. I can understand why you are unwilling to leave everything behind and move to Calcutta for good," Abdul now expressed what Isiah had told him the evening before. It was clear they were all taken by the landscape.

"Yes, this is where I grew up partially. I have a strong bond to the place and always find peace of mind when I am here. I wake up in the morning and come to sit by the pond only to hear the birds chirp and smell the blooming water lily," said Debendranath.

"You seem to live in such harmony with the people of the village. Your father has even taken it upon himself to educate their children," said Jyotish. Isiah was grateful that Jyotish had noticed this fact. Maybe it would help him look more open-mindedly on the moneyed elite.

"Yes, the only way to make people self-sufficient and allow them to form independent minds is education. Often, they have to begin hard labour at a young age due to lack of money. My father hopes some of his poorer students will go on to higher education or at least to clerical jobs."

As they were having their high tea, the sun began to set. The servant came back to collect their mugs.

"Let us go in, gentlemen. This place will be full of mosquitoes by the evening," said Debendranath.

At the entrance to the mansion were two guards who opened the gates to the four youngsters. The two-storey building was made of white marble with big arches at the front and had about fifty rooms. Like the townhouse in Dacca, there was an inner court with a stage, only filling a much vaster space. This evening, Debendranath's father had invited a well-known sarod player. Many gentlemen and a few women from the nearby villages as well as relatives who were there for the wedding celebrations had come to attend the concert. The music room, the so-called 'jalsaghar', had a black-and-white mosaic tiled floor. In the ceiling hung a chandelier and the walls were full of paintings of family members of earlier generations. The sarodist was a short, bearded man wearing a khaki-coloured salwar kameez and a black topi cap. On his right side sat a young tabla player who was there to accompany him. As he finished his alaap, the words 'kya baat' could be heard from the audience.

The next day, Isiah Cohen, Abdul Huq and Jyotish Ganguly accompanied the rest of Debendranath's family to begin the train journey to the bride's home in Comilla. Hers was also the home of landholders – a so-called zamindar family. The father was a manager of a tea estate in Darjeeling and the family owned a cinema hall in Calcutta. In those days, intermarriage was common between *zamindars*, and Debendranath had agreed to this even though he had social liberal values.

Two days later in the middle of the night, Debendranath and Chandramukhi sat on the floor in the hall room of the bride's parental home and said their vows in the presence of a priest. Isiah watched with deep curiosity as the couple walked around the fire seven times and poured rice grains on it.

"Jyotish, do you know the symbolism behind walking around the fire seven times?"

"It is known as *saptapadi* in Sanskrit. I believe it is done to wish Lord Agni for important elements of a happy marriage. Each round represents a certain element like wealth, food and children and so on," Jyotish replied.

"And the rice grains?" asked Isiah.

"They are poured on the fire to pray for a long and prosperous life," he answered.

Across the hall, he spotted Debapriya and Sathananda again. The young couple had not come from Vikrampur with them, but only arrived in Comilla on this evening. He let his mind wander again, and think about what he would have said to her, had they still been on good terms.

"So, Debapriya, do you think you will get along with your sister-in-law? You seem to have very similar upbringings."

"Yes, the only difference is that her father does not want her to have a higher education. My brother is planning to sponsor her anyway. But to answer your question, yes, I think I will get along with her. She seems to be a bit domineering. You know, she is the eldest child in her family. I tend to get along with people like that because I tend to be more on the quiet side. When it comes to my brother, I don't know."

"He looks at her very affectionately," Isiah would say. Then their eyes would lock and Debapriya would give him one of her charming smiles.

"Come, let me show you the kitchen, Mr Cohen." His daydream was once again interrupted, but this time by Debendranath's younger brother.

The kitchen was like a factory. There were cooks and caterers everywhere. In the middle of the room, bread dough was being rolled and deep-fried. Along the sides, the caterers stood with big pots of red lentil daal, pulao rice, mutton and hilsa fish. They were even making the sweet dishes themselves.

"Isn't it mouth-watering?" Narendranath asked.

"Yes, Narendra, it smells delicious," said Isiah.

"Dada always tells me I have a big appetite and I have to admit, I'm rather greedy. But don't the mixture of spices just tickle your senses, Mr Cohen?"

"You're a very entertaining young boy," He smiled at him.

Towards the end of the ceremony the bride crushed terracotta cups with her bare feet and it reminded Isiah of the Jewish traditions of crushing glass with the feet during the wedding ceremony. He liked looking for resemblances between religions and cultures. Maybe because he was tired of the prejudices of the elderly in his own congregation. He had worked hard to learn Bengali to melt in with his classmates. He had strong principles, but he was not as outspoken as Debendranath, so it usually took people years to figure him out. Because of his introvert character, he was probably the most misunderstood among the four men.

After the dinner, on the night of the wedding, Debu asked Isiah to join them for a game night. All the siblings and close friends of the bridegroom and the bride were there. It was the first time, his eyes met Debapriya's, since he had gone out on the walk in Tollygunge. Her cheeks had a crimson tone and her face was radiating. She looked more dazzling than the first time he had set eyes on the young girl in her dark blue silk saree, a few months earlier. He felt her staring at him for a long time before he looked up. Her face was flushed by now, and her jaw clenched. She was probably still angry at him for not attending her engagement ceremony, and with all rights. Her partner, whom he had not yet officially been introduced to, looked in another direction as if he could not care less of what was going on between his betrothed and the stranger across the bedroom.

"Hello," his mouth mimed, but she was still seemingly upset. Debapriya nodded towards him. For a moment, their eyes locked and her face turned into one which showed empathy, just like in his daydream. But her eyes did not linger on him, and before the lump in his throat became too large to handle, he forced himself to look away. There was no newspaper or book to shield him this time.

At 6 a.m. when all the guests went to bed, he walked down to his bedroom and read the letter Debu had brought him the day Debapriya had announced her relationship to another man. He had brought it with him in his bag to finally read it. He held the envelope to his face to see if there was any trace left of the rose perfume, but it was gone.

After reading, he curled up in his bed and cried because he felt helpless. It would have been easier if she had not shared the truth with him. There was no way he would be able to sleep now. So, he went downstairs to the hall room, and there she was waiting for him at the last step of the marble stairs. It was as if she had read his thoughts.

"Ehm, are you not planning to sleep, Debapriya?" Isiah exclaimed the moment he saw her.

"How can I sleep when you refuse to speak to me? Why can we not just act like civilised people?" she said?

The anger in her face had subsided, and it was clear she had been shedding tears.

"How did you know I would come here?" he asked.

"I know you, when something occupies your mind, you go out for a walk to clear your thoughts, just like me." She smiled towards him, but it felt like a pinch, because he knew he would not be able to have that smile to himself any longer. After a moment, he shook his head in disapproval.

"Oh no, you don't know me at all. If you did, you would never have treated me like you have," he shouted. He pointed his finger at her and his face felt warm.

"Shhhh, the whole house will wake up," she said with a quavering voice and hunched her shoulders.

"I just read your letter," Isiah said to her, still with a resolute voice, but a little quieter this time.

"Yes, there are places in life not worth exploring, Isiah, simply because they're uninhabitable."

"I see. Don't think I have any emotions left for you. You vile woman!" he said and stared her right in the eye.

She stood up and took a quick breath. Then she put her hand to her mouth and glanced at him with her eyes wide open.

"Isiah…" She tried to look him in the eyes, but he turned away his face and stared out in the open.

Without looking at her, and with a stern face, he said in an irritated voice,

"You'd better go up to your family before anyone sees us together."

Debapriya stood up, followed his order and made her way up the stairs, but she gazed at him from behind all the way to the first floor. Only when she was out of sight did he turn his face towards the stairs and repented uttering those venomous words to one of the women he loved the most.

Chapter 15

Tanushree was surprised to hear the buzz on the intercom when she rang Joshua's doorbell on Wednesday for the fifth time that week. As she walked into the courtyard to the hinterhaus and began to step up the stairs to the fourth floor flat, the anger she had felt the past weeks subsided into worry. Much was due to what Rohini had told her on the phone only two days earlier. For every flight of stairs she walked up, her heart throbbed a little bit harder. She began to imagine what had held him in his flat for two whole weeks. She had a hunch, but she waited for him to acknowledge her suspicions. The moment she pushed the bell on the door to his flat, it flung open. It was as if he had waited by the door for her to come up. He was standing by the entrance, newly showered, in a T-shirt and a pair of jeans. She had never seen him dressed down before. His face looked dazed and his bloodshot eyes gave him away.

"Hi," she whispered and looked at his face.

"Hi," he whispered back.

She could not find any other words to say, and neither could he, apparently. For a moment, they just stood there looking at each other. Then they both burst into smiles. She walked up to him and stroked his cheek and lips with her fingers, looking steadily into his eyes. Before she knew it, he put his hands on her waist, drew her closer and leaned down to press his lips against hers. It was a gentle first kiss.

"Oh, I've missed you so much," she said and looked up at him through her dark lashes.

She noticed on the stubble on his chin that he had not been shaving. His rustic side was new to her, but very attractive. After they both had drunk their cups of tea, Joshua led her to the sofa to watch a film. It was a Marguerite Duras story with little dialogue, which took place in Calcutta. She had seen it before. When it finished, she noticed he had dosed off beside her. She covered him with a quilt and kissed his cheek. Then she turned off the TV and went to the kitchen to rinse their cups. Suddenly she heard a murmur from where he was sitting. He turned his head.

"Stop hurting me. Please stop," she heard him mumble.

When she turned around, he was still fast asleep. The flat was so quiet, and it was already dark outside and a bit chilly in the flat. Her thoughts went to his violin story and how he was treated by the girl he fancied. It must have left its traces. She could not even imagine what kind of pressure he must have grown up under.

"Joshua, I'll get going. Do you want to move to the bed?" she asked.

He mumbled something in his sleep again and she kissed his cheek. Then he opened his eyes.

"I'm sorry I'm so exhausted," he said in a weak fatigued voice.

"You don't have to apologise for anything, I'm just happy to see you," she answered.

On Friday evening after her first defence rehearsal, Joshua and Tanushree met at the entrance to Hofbrauhaus next to the tower at Alexanderplatz. It was early August, but only seventeen degrees centigrade in the air. Joshua wore khaki pants and a pink striped full-sleeved shirt. His wavy dark hair was combed with a parting in the middle, and his pink lips had that enigmatic smile on them. That evening, outside the enormous pub, his eyes met hers with a sparkle. For a moment, Tanushree was tempted to kiss his lips, but not sure whether what had happened two days before was just spur of the moment. She instead gave him a hug, but dared to press her lips against his cheek. His whole face blushed slowly. She swallowed.

"Should we go inside, my lady?" he said with a grin.

His recent mood swings confused her so much it drove her mad. Before she could say anything, he held open the door to her. As often, she wore a knee-length dress, but had chosen to take stockings today. The dress was white with laces this time, and she wore her turquoise pashmina shawl over her shoulders. They sat down next to each other at a long table inside the Hofbrauhaus. A man played the guitar and sang old German Eurovision festival songs standing on a stage in the middle of the hall. The room with its long wooden benches was packed with people. Some joined the singer, but most people just spoke loudly. Joshua, who had left her alone at the table came back with a bottle of dark lager and a glass of white Merlot. After sitting down next to her again, he took a sip of his drink. Finally, it was just the two of them, no letters or diary excerpts to read, no instruments to play, and no strange mood swings to make them react in an overly emotional way. For a moment, Tanushree wondered to herself if they would be able to keep up a normal conversation with each other.

"So, if there was a place you would be able to visit when you have finished the dissertation, where would it be?" Joshua asked.

"Calcutta," she declared within the blink of an eye.

"Haven't you been there like a gazillion times by now?" he asked.

"Yes, but I was always just a tourist. Now I have connections to places through my ancestors that I've never thought about, but just have to explore. I never considered the city in that light before," she answered.

"That should be reason enough," he said, rested his chin on his hand and looked down at the table for a moment.

When he turned back to her, she noticed his eyes fixing on her lips. It must have been the bright magenta lipstick she wore. After their recital, she had made a habit of wearing make-up. She wanted to re-experience what she had felt that day. Joshua lifted up and turned the bottle in the air and took another sip of his beer, while Tanushree sipped on her wine. They sat so close her calves touched the cloth of his khaki pants. He was in a joking mood today, not a minute passed without them laughing or talking nonsense to each other. She looked at the watch, and it was 11.30 p.m.

"Would you walk me home, Joshua?" she was surprised to hear herself ask. She had been perfectly able to walk home on her own all these years, but now she yearned for him to accompany her. She looked at him intently. This evening could not end so soon.

"I would be happy to, Tanu." He smiled and straightened his back where he sat on the wooden bench.

She took his hand and led him out of the Hofbrauhaus and he made no attempt to let go until they were outside. They walked through the dark Berlin night, but every corner restaurant and bar was busy. It did not feel like close to midnight. When they entered Schonhauser Allee, he looked at her.

"Have you ever been to that club around the corner from your place?" he asked.

He pointed at the place, which had a long queue every Friday and Saturday. The place which she had been tempted to go and complain endless times over the two years she had lived at Lottumstrasse – because the music was too loud.

"I didn't know you were into rock music," she answered.

"I'm not, but I want to dance with you." He winked at her.

She stared at the queue for a second and then turned around to Joshua. They locked eyes for a moment and she could see the expectation in his eyes. She smiled at him.

"I know what we can do," Tanushree replied.

Then she took his hand and led him to the front door at Lottumstrasse. She opened it with her keys. As they walked up the stairs to her flat, she felt the world spinning around her from the wine she had drunk or possibly the feeling she had, but luckily Joshua was climbing the stairs right behind her.

"You better not fall, because I'm far too weak to do anything right now," he said.

She laughed at his expression.

"I think I might have already fallen," she answered quietly. It was the wine speaking, but it was curious how well acquainted the alcohol was with her inner wishes.

"Is that so?" Joshua said loudly with the broadest grin on his face. She smiled back, and while she struggled to take up her house keys from the handbag with her face against the door, he gripped her arm and turned her around. He grabbed her waist and pulled her body against his. Then he put his lips against hers. After a while she felt his hands stroking her back over the thin cotton dress she was wearing. She had goosebumps, but she turned away her face. It was one of the hardest decisions she had made. Suddenly she felt sober. They looked at each other.

"I'm so sorry, Tanu…"

"Stop being sorry. It's time for you to face up to reality. Is it going to be me or God?" Her voice shivered. He looked at her with his face suddenly serious, his chest pumping up and down. She put her arms around his neck again and he buried his face in hers.

"Whatever she did to you was wrong, Joshua. But you need to let her go now," she whispered.

She felt teardrops falling down her back and until his tears had dried, they just stood there in the dark in each other's arms. Then she looked up at his face, stroked his cheek and kissed it again. She led him into the flat. They went into the living room and she lit candles on the table and turned on one of her favourite salsa songs.

"May I?" he asked and took the lead.

Their feet and hips moved in pace with the rhythm of the salsa song. The music made their bodies sway from side to side in the candle-lit living room, and when their bodies touched they did not hold back.

"Will you sleep in my bed tonight, Joshua?"

"Yes, I will," he answered and smiled.

"Can I hold you in my arms tonight?" he asked. She nodded.

She allowed him to fall asleep like that on the red sofa-bed with his body against hers and his arms around her waist, but they did not finish what they had initiated earlier that night, and she feared by the morning he would go back into his holy bond with her competitor. So that night they once again lay in each other's arms as platonic as their bodies allowed them to be, while he was still allowed time to think.

The morning after their night out at the Hofbrauhaus, Tanushree woke up by the bathroom door clicking. When she turned around, Joshua was standing by the bedroom door newly showered in the clothes he wore yesterday night. His expressive blue eyes looked straight at her and his face had a grin on it.

"Good morning! I'll go and make us breakfast," he said and went to the kitchen.

When she came out of the shower she heard him humming a song. On the sofa table in the living room, there were two printed e-tickets with departure date December 16 and return on the 29th of the same month. The destination was Calcutta! He had bought tickets for her and himself! She noticed he secretly peeped out from the kitchen to see her reaction. When she turned around towards him, her face burst out in a big smile.

"So, you're really coming to Calcutta with me?" she asked.

"Yes, if you want me to be there," he said and winked at her.

"I would be honoured to have you there," she answered.

Still not completely sure what was happening between them, she took out the chia pudding she had prepared from the refrigerator the previous evening. She sprinkled strawberries and blueberries in both of their bowls. He had made them freshly brewed coffee and cheese and cucumber toasts. It was one of those serene Saturday mornings.

"If I promise to do my best never to hurt you, will you give us a chance?"

Tanushree was surprised at her own straightforwardness, but nothing she did could compare to what had happened yesterday night. For a moment he just stared at her.

"Well, ehm…"

She could not believe he was still in doubt. She was not sure her heart could take what he was most likely going to say. He looked down, but little by little his hand moved closer to hers. As their fingers touched, he looked up. He had a faint smile on his thin pink lips.

"Tanu, would you like to spend your first day of freedom with me?"

Before she had learnt 'Joshuan', she would have been frustrated by his response, but today she took his gesture positively.

After breakfast, they went out running together in Volkspark Friedrichshain. Before going there, they passed by Joshua's flat and he changed into his trainers and tracksuit while she left clothes to change into after taking a shower. The air did not feel as heavy and cold as when she went out running on her own and the runner's high made them both happy to be in each other's company. In fact, they were almost a bit euphoric.

"I'll race you to the top of the slope," she challenged him.

They both began running, but she had a head start and when he finally overtook her, he grabbed her by the waist and kissed her on the cheek.

"Cheater!" he shouted.

His arms were so strong, she couldn't get out of his grip. He was full of surprises this weekend. She liked his newly gained confidence. It was hard to imagine depression had made this energetic man recently spend two weeks in bed. She did not want to bring it up, but she knew she had to.

She took him to an organic cafe in Prenzlauer Berg. They both ordered a cup of Darjeeling tea each. She loved the odour from newly brewed tea. She sipped on her hot drink and took a deep breath.

"Joshua, tell me what was going on in your head the two weeks you were in bed." He looked a bit ashamed.

"I'm not asking to make you feel guilty. I just want to understand you better." She let her fingers stroke his cheek and then she took hold of his hand and held it firmly.

"I…" His eyes looked away.

"I was worn out. Sometimes I get these phases even though things are mostly fine. I think I tried to conserve energy to avoid getting manic. It's a defence mechanism. I'm not always depressed, just exhausted."

She could relate to it so well from the manic episode earlier that year.

"Did anything happen that made you feel that way?"

"I think it was just a mixture of anxiety and happiness. I thought about us a lot Tanu and I want you to know that. I wanted to breach my pact with God, but I wondered if I would ever be enough for you. You're so young, talented and good-hearted, you could get anyone. I know you could have other suitors. It was almost as though I was suffering from performance anxiety. This is often what happens when I go into those phases," he said.

"I don't want you to be anxious when you think about us. I don't want any random person, I want you, Joshua, because you understand me."

"I saw how some of your male friends looked at you at the recital."

She had suspected this and sighed.

"Joshua, I do not care about them in that way, even though they are close friends. You have to trust me. Otherwise, we might let something beautiful go to waste." He listened attentively and nodded as he often did.

"And Josh, I can relate to those phases very well, but I really missed you. I was worried when you didn't reply. You don't have to be on top all the time. Nobody is. I also have days when I struggle to get out of bed. I just wanted to know you were alive. Please don't shut me out next time."

She was hoping he would not take her words too negatively. The last thing she wanted was for him to withdraw from her completely. He looked down, still a bit abashed with moist eyes. Then he nodded towards her again and looked into her eyes. But she knew this was only the beginning of her fight against his condition.

He asked her to sit down on the black sofa while he was in the adjacent kitchen pouring up Chardonnay into two glasses. She could feel his eyes gazing at her from time to time. Then he came to her, handed over a glass and started stroking her cheek. His face had reddened and he looked straight into her eyes. She had no desire to resist him when he tried to approach her, because somehow she knew she had the upper hand now. Before she knew it, he bent down to touch her lips with his. It was a long kiss this time and very enjoyable. She felt someone had finally freed her of her shackles of guilt. After all, she had made a phone call to her parents that day to tell them she had met a man, even though it was questionable whether they had agreed or how they felt about her relationship. Joshua and Tanushree both smiled after the kiss and continued the evening with dinner. They sat down to eat at the wooden table overlooking the concrete building opposite to them. Joshua had made fried oysters and boiled potatoes with asparagus. The night was pitch-black and the

135

little tea candles on the table had almost burnt down. They both kept unusually silent during dinner, but there were gazes between them every now and then.

"You're a very good cook, Professor Salisbury."

"Thank you, soon-to-be Dr Roy Chowdhury. I'm glad you liked it."

He let his fingers stroke her hand lightly. Then he pulled his hand back, went out in the living room and brought a letter for her to read.

Dear Isiah,

There is no easy way of saying what I am about to write. I understand that you are upset with me for this horrible fault I have made. But you must know my feelings for you are true. My body and mind crave you every day. Every time we talked about life and literature I felt a little bit wiser. You made me grow as a person. I have no such connection with Sathananda. Ours is a match made for the benefit and convenience of our parents. You have to know that every time my hand touches yours a small fire begins to burn inside me. I get nervous and I begin to talk, but in fact, all I can think of is exploring every little inch of your glowing olive skin, but I know we are both dignified people. I am quite sure I will never feel this way about anyone ever again, but duty calls Isiah, and I hope you will find it in your heart to forgive me for falling in love with you. I just cannot defy my parents. Such is the life of a Hindu woman of a zamindar family. All I ask of you is to part as friends and try to restrain ourselves from our bodily lusts. I am so much looking forward to hosting you, Abdul and Jyotish in our ancestral home. There are plenty of things I want to show you from my childhood. On this note I end this letter, and I hope that you will understand.

Yours sincerely,

Debapriya

When Joshua looked up at Tanushree after she had finished reading the letter, she noticed his eyes were moist again.

"I want to give us a chance, Tanu. I don't want to lose you," he said abruptly and looked steadily into her eyes. Her head, which had not yet digested the contents of the letter, made a leap to the here and now. Apparently, he had pondered on her words from previous conversations, but she never expected a letter from more than a century ago would make him speak out his decision.

"I want to give us a chance too, Joshua…and I'm not going anywhere," she said and smiled with her whole face beaming at him.

She walked to the other side of the kitchen table and put her arms around his neck. When his lips burst out in a broad smile, she kissed him on the cheek.

"Come, Tanu!"

He held her hand and they walked into the living room. Just like that previous night when he had slept in her bed, they lit candles and turned on the salsa song. As they danced closely together, she felt his whole body wanting to become one with hers. For the first time, she knew she was allowed to express her feelings and conquer every inch of him.

Chapter 16

"This is my dear classmate from Presidency College," Debu's cheerful voice said to his wife Chandramukhi. But it was only when he put his hand on his shoulder that Isiah, who was deeply immersed in his book, looked up. The newly wed woman put her palms together and gazed into his eyes. A bit startled, he stood up, put his book on the chair, and did likewise. The first thing he noted about his friend's spouse, now that she was next to him, was that she did not have the slender physique of Debapriya. On the contrary, she was quite plump, and her belly bulged out over the lower part of the heavy silk saree in magenta, which was tucked into the petticoat. But to compensate for what she lacked in physical appearance, her long-lashed kohl-rimmed eyes radiated a kind of warmth he had seldom seen in younger women.

"Nice to meet you, Isiah."

For her young age of sixteen, she had a heavy voice. It was almost a bit masculine, Isiah thought.

"Nice to meet you too, Chandramukhi."

They smiled towards each other, and there was not a sign of the coyness of a new bride in her. While Isiah was busy greeting Chandramukhi, Debu picked up the book from the chair his friend had sat on the past three hours.

"I see you're reading Ram Mohan Roy's writings on sati. How come, old sport?" asked Debu.

For a moment, Isiah did not know what to say in return. He could not possibly tell him the unfortunate fate of his little sister had inspired him to read about the rights of Hindu women. Instead, he turned into his intellectual self.

"Well, I find his travels to England to ask the Queen to ban sati quite honourable. I think he's one of the greatest revolutionary thinkers of Bengal."

At the moment, he spoke those words, Debu and Chandramukhi both looked at him with sparkling eyes.

"I do agree with you," she said.

It was from this sentence he realised that just like his own friendship with Debu, the man had also chosen a life-partner who was interested in the same topics as himself.

"I hear you will be joining your husband in Calcutta. Is this true?" asked Isiah.

"Yes, it's true," she answered.

"What are you planning to do while Debu spends his days at the college?" He asked a leading question.

She smiled towards him, but seemed reluctant to tell him the truth.

"She will be undertaking her intermediate school studies at the Bethune College with my sister," Debu announced proudly while his wife looked down at the marble floor. Isiah wondered why she seemed so troubled, but then he remembered something Debapriya had told him about her future sister-in-law.

"Is it common for women in your family to partake in higher studies?" he asked inquisitively while Chandramukhi's eyes were still fixed on the floor.

"She will be the first female in her family to attend college," Debu said loudly and put his arm around her neck. It was funny how a person who had seemed so confident at first glance, seemed to have lost her voice only because of one simple question.

"My brothers are not all too happy about it," she said quietly after looking around her to see if someone was eavesdropping. She uttered those words with a serious face, and Isiah's eyes met Debu's, whose face had turned from proud to compassionate.

When Isiah first saw the perpetrator to whom Debapriya's heart now belonged that evening, her fiance stood and talked to his father-in-law in the hall room. On his face was a broad grin, and his teeth were clean with a complexion close to white. From his gesticulations and rapid mouth movements, it was clear he was a very dynamic man. A younger male family member of the Roy Chowdhurys' came up to him and put his hand on his shoulder.

"Long time no see," Isiah heard the family member exclaim, so it was clear they knew each other from before Sathananda had gone to England. They embraced in a way, which made it evident both men were long lost friends. He was all the things Isiah was not – newly arrived from London, sociable, a dashing young man and a zamindar's son. How could he even consider competing with this man? Debapriya came up to her fiance and he put his arm around her neck. Isiah felt a sting in his heart. Then he watched the couple walking towards him while trying his best to push away all negative thoughts.

"This is my fiancé, Sathananda," Debapriya announced proudly to Isiah with a smile on her face.

It was apparent she was happy in his company, but Isiah wished she would play it down just a notch. Did she not have any sympathy left for him at all? Did she really think all his emotions were gone just because he had told her so? He tried to tell himself it was only the honeymoon phase, which made her so content. The next moment when he looked at her face, it was like someone had wiped away her smile. She stared at Isiah as if she studied his face too. But her dandy-like life companion went on talking cheerfully.

"You must be Isiah – a friend of both Debu's and Debapriya's, I hear. Very nice to meet you."

He swallowed down a lump in his throat and stretched out his hand to shake the hand of Sathananda.

"Yes, that's correct. Nice to meet you too. I've heard a lot about you," Isiah said, but he did not reveal in which context.

"I've laid eyes on you a couple of times the past few days, but unfortunately no one was there to introduce us to each other," said Sathananda.

Isiah nodded in response, but knew what not to say. It was unfathomable how Debapriya had chosen someone so focused on appearance and show off. He who had always considered her a girl of emotional depth. Sathananda began to look around him, almost as if he searched for someone new to talk to. Then he sighed and turned towards his fiancée.

"Should we perhaps give your parents a hand with the gifts?" he asked her.

Debapriya, who had stared at Isiah's face ever since she walked up to him, now turned to Sathananda.

"Sure," she said in a mellow voice, but her eyes looked sideways to the floor. Sathananda looked down at the face of his future wife, looking a bit flustered about her sudden change of mood. Then he looked up at Isiah again with a smile, but not a single crinkle was visible in his face. It was hard to know what to make of the man. Maybe he was just a phoney.

"Will you excuse us?" Sathananda asked.

Isiah nodded his head, and the couple moved towards the entrance to the hall room, while Debapriya looked back at him over her shoulder.

The sitarist strummed his strings one by one to begin the slow-paced introductory alaap of the heptatonic evening raga Yaman. It was at that moment that Isiah changed his weight from his right hand to his left where he sat on the floor. The music salon at the bride's house was chilly and the black patterned mosaic floor felt like ice against his legs. He could sense the cold through the jute mat he sat on, cross-legged beside Abdul, in front of the stage. The crisp cold air, which came in through his nose and the partially open mouth, stung his throat and he coughed. When he looked around him, almost the whole audience was wearing woollen shawls like himself, some of them with their heads covered. He fidgeted once more, but it did not make the sitting less strenuous. Nor did it help that he looked into the deep neck of the newly engaged Debapriya, and she had her fiancé sitting next to her. When the former touched the hand of his future wife at the end of the last raga, the lump in Isiah's throat tightened. He thought about how she had laid in his arms only weeks earlier. At the time, he had even begun to think about different ways of disclosing his romantic liaison to his parents and grandmother. Just like then, he could smell the perfume oozing out from her body, and just like then, it bewitched him. When the pressure became too much for him to handle, and his ears had stopped listening to the music, he stood up. Abdul looked at him with concern, where he sat beside him on the mat. Isiah whispered in his ear that he needed fresh air, and his classmate's facial expression turned into pitiful. He knew very well what had happened between Isiah and Debapriya, but he pretended not to react, probably to save his friend from negative emotions. The moment Isiah stood, the newly engaged couple turned towards him. One had a face looking like a question mark, and the other had eyes full of compassion. There were probably other members of the audience who turned to look at him at the moment he stood, but those two were the only faces he registered. Nevertheless, he neglected them, and walked through the crowd and out through the doors to the first-floor hallway. He hurried down the stairs and immediately dashed into the back garden. Then he walked up to the fountain at the lower end of the gravelled path, leading down to the back of the garden from the house. There he released his emotions and let the tears at the corner of his eyes run down his cheeks. It was dark outside, and no one was to be seen in the garden, so it was safe for him to subside to his unmanly side here in this oasis. His feet paced up and down the gravelled path, while his head gave way to all kinds of thoughts. Was it too late to talk to her? She still had sympathy for

141

him, he could see it in her eyes. Should he ask her to elope with him? They could live in a foreign land where no one interfered with their mutual life. The next time he reached the statue and the fountain, he stomped his feet hard on the ground, almost as hard as she had stomped on his heart. Except that it was not her fault. It was this darn society with all its expectations and double standards. For a while, he thought about the visions he had shared with Debendranath. Would they succeed to contribute to a better world one day? Will she like him better then? His mind was running wild in the crisp cold of the night. He walked a lap around the garden, but was careful to stay out of the light of the lanterns. He stopped and coughed. Breathing the cold air so fast was hard on his lungs. While he wiped away the mud under his shoes against the grass, a shadow appeared at the back entrance to the palace. The shadow had shoulder-length curly hair and wore a saree. She began to walk towards him. In the background, he could still hear the sound of the sitar and the accompanying tabla. As Debapriya came closer, he saw the tears running down from her amber eyes. Her face was pale. All the anger, her betrayal had caused him went away for a moment. Left was her doll-like face, which stared at him in the still of the night. She had stopped a few yards away from him and he waited for her to open her mouth.

Part II

Chapter 17

The year was 1925. For the tenth consecutive year, Isiah had come to spend his summer vacation with Debendranath and his family in Vikrampur. Celibacy had made it easy for Isiah to leave Calcutta and travel to East Bengal from time to time. The second-largest city in the British Empire had lost its role as capital to Delhi fourteen years earlier and Bengal had been reunited. The Paris of the East was without its role as the administrative capital of British India, and the city had become another name for activism and nationalist terror. Jyotish Ganguly had been right in his prophecy about the relationships between Hindus and Muslims that time at the tea stall when the four men were freshers at Presidency College. But to the great satisfaction of Debendranath, for the second time, a woman had taken over the office of president of the Congress Party.

"Uncle Isiah, can I ride on your shoulders?" Debendranth's eight-year-old daughter begged her father's close friend.

"Of course you can, Shilpa."

He bent down and let her climb upon his shoulders. The short and meagre lawyer held her legs in a firm grip and began trotting on the lawn to imitate a horse. Her loud shrill laughter penetrated the fresh thick morning air.

"Be careful, Shilpa, or you'll fall and hurt yourself," Chandramukhi cautioned her daughter.

"Isiah, don't let her talk you into anything. She has been far too pampered by her father. Besides, Shilpa, it is time for your singing lesson."

"Do I have to, Mother? I want to play in the garden," Shilpa protested.

"Your singing teacher is waiting for you in the drawing-room. No matter what your father says, girls should learn to balance their lives, not only doing sports like little boys," Chandramukhi said in a rigid voice. "You will thank me when you are older," she added.

145

Debendranath and his English colleague, Mr Iverson, came in through the high gate at the entrance of the garden.

"How do you do, Mr Iverson?" Isiah stood up by his chair and put out his hand to greet the elderly gentleman. The man shook his hand gently, but his eyes tried to avoid Isiah's. When he looked up, Isiah noticed the crimson colour of his cheeks.

"Please, sit down," Isiah heard Debu sigh.

"I have come here solely to get an explanation, not to join your tea party, Debendranath."

The old man's face became more and more rigid. Isiah was not sure what kind of explanation the elderly man wanted to have, but he suspected it had to do with Debu's job situation.

"Then, I should leave you to it," Isiah said and stood up hastily to leave the fruit garden. He went inside the palace and sat down on a rocking chair on the veranda. He looked out through the arched window from time to time to follow Mr Iverson's and Debu's dialogue, but he was too far away to hear their agitated voices. Instead, he listened to the young girl singing the ascending and descending scales of *Raag bhairav*. She sang in C minor and hit the D and B flats perfectly. The evening before he had accompanied her on the harmonium. Isiah who had been trained in western classical piano from the Calcutta School of Music knew by now that bhairav was the mode that corresponded to the minor scale and vilawal the mode that corresponded to the major scale. The other modes of Hindustani classical music still confused him. They seemed out of harmony to his ears, but he enjoyed listening to them.

When Debapriya's family came into the garden, Isiah was coincidentally standing next to the fountain where they had said their last goodbyes that fatal night twenty years ago. The young advocate, who had remained a bachelor, watched while the romantic partner of his youth walked down the gravelled path next to her husband Sathananda. Her skin was just as dazzling as it used to be and her light brown eyes sparked when they met Isiah's, but the Dasguptas were far from the youthful couple he had encountered at Debendranath's wedding. Perhaps parenthood changes people with all its musts, Isiah thought to himself. He stretched out his hand in a modest manner and then turned his gaze towards the twins.

"Jogesh and Suresh, this is Uncle Isiah," Debapriya explained to her sons.

"Hello, Uncle," the boys said in unison, while Isiah nodded his head towards them. Sathananda had already found himself a chair in the shadow of a tree next to his brother-in-law. While Isiah walked in their direction, he saw the two men had already engaged in conversation, and Mr Iverson seemed to have left.

"Let's not forget how much the British have contributed to this country, everything from railways and schools to hospitals. I find it difficult to see how native Indians will set up the administration and infrastructure to continue on this work," said Debapriya's husband.

It was July and monsoon season in Bengal. The two siblings Debendranath and Debapriya had brought their families to meet relatives in Vikrampur.

"I do not belong to the ones who deny our history Sathananda, but let's not forget how much oppression the British have brought upon us. It was not until the middle of the last century that we could work as civil servants for our own country. We still have markets and country clubs that are only open to the white population, solely because they don't want to brush shoulders with us. I know these things are difficult to see for someone who has been educated in England," said Debendranath.

"Dada, let's be fair, we all know England has never been a bed of roses for Indian students," Debapriya interjected to support her husband.

To the dismay of Isiah Cohen, Debendranath's younger sister married one of her lecturers while at college. Isiah had never dared to admit his feelings, but after becoming aware of Debapriya's decision to marry Sathananda Dasgupta he had gone into a frenzy of practising the piano hour after hour upon coming home in the evenings. Right before it was time to revisit Vikrampur to attend her wedding, he fell sick and could not get out of bed for two weeks. Sathananda had returned to Calcutta from England in 1905 and upon the sudden demise of his father, the couple had recently relocated to Rangoon to take care of the family's teak business.

Chandramukhi put a clay pot full of home-made *rasgullahs* in the middle of the long mahogany table. Shilpa leaned over the pot and fished out a round, curd ball with her fingers. She put the whole thing into her mouth and chewed it. It was full of syrup and her mouth became so full it felt like her cheeks were going to burst. Her five-year younger brother Nilesh and cousin looked at her round red cheeks and began to giggle.

"Shilpa, where are your manners?" Chandramukhi asked.

She swallowed with a gulp.

"You're a big girl now, you should act as a role model to your younger siblings."

She gave her husband a strict glance for not telling off his daughter. Shilpa's mother served all the guests *rasgullahs* in bowls and tea in little blue Chinese porcelain cups with flowery patterns which Debapriya and Sathananda had brought from Rangoon. Isiah could hear the rain pouring down outside and felt a light breeze.

"My daughter has been learning Greek mythology lately."

Debendranath was very proud of his daughter Shilpa, and her talents were often shown off to friends and family.

"Do you remember the Ode to Psyche by Keats? Will you recite it to us, Shilpa?"

She was not necessarily very fond of reciting poems to others, but she knew by now there was no use in showing resistance.

"O, Goddess! hear these tuneless numbers, wrung. By sweet enforcement and remembrance dear..."

Her voice was still very childish. After all, she was no older than eight. She stopped after the first stanza and looked at her father.

"That's adorable!" exclaimed Sathananda. He clapped his hands in appreciation. His wife smiled and gave her precocious niece a kiss on the cheek. Shilpa looked down at her sandals and clenched her fists. Sometimes she pretended she was a clown who was there to entertain her audience. Often the adults would laugh after her performances. It would make her sad when the adults laughed as she did not understand why, and she could not always pretend. Each time, her mother assured her grown-ups always laughed at children when they found them cute. Shilpa's younger brother and cousin were playing tag on the backside of the house. The young girl looked out longingly to the garden.

"Don't even think of it, Shilpa. You will spoil your frock," Chandramukhi said strictly.

She had seen her daughter's mischievous eyes looking out through the window.

"Let your uncle and aunt hear the bandish of raga bhairav. Have you learnt the tans by heart yet?" She was very strict with her daughter's musical education. To her, the practice of singing was an activity which added to her daughter's feminine side. She was seriously worried about Shilpa's preference to spend so much time running around in the garden and playing sports. To her, those were boyish activities. Their eldest daughter was the apple of her father's eye and Chandramukhi often blamed him for spoiling their daughter. Even though she belonged to the highly educated fraction of women in British India, she still had a very traditional view of how girls should be brought up. On top of it, she tried to fill her daughter's daily schedules with meaningful activities, much in the same way she had been brought up herself. Shilpa would often think it unfair when she saw her cousins and younger brothers playing. Both her parents tried to instil into her that the eldest sibling should be responsible and show good leadership.

Debapriya, who had often been shown off in the same way as her niece when she was a child, came up to the window sill where Shilpa sat and hugged her niece.

"Dry your tears, Shilpa. You are very talented. We are all proud of you. Such a beautiful voice and sharp memory. Your parents will know when you come home with the highest marks in all subjects in school. I can assure you that."

For the first time since she was asked to recite the poem, Shilpa smiled with her face glowing towards her aunt.

Five days later, Debendranath, who had lost his post as a district magistrate in Hazaribagh, took the train to Calcutta together with his family and Isiah.

"Have you heard from Jyotish and Abdul, Isiah? Jyotish has been ignoring me for quite a while now. He seems to think I will join the martyrs and let myself be killed by shots from the British. To be fair, he has always viewed my involvement in the swadeshi movement as an unfathomable quirk." He smiled to himself. Isiah, who had been quietly contemplating the past hours cleared his throat.

"Yes, Jyotish has kept away for quite some time now." Isiah knew very well it was due to his own tight relationship with Debendranath, but he spared his friend of this information. "The last month, on the other hand, I was invited for dinner to Abdul's Park Circus home. Much like East Bengali Hindus, Calcutta Muslims have reasons to worry these days, so this pressure is lying heavy on his shoulders. He is still practising in court and trying to keep his family calm, but living in Calcutta today makes it difficult to remain uninvolved and unaffected. Why don't you go and visit him Debu? The poor fellow seems very troubled."

"Maybe I should accompany you to his home on your way back to Calcutta. I have invited Abdul to Hazaribagh several times, but it seems like the family has little funds."

"He has five children, Debu and three of his sons attend St Xavier's Collegiate School. The fees are quite high in those schools."

"How is his health?" Debu asked.

"His physical health is fine, but he's breaking down mentally. Some time ago, the doctors told him to go on vacation, so he could get rid of his sleeping problems, but he has become an obsessive worker."

It was hard for Debendranath to imagine his friend's condition as he had always been someone who could tackle hardships.

They parted at Sealdah station, where Isiah went home to his parents and the Roy Chowdhurys took the commuter train to the garden house of Chandramukhi's parents in the southern suburbs.

In the evening of the day they arrived, Debu and Isiah took the tram to Park Circus and knocked loudly on the mahogany door of Abdul Huq.

"I'm finding it increasingly difficult to support my family, Debu. Hindus of the city show distrust against Muslim lawyers. I'm getting fewer and fewer clients these days. I will soon have to find a new school for my sons. On top of it, my family owns no land. Everything we own is between these four walls and I am not ready to sell my house," Abdul Huq explained in a sullen tone.

Isiah knew Debu was yet to witness the segregation and racial feelings that had spread in the city of Calcutta. He must be feeling it was unfair. Abdul Huq was a liberal Muslim. He had fought hard to gain British legal training and had melted in well with the Hindus. Why should he be affected by anti-Muslim sentiments?

"Only centuries earlier, Muslims were the leaders of Bengal but due to their boycott of English education their possibilities had become limited," said Debu.

"Abdul, I own some shares in the Dhakeswari Bastralaya company. Let me sell them to fund your family for the coming years."

"Debu, I cannot begin to say how grateful I am for your gesture. I promise to pay it back to you when the political climate has gone back to normal."

150

Despite the confidence in his voice, Abdul looked down at the mosaic floor doubtfully.

The otherwise optimistic and zealous, Debendranath, felt Abdul Huq's desperation. Isiah could see it in his eyes. He put a hand on his shoulder and looked into his friend's hollow and sunken eyes, which were rimmed with wrinkles and black lines.

"You have to keep faith for the sake of your wife and children Abdul," said Debendranath.

The worried 38-year old man nodded to show he agreed. Then he put his palm over his face to hide the tears at the corner of the eyes. At that moment, it dawned on Isiah that he himself had been living in a haven protected from the political happenings in the real world for much of the past decade. Who was he to give consolidation to those that fought with everyday life? As Debendranath Roy Chowdhury left Park Circus that night, Isiah could see a serious, pale and slightly traumatized expression on his face. His long-time dream that Muslims and Hindus would continue living side by side had been shattered. The city they walked into was gloomy and dark and sent shivers down his spine. Even the convenient shops had closed. He groped for something familiar to hold on, but all he was met by was hostility. The city of Calcutta had become their adversary.

A couple of days before the famous freedom fighter took his last breath in Darjeeling in June 1925, Isiah took Debendranath to Calcutta Club with one of his clients. Two decades earlier the whitewashed building next to the Maidan had been the first country club to open up its doors to the indigenous population. The atmosphere in the city was uneasy now that the nation was about to lose one of the few leaders who knew how to unite Hindus and Muslims.

"You, Mr Cohen, must be hoping your British brethren will stay in power," said the colleague of Isiah's client.

He looked up in surprise at the old man's judgemental comment.

"I am not British, Mr Chatterjee. I'm a Baghdadi Jew, my forefathers came here from Iraq. And no, I do not wish the British to remain in power in India. I think it's every nation's own right to be sovereign. More importantly, its citizens should all be equal." For the moment, he let it be unsaid that he was an ardent member of the Congress Party. He was used to being misunderstood. In his younger days, he would not even correct people, but age and his close friendship with Debendranath had shaped him into someone who spoke up when necessary.

"Ehm…I hardly think our freedom fighter will survive this time; quite a character that one!" The old Mr Chatterjee continued, neglecting Isiah's words.

"He gave up his law practice to dive into politics."

"Yes, he met some of our prominent political leaders while studying in England. He supported the first Indian MP for the Liberal Party of England," Isiah said.

Mr Chatterjee became quiet and looked at the well-dressed slender lawyer in awe.

"I hear you are well-versed with the Indian freedom struggle."

Isiah nodded and looked at Debendranath, who seemed indifferent.

"Yes, Mr Chatterjee, I'm a member of the Congress Party."

"I hear he used to send his clothes for dry-cleaning in Paris but stopped that the moment he joined the Home Rule movement. He burnt his Western clothes and began wearing Khadi clothes."

Isiah had heard all those stories from Debu who had his origins in the same town as the political leader. He knew Debendranath's father had taught many of the politicians' family members but he remained silent. Now was hardly the time for gossip. A man wearing a turban came with a tray of sandwiches and tea. After Mr Chatterjee left the two friends, Isiah turned towards Debu.

"You have withdrawn from us since you came to Calcutta, Debu. Is everything alright?"

"I'm scared, Isiah. I don't know what is happening to this city."

Both men took sips of their coffee.

"Yes, I understand. I feel the same way."

"There is one more thing, Isiah."

"Yes, Debu. What is it?" Isiah asked.

"I am close to bankruptcy. All my investments in East Bengal are out of reach… At this age, it is also very difficult to start a career over from the beginning and find new clients."

The man was a stranger to the situation of asking for financial assistance.

"Why haven't you told me before, Debu? You should absolutely come and join me in my law firm. I have already invited Abdul."

Early the next day Isiah put up a board on top of the heavy mahogany doors with a light green background saying 'Cohen, Huq and Roy Chowdhury solicitors' in black letters. His friend climbed up the red coloured stairs and was met by the signboard the first thing before he entered the office. Debu was moved. For the first time since he left behind the life in East Bengal and Hazaribagh, he did not feel like a stranger in the city where he was made into an independent thinker and a lawyer more than a decade earlier.

That evening Chandramukhi and Debendranath were invited to Isiah's family for a Rosh Hashana feast together with the family of Abdul Huq. As they entered the dining room of the apartment in Brabourne Road, lying on their plates were peppers stuffed with rice and chicken together with deep-fried potatoes.

"These are known as *mahashas*," said Isiah's sister Hannah and pointed at the bell peppers,

"And those are *makalahs*," she said pointing at the deep-fried potatoes. She served the couple some cucumber salad and beetroot salad with onion. Isiah who wore a kippa for the occasion passed around a dish with *fish shooftas* and stuffed dumplings. Then came fish pulao. Isiah, his sister and her husband Avram said prayers in Hebrew before they began the dinner. Debendranath and Chandramukhi relished the food. They had visited Isiah's home many times before as students, but in the past, Isiah's parents had often ordered food from a local restaurant in fear that they would not appreciate their traditional dishes.

"We were visited by a Kabuliwahllah yesterday, so we have dried dates for the occasion. Please, have some pomegranate and do taste the carrot cake I have made."

"I understand your family has spent some time in London, Avram," said Chandramukhi.

"Are you planning to move back?"

Hannah looked at Isiah and Debendranath's best friend looked with a troubled gaze at Chandramukhi. Right there and then it dawned on her she and her husband would not much longer have the pleasure of having the company of Isiah in Calcutta. She looked down at her plate again. All three of them were relieved Debendranath missed the swift non-verbal communication between them. They were all worried about his well-being and Isiah's already fixed plans would be a shock to him.

"We will see what the future has in store for us," Hannah lied.

Chandramukhi nodded and tried to come up with a different table topic.

"The food was absolutely delicious, Hannah. Don't you agree, Debu?"

Debendranath woke up from his thoughts. He often kept aloof in social situations these days.

"Oh yes, I very much enjoyed it. Thank you for inviting us, Hannah."

"It's delightful to have you here, Debendranath."

"I hope you will enjoy working in our office, Debu. I know the size of the law firm is very humble and you are used to larger enterprises, but we all have to begin somewhere," said Isiah. Chandramukhi looked into Isiah's eyes almost as if she wondered why he had started a law firm if he knew he was moving to London soon, but he knew it would be a good work opportunity for her husband.

Isiah turned to Abdul, but the only question that came to his mind was whether his family would stay in Calcutta or not. He decided to keep his mouth closed not to cause any discomfort.

"You should all come for dinner at our place soon. I know we live under very sparse conditions far from central Calcutta, but I hope you will not be too uncomfortable," Chandramukhi said.

"Don't worry, Chandramukhi. When our forefathers came to Calcutta, they did not even own homes here. They also had to begin businesses from scratch," said Hannah, in a comforting tone. Isiah had never thought about it that way before. In fact, at that moment, he realised all immigrants left their homes and jobs to start anew in the place they go to.

Chapter 18

Tanushree slowly poured a bowl of hot water over her head and rubbed her belly with the other hand to get rid of what was left from the olive soap. Then she took her thin red and white chequered towel and wrapped it around her waist. When she opened the door to step out from the steam bath, lukewarm air bit her warm face and bare legs. She took a cold shower, and shivering, she went up to the lounge of the Turkish Hamam. Her skin was still red and ached after the elderly lady had given her a manual peeling using her whole body weight to rub Taushree's skin vigorously with a hard glove.

"Could I have a cup of tea, please?" she asked quietly.

The woman sat at the cash desk handed her a Turkish teacup, and she poured herself the black tea, which was in the pot. Then she sat down on a lounge chair. For a moment, she just wriggled her toes, but decided she should give herself some reading time. After bringing a light green aerogramme from her backpack in the changing room, she sat down on the same chair and took another sip of the tea. In her hand was a letter written by Debendranath to Isiah sent in late 1925.

Dear Isiah,

I hope this letter finds you well. I expect you to have settled in London by now. First of all, I cannot begin to thank you for allowing me and Abdul partnership in your law firm. We are trying to keep everything tip-top in your office, so you can just come and initiate your work as soon as you are back in Calcutta. Jyotish is doing well in his own practice, so I do not think you need to worry about him. Also, thank you for caring about my mental health, I am doing much better now. Working in Calcutta was a good idea, and we are now having a little house built in Dhakuria, where our family can live. So, we are leaving Narendranath and his family behind in Tollygunge. But sometimes I worry about what will happen if we do not get enough clients. Only the week before you employed me, I sat at the bar library smoking my pipe and looking for potential new colleagues. I had gone there every day for the past month, but to no avail. As the evening dusk began to fall over the city that day I went home to finish my daily walk around Dhakuria. For a moment, I stood by one of the black ornate street lanterns by the man-made lake to catch my breath. I often find myself out of breath these days. Then I walked down Lancedowne Road towards the market to buy groceries for supper. Funds were sparse before I began to work, but fortunately, I can still afford to pay for our cook. In fact, the elderly servant is a man we have brought with us from Dacca.

"Fresh hilsa fish!" I could hear the vendor shouting.

The narrow pathways in the market were crowded. There was a strong stench of fish. The vendor lit a candle to brighten up the space where he sat and scaled them. I knew there was nothing to celebrate, but the mere sight of the silvery skin and the reddish flesh of my favourite fish tickled my taste buds. It would be perfect with mustard powder I thought to myself.

"May I have one kilo of hilsa fish, please?" I heard myself asking.

I turned towards the vendor who picked up a couple of middle-sized hilsas and put them into my bag, and I gave him the change. Next, I passed by the fruit stand. Everything seemed enticing to me that day. Something had made me regain an appetite for life, even though I was officially unemployed. I picked up and smelled the fresh sweet yellow mango, Isiah.

"This takes me back to Vikrampur," I told the vendor and closed my eyes.

"Babu, would you like some mangoes?" the vendor said to me loudly.

The sound of the loud voice woke me up from my thoughts and I nodded.

I went home that evening and sat on the veranda in Dhakuria looking out on the street with my teacup in one hand and a Parle-G biscuit in the other. I dunked the biscuit in my tea and watched a group of young boys playing cricket in the street. The neighbourhood is sparsely colonised by houses. On the plot beside ours is still a large playground. Just as I was going into deep thoughts again, Chandramukhi came and asked with her soft voice:

"Any luck at the bar library today, Debu?"

"No, I did not meet a single lawyer today. Nor did I find any clients," I answered her.

"And yet we are having hilsa fish for dinner!" Chandramukhi exclaimed.

"Yes, I thought we needed some change from the monotony of everyday life."

156

"You know we have to become more frugal, Debu," she warned me.

I know she has noticed her husband's recent vices, so she knew very well I tried to compensate for my unemployment. Isiah, I wish one day I will get out of this uncertainty and feel joyful for the little things in life again just like that day at the market. I do not like counting every single coin, but somehow it helps me that Abdul can understand my situation and we can help each other through the bad times. Now, please let me know how your first few months in London have been.

Best wishes,
Debu

The waiter who was standing beside the bar desk gave Tanushree the eye, where she sat behind her computer in one corner of the half a century old Indian restaurant. It was close to Savignyplatz, the part of Berlin where she only allowed herself to go during weekends, much because the long travel time. Suddenly, a man she had never seen before during her earlier visits to the restaurant appeared by the table. His colourful sweater and black smart pants told her he was not part of the staff, who all wore white shirts.

"May I sit down?" he asked to Tanushree's surprise.

Before she had the chance to answer, he pulled out the wooden chair. He stretched out his hand.

"I assume you are a student, since you are working on your computer in a restaurant."

Tanushree blushed, suddenly remembering her manners.

"Where are you from?" he asked.

"Sweden."

"How curious. I thought Swedes were blond and light-skinned."

At first, she chuckled at the man's statement, but after noticing that his thin lips had remained stiff, she stopped her laughter abruptly.

"Has your family always lived in Sweden?"

"Not always. My father was a trainee and studied at an engineering school in West Germany in the sixties," she replied.

"How interesting, I came around that time myself. I assume you're Bengali then."

Suddenly, what had seemed like offence, opened up a dialogue between the two of them.

Joshua appeared behind the man and smiled at Tanushree.

"Oh, hello," the man turned and scrutinised him.

"Is this your boyfriend?"

"Yes," she answered with her face beaming towards Joshua.

"Nice to meet you," he again avoided mentioning his name.

"I shall leave you to it. Hope you enjoy your soiree."

As they ate the daal soup as an apperatif, Tanushree asked Joshua to read the letter from Debu.

"He seemed so carefree despite being jobless. I wish I could look at life in his way," Joshua said.

"Have you ever been unemployed, Joshua?"

"Yes, after graduating from music college, I fought like a fool to get a job, but I only got little gigs every now and then."

Tanushree said nothing, but remembered how critical her surroundings were towards his choice to study music.

"But you got a first-class!" she exclaimed.

"It didn't help much," Joshua said and put the bowl aside.

"It must be hard to be a scientist too," Akash had finally arrived. Tanushree thought it would be good if the two of them would get to know each other. For the first time that evening, he turned towards Joshua, who looked back at him with a sullen facial expression.

"Most of my friends fled from academia once they were done with their doctoral studies. Management consultancy is so much more well-paid and yet you work the same amount of hours as a PhD student."

Joshua looked back at Akash for a moment, as if he was preparing a rebuttal.

"I don't like my liberty to be challenged," he replied bluntly.

"Doesn't poor economy challenge your liberty?" Akash asked.

"I'm talking about the liberty of my work," Joshua retorted. His eyes glared at Akash this time.

"Would you excuse me for a moment?" he asked.

Joshua went up to the bar, A few moments later Tanushree heard the sound of boiling daal from the kitchen stove. She turned around and leaned back on her chair in the restaurant and saw Joshua looking out through the window at the bar.

It was 3:30 p.m. when they drove into the parking space next to the town house. The car journey from the airport had gone smoothly, but not a word had been uttered by anyone. On a phone call only a week ago, Tanushree had informed her parents that she had a boyfriend, which had been met by the same silence as today. The first sign of kindness was when her father offered to carry Joshua's suitcase to the door. While Joshua was busy getting settled, Tanushree prepared tea.

"Have you ever been to Sweden before?" The first question came out of her mother's mouth.

"No, I haven't," Joshua answered a bit nervous.

After a while, he opened his mouth again.

"Have you been to England a lot?"

"Yes, we have relatives there, so we do tend to visit once in a while."

"He knows Rohini very well, Mother. They were classmates in higher secondary school," Tanushree said cheerfully.

After a while, her father opened his mouth and told Joshua about his first journey to London in the early sixties. That is a good sign Tanushree thought to herself.

"What do you do for a living, Joshua?" Tanushree heard her mother asking while she went to fill up the teapot.

"I'm a theoretical acoustician," he answered.

"I suppose that has something to do with music," Menakshi Roy Chowdhury said.

"Sort of, but more Physics I suppose," he answered calmly.

"Then you're not a doctor," Menakshi said quietly, but Tanushree saw from Joshua's face that he had overheard it.

"Does everyone have to become a doctor, Mother?" Tanushree asked at last.

"Well, it gives you more stability in life," she replied. Tanushree rolled her eyes. She wondered how many times he had to have this kind of discussion with people.

"Why don't we go out for a walk, Joshua? I have so much to show you from my younger days."

They took their jackets and walked up to the hills she knew so well, the place where she used to go every time she needed a moment to herself when she was growing up. She stood at the top of the slanting meadow and looked out over her hometown. All those steep streets lined with trees and wooden houses had a special beauty. Just standing there and breathing fresh air felt like a privilege. A day earlier she had been standing in front of her thesis advisor and explained her insights on moods and musical modes. Her head was heavy after the cross-interrogation but she was finally done with writing her thesis! When they came home it was already dusk.

"We were zamindars and owned an estate in Vikrampur. The school I attended when I was little belonged to our family and my grandfather was the headmaster. We also owned several temples."

"I know all that, Father. That was not my question." Tanushree sighed, tired of his materialistic thinking. After coming back from the walk, she felt refreshed and cut right to the chase.

They sat around the dinner table in their Gothenburg town house, where she was brought up, Tanushree, her parents and Joshua.

"Why do you have to turn everything into a bed of roses? Our family fled from East Bengal, didn't they?"

"Technically speaking, we were not refugees. We had somewhere to live in Calcutta. My grandparents lived there and we owned a home there."

"Grandmother fled from Vikrampur in the middle of the night with you and Uncle Dhanesh," Tanushree said adamantly.

"Do you remember?"

"What are you going to do with that knowledge Tanushree? It's all in the past. Focus on your own work," her mother replied.

"Don't we have a responsibility to our ancestors, to tell the truth rather than making up stories?"

Her father looked up at her in wonder.

"How do you know all this Tanushree?"

"I read my grandfather's letters to his best friend Isiah Cohen."

Her father's pupils dilated and he gaped in silence as if he had seen a ghost. Her mother raised her eyebrows and Joshua stopped eating.

"I met Isiah's only grandchild, who lives in London and some time ago, his parents, Judith and Steven, invited me to their place. They have saved century-old correspondence between Debendranath and Isiah and pictures. Joshua is his grandchild!"

She felt all three of them staring at her now, but Joshua's lips had a faint smile on them.

"Something bad happened to our family. It was not only the expropriation. Grandfather lost his family members in the Japanese bombings and his brother was killed in clashes between Hindus and Muslims in Dacca town. After coming to Calcutta, he lost another one of his loved ones. Do you remember?"

"I remember, I told you about the uncle you lost, didn't I?" her father said quietly.

"You told me about him but you forgot to tell me about the emotional state of your family members after all these negative events."

"He never shared his feelings with me. It was your grandmother who raised me, almost single-handedly. He only came around when it was time for reprimanding."

"Did you ask him about his feelings?"

"Tanushree! That's enough!" her mother said in a strict voice.

"Sorry, I don't mean to make you feel bad, Father. I know you've shared all you remember with me and I'm very grateful for that. But you were only a child back then. Things were more complex than they seemed on the surface and it's clear from his letters."

She ran up the stairs to her room and took out the letters and pictures from her suitcase. Then she walked back down with her arms loaded. The following few hours they sat in silence and read her grandfather's letters. She showed them the pictures and told them everything Judith had explained to her. Her father shed tears from time to time and the others were contemplative. Even her mother, who always thought it was so important to move on and forget about the past, seemed a bit moved. Tanushree often wondered why she was like that. She had hardly lived outside Calcutta when she was younger, but her family also had strong ties with East Bengal. Her father had been a co-owner of the flight company that saved refugees from both sides.

"I need to get some air," Tanushree said.

"How could you take such a heavy load on your shoulders without telling us?" Alokesh asked.

"It's OK, I could talk to Joshua. I needed to digest a bit before I told you."

"You could talk to Joshua?" her mother asked raising her eyebrow.

At that moment, her family looked up again. She had not told them about her relationship with Joshua and she decided to keep it to herself until very recently.

"Yes, Mother, he shares my curiosity about the yesteryears of India."

Chapter 19

Four months later, Debendranath embraced his college classmate Isiah Cohen and bade him farewell. He had accompanied Isiah's little sister Hannah, her husband Avram, and her two-twenty-something year old sons to see Isiah off at the Dum Dum Airport.

"I shall miss you, Isiah. I wish you would reconsider your decision and stay here instead of going halfway around the globe to do barrister training."

"And I shall miss you, my dear friend. Take good care of your health and do look after the law firm for me. Who knows, maybe in a few years I will come back," said Isiah and embraced Debu.

Isiah Cohen wore his spectacles on his head as he read the airport signboards. He was far-sighted, so he did not need to wear them all the time. That morning he had put on an elegant grey suit and a navy-blue tie, but the tears that rolled down his face were now landing on the suit leaving little marks of sadness. The Cohen family had recently sold off part of their jute business for Isiah to have enough money once he reached London. He, in turn, had got rid of all his belongings and was now about to board a plane to England carrying nothing but a suitcase. As he made his way towards the check-in counter, Isiah considered his friend's suggestion once more. The decision had not been easy. It made him sad to think of how society had changed around him over the years in Calcutta. His plan had not always been to leave the country. On the contrary, when India had taken up the fight for independence, Isiah too was elated and full of idealism. He joined his Hindu, Muslim, Buddhist, Christian and Parsee friends from Presidency College in the erstwhile demonstrations. They wanted an independent India free from colonial rule. Debendranath had introduced him to his party fellows.

"You should absolutely go and visit him, Debendranath," said Hannah and kissed her brother on his cheek. But they all knew a trip to Europe would not be possible as he was still fighting with his financial situation. It would probably be the last time he would see his dear friend. Isiah felt a lump in his throat.

"Will your cousin receive you at Heathrow, Isiah?" Isiah's cousin had moved ahead of the rest of the family to make practical arrangements in London.

"Yes, I believe he will," he replied.

The two-decade-long friendship with Debendranath had meant a lot to Isiah. Most of all he felt included in the Bengali culture. He abhorred how the older parish members sometimes looked down on the 'Bengalis' even though at home he had always learnt to be grateful about being born and brought up in Calcutta. His mother would tell him repeatedly it was one of the few places where anti-Semitism was almost unheard of and the Baghdadi Jews had prospered and done very well in society. A few decades from now, many parish members would make 'Aliyah' to the newly formed Israel. Others would go to try their luck in the land of the King or America. Many international companies would close down, unsure of how the economic situation would look like after the new socialist government took over. At the same time, Calcutta would become overpopulated with refugees. In the year 1947, the city would witness turmoil. All this would plant a seed of fear into the whole Cohen family and finally lead them to make the decision to move to England.

Twenty-two years before the Second Partition, Isiah turned around one last time and waved to Debendranath. The man shed tears as he watched his friend walk towards the aircraft.

"Goodbye, Isiah!" he exclaimed.

Isiah's gesture of inviting him to work at his law firm had been the first action that made Debendranath feel at home after coming back to Calcutta. Isiah was one of few friends who had insistently kept in touch with him through his ups and downs over the years. Also, when his mental state changed radically after losing his job in Hazaribagh, his former classmate stood by his side. Debendranath knew by now he would never move back to East Bengal. His birthplace had been lush green and full of natural beauty. It had been the land where Muslims and Hindus lived in peace. Never had he imagined the demonic cruelty that would soon kill his brother. With that act, the land of his former home would stop existing to him. On top of it, the zamindari system would be abolished by the state, so he would have no property to return to.

"How are you, Debu?" Chandramukhi knew this day would not be easy for her husband. He sat on the porch as usual with the Statesman in his hand. He pretended to read but his gaze was somewhere far away. The evening was dark but kerosene lamps in every home were lit to brighten up the neighbourhood. Outside, one could hear the sound of moths. She knew he listened to her advice often, but she would never be able to replace the pragmatic side of Isiah.

"You have to be brave for Isiah. Keep your focus on the law firm, dear. You owe it to him." She instilled courage into her husband.

On the Shabbat two weeks after arriving in England, Isiah visited a synagogue for the first time in his new country. It was housed in an old red brick building in East London. As he entered the building on Saturday morning a tall man with chestnut brown hair and thin green eyes walked up to Isiah. His scrutinising facial expression was serious and judgemental.

"Are you a member of the parish?" he asked Isiah without even greeting the man. His tone was hostile.

"I hope to become a member, sir. I have recently immigrated to London from the city of Calcutta in India."

"Are there Jews in India? I didn't know our people could be dark-skinned."

At first, Isiah did not know what to reply. People rarely called his skin complexion dark in India but he looked around him. In fact, most members of the congregation were more fair-skinned than himself. Some of them were even blond and had blue eyes, very different from the Magen David parish in Calcutta. He could have given the man a long speech about the Jews of India, but he realised this parishioner was not susceptible to such information.

"My family hails from Baghdadi Jews who immigrated from Iraq to Calcutta in the early 19th century."

The man looked sceptical upon Isiah's reply, but became quiet and left without a word of welcome. The rabbi took out the Torah rolls.

The first period in London brought many similar shocks to Isiah. It was tough for him to endure. He wished he could have someone to confide in. His cousin and his wife seemed to have a very different experience to his in London. The preparation time in London had been very successful for Nathaniel. It became increasingly difficult for Isiah to describe to them how it felt to be jobless with little social contacts in his new home town. He began to feel like a scavenger in their home.

In the evening after coming home from the synagogue, Isiah took another spoon of the thin broth and a bite of the rye bread. His cousin's family still had too little funds to buy proper food. Living on one man's income was hard. The rent of the small terraced house in Golders Green was high and their savings account almost empty. Unlike other immigrants from the Commonwealth, they at least did not have to live in immigrant camps. Nathaniel had already made arrangements for a home for them before they arrived.

Isiah sat shivering in the living room. Up until now he had got by with his raincoat, but he needed something with more lining to keep him insulated from the cold. He decided to go to Harrods to buy an overcoat. Walking down tree-lined street that afternoon he suddenly felt observed. It was an elderly lady who walked towards him on the pavement. There was nothing vicious in her manner of staring but rather curiosity. Isiah turned to her with a courteous smile.

"Hello, sir, would you mind if I touched your hair?"

It was a simple question, but Isiah was so unused to getting this type of attention that he did not know how to respond. He decided the question had just been an act of innocence on the woman's part, so he let the elderly lady touch his hair.

"I hope you don't mind. I have never seen a brown person before."

"No, not at all."

Despite uttering that sentence, he felt very uncomfortable. It was almost like being a puppet. But he did know how to differentiate between malevolence and curiosity.

One day in the first half of Michaelmas term a timid red-haired girl knocked on his door. She began to ask questions about Jurisprudence. The questions were well thought through, and he thought to himself it must have been in response to his tuition ad at the local grocery store.

"Please come in, Esther." She stepped in and bent down to undo her laces. Her every move was gentle. She reminded him of Debapriya, a bit precocious but shy. They spent an hour of tuition. She was his first student since he had arrived in the country. From this day on, they would meet every weekday for three months to come.

"If you ask your questions in class, then the other students would benefit also from the answers," Isiah said.

For a moment, she stared at him intently. His words had spoken to her. The timid red-haired girl then smiled, thanked him and bade him goodbye. After coming home from court, the next day he waited for her questions. She stimulated him intellectually. The young girl read his facial expressions and told him she had felt encouraged to put up her hand in class. He could hear an accent when she spoke. It was German if he was not mistaken. He knew her name was Esther Katz. She must be Jewish too, albeit Ashkenazi and not Sephardic as himself. The red-haired girl must have come as a refugee during the war. Was it the accent that made her refrain from speaking in class the first day? He knew how evil youngsters could be to those that did not fit the societal norm. As he taught her that afternoon their eyes met again. Her blue eyes expressed open-mindedness and a deep willingness to understand what he was saying. He caught himself lingering a little bit longer than necessary. She gave him a sense of safety. When she spoke to him he had to lower his gaze not to show his infatuation. As the days passed, she became like an enigmatic muse to him, who inspired him to become a better teacher. He had sat isolated with his work for many months now and getting that kind of inspiration from another human being was something he had never felt before.

Almost three months had gone since Isiah had moved to London. He had remained a bachelor and continued living with his cousin's family in the terraced house in Golders Green. He was able to contribute to the family economy and felt better about himself these days. He had reached the age of 39. Things had become better at work. He had grown quite successful with his research on the causes of youth pilferage in inner-city London. At the same time, he went on working as a lecturer and practised the piano when he came home in the evenings. By the age of a pension holder, he felt rejuvenated.

"What is behind the smile on your lips?" Nathaniel asked.

"There's nothing. I just thought about something funny that happened on the tube today." His cousin was glad to hear he finally enjoyed life in London so much it could bring a smile to his lips even at the dinner table.

They were interrupted by a knock on the front door.

"Hello, my name is George Smith. I'm your new next-door neighbour." The elderly gentleman stretched out his hand.

"Nice to meet you, Mr Smith. I'm Isiah Cohen and I live here with my cousin Nathaniel and his wife Ada."

"Mr Cohen, I'm actually here on an errand. I'm an amateur cellist and I'm looking for a pianist to accompany me at a concert a month from now. It seems like someone in your home practises the piano every evening and it is quite an enjoyment to the ear."

"I am honoured that you feel that way, Mr Smith. I usually just play to keep myself happy," replied Isiah, who had never performed to an audience before.

"It is a Sicilienne by Gabriel Faure that I want to recite. It's not a very hard piece. I can bring you the musical score by tomorrow evening. Will you be free to rehearse then?"

"Yes, Mr Smith, I do think I will. You are most welcome to come by."

Just like Tanushree and Joshua 97 years later, these two men found each other through music and Isiah was finally going to be acknowledged for his skills. The life events that are so common during younger years for most people of his calibre seemed to come to Isiah late in life. Was it because he always kept his character and his talents to himself?

The evening finally came. The two of them were on the stage and in the audience sat around 200 people. Isiah was tense, but ventured to look out at the audience before they began. On the second row, he saw the face of someone he recognised. For a moment, he just stared in awe. It was Abdul! His old acquaintance noticed him and smiled at him. He felt elated as he accompanied George Smith that evening. The old man came to shake his hand after the piece ended and the audience applauded. He felt a pair of blue eyes looking at him and then slowly turning for the door. His eyes lingered on Esther as Abdul came up to the stage.

"My friend, how did you find me and what brings you back to London?" They embraced each other.

"I am training to become a barrister at old age, Isiah. I found an advertisement for this recital in a coffee shop in town. You seem to be doing very well. There is a radiance in your face. Why have you never performed for us? I'm sorry it took such a long time for me to find you. I had to look up the British phone book finally. I am going back to Calcutta next week."

"I see. Well, please join us for dinner. Also, please send my regards to Debu and Chandramukhi. Tell them not to be worried, I know I haven't written to him for a while, but I have been busy with work and had little news to come with."

"Little news? Are you sure about that? Who was the lovely woman your eyes rested on after the concert, Isiah?"

Isiah smiled, but let the rest be unsaid. After all, the feelings he had were ungodly.

Chapter 20

Tanushree's eardrums ached. When they had decided to join her parents for an Indian celebration earlier that evening, she had not expected the sounds of an unknown upbeat melody to evoke emotional turmoil in her. Perhaps, had she become pampered by the weekly Indian classical concerts in Berlin, the city where she had lived the past four years – those Thursday concerts when she was part of an audience who listened and appreciated Indian classical music. The Bollywood song began ringing noisily in her ears again and she fidgeted. She wore a maroon salwaar kameez with a grey churni. For the second time in a year, she wore make-up and was dressed up. She had stopped caring about her looks, the more isolated she had become the past year. People she had never seen before walked up to the stage and began to dance to the music now. She had come to pay her respects to the country where she had her roots, not because she was patriotic, but because culturally she still identified herself as an Indian. It was the first time she had attended this type of celebration in her home town for more than a decade. Hundreds and hundreds of people had joined forces with the once meagre community of Indians in the city. Growing up, she seldom had the opportunity to attend Indian celebrations. She rather identified with the Muslim community of the country she was born in, more than the next to non-existent Hindus.

That evening in the middle of the song, something stirred up emotions in her. Suddenly, she clenched her handbag, stood up and left the front row seat. She knew Indian culture in this city often meant light music, but yet she had expected something more civilised. As a musician, she was particularly sensitive about it. She had not come to attend a disco! When she felt her tears coming, she bit her lower lip and walked away even more hurriedly. Her feet paced for two reasons. One was to have peace and quiet, and the other was to forget what the music reminded her of – Those horrible days when she was an outcast of the Swedish Indian society. Those days when all the Indian children went to "Indian" parties and she sat at home. Those days when they made friends with each other and she wrote stories to have an imaginary world to elope to over weekends. Her drawers were still full of short stories about Iranian girls who were brought up in the north-eastern parts of the city and fell in love with ethnically Swedish boys who grew up in the more affluent neighbourhoods of the city and lived happily ever after. One day, after a long discussion in school about how highly educated immigrants never got the jobs they deserved, her immigrant classmate had left the room in frustration, much to the surprise of the other classmates. It had dawned on Tanushree then she was not the only one harbouring such emotions, even though she had sat there watching as a quiet observer. That incident had fuelled her interest in women's rights around the world, so in the afternoon she went to the library and borrowed all the books she could find on the topic. Her Swedish teacher had asked, "Why are your female protagonists always Iranian by ethnicity and never Indian?" The 15-year old Tanushree sat there dumbstruck. Her teacher wondered why she did not write love stories about girls with whom she could identify better. Tanushree could not possibly tell her she was not the kind of girl who attracted boys. Those were also the days when she had stopped jogging, gained weight and become more and more convinced no one would ever look her way. Or should she maybe tell her teacher that to her, Iranian girls were beautiful and street smart just like those Indian girls who went to the bhangra parties?

She remembered how she had always felt left out when the loud music began at the end of the Indian functions in her young days. This was when all the young people walked up to the stage and began dancing. She secretly dreamt of dancing with them, because she wanted to be beautiful and smart like the other girls in her community. But there was never an invitation, and so she had always fled so as not to humiliate herself. Her friends in those days would scold her for being haughty. Tonight, she was happy that the boy with the friendly eyes had acknowledged her. That small gesture was all she had craved to feel included.

Oh, how she had felt like an outsider growing up in this city. Twenty years later and still single, how she had loved going to the Berlin functions where she was a part of something. But there was yet another reason why Tanushree ran out of the theatre that evening. It was her mother. She had never been able to establish herself as a classical musician because she lived in a city which could not appreciate her art. Have courage, she told herself as she walked out of the hall. Then she thought about the PhD thesis which lay on her desk. It was her attempt to translate the importance of Indian classical music to the audience she grew up with, both western and ethnically Indian. She had not been able to finish the corrections for months, but this soiree and its shortcomings had made her more determined that she would finish it. It was her way of showing how the different cultures completed each other.

After walking out the door to the hallway, she felt someone watching her from behind. It was him, the man she had brought to the soiree to show off her community. He stood with his back against the wall. His blue shirt and ironed black pants suited him well. His face was clean-shaven.

"How are you?" Joshua asked when she turned around. For a moment, she wondered, however, she would begin to explain.

"I am fine, thank you." The lump in her throat tightened as he looked deeply into her eyes. He came forward and wrapped his arms around her. As they went to open the door she smiled. She exhaled into the Swedish summer night. But before the door closed behind her, one of the aunties she had met a few times in her younger days, grabbed her arm.

"Tanushree, so nice to see you. What are you up to these days?" the elderly lady asked.

"I am about to finish my PhD, Aunty," she replied in her humble tone. "How are…"

Before she had the chance to finish her sentence, the conversation had evolved into something she had feared the moment the elderly lady came up to her.

"You know, beti, all of my relatives are successful doctors, lawyers and engineers – just like yours! My family owns a three-storey house in Lahore."

Deep down, Tanushree knew these kinds of words only came out when people felt frustrated. It was a way of feeling better about themselves. She purposely stayed away from the lot who could not acknowledge their deprivation. She knew the elderly lady had been forced to live under much more stringent conditions in Sweden than in her native town. Her qualification was never acknowledged by Swedish society, but that was not what she wanted to convey. The lady did not speak about the emotional journey she had made in Sweden; neither did she attempt to educate her listener. At one point, Tanushree

171

stopped listening and looked away towards the hall from where the Bollywood music was still belting.

On the way home in the car, nobody spoke, but once they reached the Roy Chowdhury residence, Joshua asked Tanuhsree to sit in the garden. Now felt like the time to ask him about his childhood to her.

"Tell me about your childhood best friend again. Where did you meet her?" asked Tanushree.

"Oh, I met Cornelia in secondary school. She was really fun to hang out with. She loved sports just as much as our male classmates. We would play football almost every recess," Joshua answered.

"So you were well-integrated with them at that age?"

"Yes, I was still normal if I may call it that, and she was lovely," Joshua replied.

"Tell me what made her lovely apart from her interest in sports," she begged.

"I didn't have to explain things; she just knew by the look of me."

"What went wrong?"

"We began our A levels, and I took a step back," he replied.

"Why?"

"I was going into manic phases. I walked hour after hour and stayed awake night after night thinking about all kinds of rubbish. I knew something was wrong with me."

"Is this when you began to get bullied?" Tanushree asked.

"Yes, I put on weight, became plump and had pimples on my face. I also became more and more anti-social. I felt like I had no one to confide in. One day the boys plunged my head in the toilet and flushed."

"Didn't Cornelia come to your rescue?"

"I'm not sure she knew. She had stepped away more and more, because every time she defended me people began teasing her, but most girls were on her side. So, when I tried to catch a glance, she seldom looked back."

"Didn't you feel unmotivated to go to class?" Tanushree asked.

"I was regularly late for class, but I did well on my exams."

"Did you ever have an eye to eye talk with Cornelia again?"

"Yes, one day I called her on the phone in the middle of a manic episode. I told her I loved her."

"What did she respond?"

"She said she was in love with her cricket instructor and they were in a relationship."

"I'm sorry, Joshua," Tanushree put her hand on his shoulder.

"Well, it has been a while, Tanu, and I have you now." he smiled and drew her near him.

"So, out of curiosity, why did you run out of the hall today?" Joshua asked.

"I don't like loud parties. I often react like that – because it reminds me of my younger days. I was always the odd one out at those parties. My place was at my desk at home, not at a disco with people I knew nothing about."

"So, you know what I'm talking about then." He grasped her hand.

On the flight back to Berlin, Joshua held her hand. It made her feel safe, an emotion she had longed for the longest time. She put her head on his shoulder and closed her eyes. She dreamt she had just boarded the flight from Calcutta. She used to spend the first two hours on the flight shedding tears, and she was not the only one knowing she had to wait a year to see her family members again. There would be no rowdy family parties within that time, and perhaps by then one or two of the elders would be gone.

London used to be the end of the journey after thirteen over hours they of travelling with American, Canadian and British Indians. Some of them she had come by at Calcutta Club and musical functions at larger venues. She had taken a liking to their accents, it made her think about the last time she had seen her Californian cousins. No matter how many times people would laugh at her funny accent she would have fun with them. She remembered her cousin's wedding in LA. A woman had walked up to her and told her she had been in the same class her aunt. Another woman told her she had heard her mother sing before she left Calcutta. Those comments had made her feel something she rarely felt in Sweden, where there was only one family with ties to her family from prior to moving from Calcutta. The last flight, albeit only two hours from London, felt extremely lonely. She knew she was heading back to being of a minority again. No looks of curiosity even though people had questions. A few days she would be able to keep herself happy from the last few common waves of laughter in Calcutta and the cosiness from the flight.

"How can you feel so close to people you only meet once a year?" her classmates would ask when she was back in Gothenburg, and she would go through the trouble of explaining.

"It's different, because we see all our daily routines, from the morning fried eggs to the evening dinner combined with loud discussions. It's not like only spending a few hours together."

Chapter 21

He was gone again. Of course, he was gone! Tanushree could tell what had happened this time. Akash and her mother had stepped on his toes and Joshua's insecurity had taken over. She held the key to his apartment in one hand and the banister in the other. When she opened the door to the flat and stepped in, there was pin-drop silence.

"Joshua," she called his name a few times, but no one answered.

Then she took out her phone from the backpack and called him, but there was still no reply. She called a couple of times, but to no use. She hated it how he could just walk out of her life with no warning. It gave her second thoughts, even though this time she knew exactly why he had disappeared. She felt very little compassion. Why could he not just have stayed and talked to her about what he felt? And why did he not answer the phone? She walked into the empty living room. Only the bed, a closet and a sofa were left. She feared the worst – that he had taken the morning flight to London. Maybe it was his way of breaking up…

"He hasn't answered the phone for over two weeks. It seems to be out of battery."

"He's so irresponsible. Don't tell me I didn't warn you!"

"That's not my impression at all."

"He used to be in love with one of our classmates."

"I know; he has told me all of that."

"She fancied him too, but he pulled away."

"Have you ever considered that there might be a reason?"

"I know that the other boys used to tease him sometimes."

"Teased? Would you call holding someone's head down the toilet bowl teasing?"

"I didn't know about that," Rohini said defensively.

"We talked about that the other day. He began to feel very bad about himself."

"I'm sorry, Tanu, I didn't know too much about what he went through in school."

Tanushree began to feel really upset with her cousin at the same time as she felt pity for Joshua.

"It makes me sad to hear that nobody cared."

"He made the funniest choices," Rohini said quietly.

"What were they, if I may ask?"

"He aced the Physics and Mathematics exams, but instead of applying for Cambridge or Oxford, he began studying music."

"…at a very good institution, if I may add…and so did I. Is studying music such a crime, Rohini?"

"It doesn't exactly bring in a lot of money. Everyone knows that."

"Well, I've played with him, and he's quite skilled."

"Stop defending him all the time. The man hasn't called you for two weeks…"

Rohini's face became serious as if she suddenly remembered something. Tanushree inhaled quickly.

"Tanu, there is something he hasn't told you. I think you should contact his parents."

Joshua's mother took off her turquoise flowery scarf and hung it on the backrest of the chair. She was an elegant elderly woman with short brown curly hair wearing a pearl necklace. For her age, her skin was unusually unblemished, and her eyes were the same light blue as her son's. She had expressed a wish to see her when Rohini told her she was trying to get in contact with Joshua. So this weekend, she had made another one of her train journeys from Paris to London.

"You probably find it odd to meet me. After all, you have only met my son a couple of times. I just came to give you a word of warning, Tanushree. He is not like everyone else."

"Being fed-up with the culture of bragging about your children that she was often exposed to as someone with Indian roots, her honesty was very refreshing to her. Although, from Rohini's words and by studying Joshua's behaviour, she had already figured out he was different."

"In what way is he different, Mrs Salisbury?"

"Please, call me Judith, Tanushree. He has always spent a lot of time on his own and sometimes he can be withdrawn in social situations. When he works, he can spend hours and hours in silence because he needs to concentrate. But he can be incredibly thoughtful and caring when he is on his own with you. He just has his own ways of showing emotions. He can also have a wonderful sense of humour at times if I may say so. I am sure you have already noticed some of these sides."

She had a smile on her thin lips and Tanushree smiled back at her. She could not help but picture how she would be as a mother-in-law. Then her facial expression became serious. She leaned towards her over the table and lowered her voice.

"Tanushree, my son was diagnosed with bipolar disorder when he was eighteen and as a consequence, he has developed social anxiety. We usually don't tell people, because I don't want him to be looked upon any differently. It's enough that he's aware of it. But I came here to ask you to not be angry with him for not responding to your phone calls and emails."

She was not surprised, so she hardly reacted, but she began to understand why she had felt such a connection. As a classical violinist, she had come across many bipolar personalities along the years.

"Judith, I actually had a manic episode myself three years ago."

She touched her hand and looked into her eyes with what seemed to her to be empathy.

"Then you know what the condition is all about Tanushree. But you probably also know that the disorder can express itself in many different ways."

She nodded.

"My son has a rather severe form but he's under medication since many years back. It does its work most of the time except under strong emotional stimuli. My question to you is — are you ready to take on the challenge this means, especially since you have yourself suffered from mental illness?"

It felt unfair that she should be judged because she had had an episode of mania in the past when she was still capable of leading a normal life.

"I would do my utmost to try to understand him and be patient Judith. I am convinced suffering from a similar condition can make it easier to understand the other person sometimes. But he also has to understand me. We have to find a way of supporting each other equally. I got really worried when he didn't respond."

177

"I like your way of thinking, Tanushree, and I'm certain you will try sincerely. I'll bring you to his flat and then you can talk to him in person or just be there for him. I remember that evening in Cadogan Hall two years ago, I saw how he looked at you when the two of you were talking before the concert and I noticed you were accompanying Rohini. I was hoping he would bring you home one day, but he never did."

She smiled and Tanushree blushed. She drew a deep breath. She could feel how her chest cavity filled with air and then she exhaled with expectation. This woman was really quite something, just like her son.

"How did you figure out he was bipolar, Judith?"

Tanushree poured some tea into her cup from the porcelain pot which was on the table.

"He had depressive phases and social anxiety from a young age. I knew something was different from the beginning, so my father stayed at home with him when he was little. During his first year in school, he didn't talk to any of his classmates. His teacher sent him to a speech pathologist. We tried to explain his behaviour and social withdrawal, but they wouldn't listen to us. Around the time he began his A levels, he went into manic phases. Sometimes he stayed up all nights several days in a row to study, or woke up at dawn to practice the piano. He could walk relentlessly for hours and hours. Sometimes, he would call all his friends in the middle of the night, which was unusual considering he never liked talking on the phone otherwise."

"Did his friends understand him?" she asked.

"Very rarely. In the beginning, they thought he was drunk when he called, but with time they realised something was different about him and his classmates began talking behind his back. It was a very tough period for him, because his manic behaviour was out of personality and he never had the chance to explain to anyone. He was really just a shy young swotter."

She thought back on her own first manic episode. Years of solitude in a foreign country with no one to confide in had caused emotional stress, lack of sleep and multiple depressive phases. Her body had played around with her neurotransmitters and hormones, which finally caused mania. Suddenly, she felt anger against her cousin Rohini, who had described Joshua as an oddball. She had never taken the time to try to understand him.

"But, Tanushree, you won't have to worry too much about this. He very rarely gets manic these days, but sometimes he does shut himself up to conserve energy just like he's doing now. You may end up feeling very lonely at times. I hope that's OK with you."

She took the last bite of her date and walnut loaf. Then she looked at her and nodded to show that she was ready for the challenge.

"There's one more thing, Tanushree."

Her tone worried her, and she prepared herself for the worst possible scenario.

"Did you say your surname was Roy Chowdhury, Tanushree?"

"Yes, that's right."

"That was all I wanted to know, dear. I'll see you tomorrow in West Kensington."

She was perplexed. What was so important about her surname? She grabbed her handbag, stood up and kissed her goodbye on the cheek.

That evening, she found the name Joshua Salisbury in her inbox.

Dear Tanu,

First of all, I would like to apologise for not being in touch for a long time, but I hope this email finds you well. The truth is that I have had one of my low phases. I was in bed for two whole weeks and hardly left home. I tried to work, but my body just wanted to sleep. I found no motivation at all. How are you? Is Berlin treating you well nowadays? I have been thinking a lot about you, the little time we had in Berlin and Gothenburg, and the recital felt magical. It was my first public performance since music college and you made me feel really relaxed about it. If you are not too busy during the coming weekends, why don't you come by one of these days? I really enjoy our conversations and I am looking forward to seeing you tomorrow.

Josh

Chapter 22

The July morning in 1926 when he saw Esther again, Isiah sat at the Savoy, just a stone's throw from her university. He drank his tea and munched on a cheese sandwich. The term had finished. He was correcting papers, but Esther had caught his attention. She sat in the far corner towards the window with a book in her right hand and a cup of tea in her left. He leaned down to see what she was reading but without success.

The place was quiet. The only sound he heard was the waiter washing cups behind the bar. Apart from Esther and Isiah, there was only one other customer there.

Esther was wearing a long dark blue coat and under it, he could see her black silk stockings. In his eyes, she had the excruciating beauty of a young woman. Her skin was pale and smooth without a blemish, and the sun rays coming through the window caused her silky red wavy hair to shine. Her cherry lipstick made her lips look lustrous. He tried to restrain himself, and turned his gaze to the floor knowing he should not be thinking those thoughts about a woman 20 years younger than himself. Until very recently she had been his student, he could absolutely not allow himself to think this way about her – and yet he did.

For a moment, he left the building to go out and smoke a cigarette, but his eyes rested on her.

"How are you, sir?"

He startled. As he came back into the hotel, he turned to notice the friendly waiter with a French accent. The waiter made attempts to talk to him every Friday when he came to the hotel, but as the man of few words he was, Isiah did not linger for small talk.

"I'm fine, thank you."

He gave a smile. Then he walked over the floor of black and white marble tiles to go back to his seat as discretely as he could, careful to stay out of

Esther's field of view. He wondered to himself what would happen if she spotted him. What would such a young girl talk about with an old man like him? Would she be interested in his many life anecdotes? Isiah did not think she had noticed him as he was walking back to the table. Only when she could glimpse him at the corner of her eye, did he shift his gaze to look down at his well-polished black shoes, but it was too late. She smiled towards him and as he went to sit down he felt a tap on his shoulder.

"Hello, Professor Cohen. Nice to see you here."

He admired her guts. Never would he have dared to walk up to her himself.

"Hello, Esther. Please, call me Isiah. We are no longer in the company of your fellow students and nor am I any longer your professor."

Now that she was standing closer, he could see the book she held in her hand was Geetanjali. He could smell the rose scent she wore. As surprising as it was to him that she was reading the great poet of his youth, it gave him a sense of connection to her. His initial nervousness and doubt of whether they would have something to talk about disappeared.

"I have seen you a few times at the synagogue. I did not know you were a member of the parish, Isiah. In fact, by the judgement of your academic merits, I would have guessed religiosity was not your cup of tea," Esther continued. She spoke with the same intensity and curiosity as she had always done in class.

"I always thought science and religion were good complements to one another, and with science, I obviously mean the Social sciences. Little do I know if you would expect the same answer from someone who studies the Natural sciences," said Isiah.

"I have always loved your wit, Isiah. There was a reason why I enjoyed attending your lectures."

Not that he had not noticed her in the synagogue. He had seen her there many times with her family, but he kept a low profile. He did not want her to think he could do whatever he wanted to his students because of his position and stature. Sometimes when he looked at her in the synagogue, he could sense his sister's eyes at the back of his neck. His family had always been wanting him to find a partner, and seeing him observing the same young attractive woman week after week certainly caught their interest. The only thing was that they did not know how young she was.

"Do you enjoy reading the works of the Bard of Bengal?"

"Oh, do you mean Rabindranath Tagore? I wish I had had the luck to visit Calcutta. Isn't that where you're from?"

"That's right."

He smiled at the thought that she wanted to visit his home town.

"Do you miss it?"

"I do at times, yes."

"What is it you miss about it?" She was very persistent with her questions as always.

"I miss being equal with the average man." Something made Isiah open up to her.

"You know, Isiah, when my family came here we did not even have a home. I was in my teens but did not speak a word of English. My classmates could say the meanest things. I missed Berlin every day but I knew I would most likely be taken to a concentration camp if I returned. I was lucky to have both my parents and my siblings with me, but many of our relatives were killed. I always think one should ignore the ignorant, Isiah. Otherwise, they will pull you down with their assumptions. Besides, you are a scientist Isiah! Scientists shouldn't believe in other people's assumptions." Isiah listened to his former student's words intently. The difference between them apart from the age factor was that his home town would never send him to a concentration camp.

"Thank you for encouraging me, Esther."

She smiled.

"I just wanted to share a way of thinking that helped me when I came as an immigrant to this country. I have to go, Isiah, but I hope to see you soon again. I want to hear all your stories about Calcutta."

"I would be happy to share them with you, Esther."

Esther walked up to the till to pay. She too seemed familiar with the waiter. Unlike Isiah, she engaged in conversation with him, but he could not hear what they were talking about.

While he was preparing to leave for the day, Isiah heard someone knocking on the door to his office. It was past five o'clock and the classes had finished a long time ago. As he opened the door, he was met by Esther's youthful face.

"Hello, Esther. What brings you here this evening?"

"I was wondering whether you could give me your view on my assignment for the Criminal Law course."

"It is certainly not my speciality, but let us see what we can do."

"I thought you worked on youth pilferage in the city."

This woman never ceased to bewilder him. She must have looked up his work secretly. He smiled at her. Esther took out the papers from her brown bag, sat down in front of him on the chair which was padded with a red cushion and started reading aloud. They had a long discussion about her paper, and as always, Isiah was satisfied with her work. He was not only impressed, but he was actually proud of her. When they had gone through the whole paper, Madeleine became quiet, her eyes turned to Isiah's hands. He cringed, wondering what she was thinking.

"Why aren't you married, Isiah?" She was just as blunt as Debapriya had been two decades earlier.

This girl was certainly more direct than she had given the impression of being the first day she had walked up to him in class. Isiah's whole face turned crimson.

"I suppose no one has ever fallen for me." He stammered and his voice was trembling. It was a very sensitive topic for him.

"Surely someone has. You are far too good-looking and intelligent to not have been noticed."

He smiled to himself at the thought that she should think that.

"Well, thank you for saying that."

"No, I really mean it. You are such an emotionally stable and witty man, Isiah, even though you keep a lot to yourself." He had never looked upon himself as an emotionally stable man.

"What is your own answer to your question, Esther? Are you seeing anyone?"

On the spur of the moment, he had decided to ask. Isiah had been gathering the courage to ask that question for a long time, but never dared to. In fact, he had never dared to ask anyone that question after the love of his life married another man without even giving him a word of warning. Now that they were speaking on a personal level, he thought it would be a good time.

"I was seeing someone until three months ago, one of my own classmates, but he went behind my back with another girl." Her voice became mellow and she looked down at the desk.

"I am sorry to hear that. I don't understand why anyone would want to treat you that way."

"No, you don't understand because you are good-hearted and too much of a gentleman, Isiah. I bet you would never do that to any woman. Younger men think they can do whatever they want and get away with it."

She sighed and then looked him deeply in the eyes. Then she lifted her hand from the chair handle and let it stroke his slender fingers. For a moment, Isiah gasped for air. There was no need for pretence anymore. She reciprocated his feelings just as he had suspected. He leaned over the desk. His fingers trembled as they approached her face for the first time. The touch left her pale cheek blushing. They let their eyes linger on each other's faces. He leaned forward once more and let his lips touch hers. It was the first time ever he had experienced the bliss of a kiss in his lifetime of 39 years.

The following Saturday at the synagogue, Esther introduced Isiah to her parents. He recognized her father immediately. It was the man who had asked him about his origins the first day in synagogue four years earlier.

"Isiah was my Jurisprudence professor, Vater."

"Do you call all your professors by their first name, Esther?" her father asked.

The middle-aged man who was probably around the same age as Isiah, did not look happy at all. He had already sensed something was the matter between his daughter and this very atypical Jewish man from their many affectionate glances the past months. Hannah noticed the man's reaction and looked at her brother's face. She knew how much Isiah had fought his romantic emotions in the past and remembered all about Debapriya. Falling in love with a twenty-year younger student was not ideal, but she just wanted her brother to experience the happiness he had always sought during the remaining years of life. Why did he always have to take on impossible missions? The face of Madeleine's father grew redder and redder in anger.

"I suppose you are looking to marry to gain British citizenship, Professor Cohen."

No one had uttered any words of marriage. Isiah, who was usually good-tempered, felt provoked by the man's ill manners and lack of knowledge. So, now he was going to do just as the man's daughter had told him. He was going to ignore the ignorant but as a teacher, he felt a need to educate them too.

"In fact, Mr Katz, I have a British citizenship from India, so no, that type of marriage does not interest me."

"Let's go home, Esther," the man said in a bitter tone, grabbing his daughter's arm and leading her away from Isiah's family. She turned around to look at Isiah before she was forced to leave.

Part III

Chapter 23

Dear Isiah,

I hardly know how to begin this letter. A few days ago, I experienced the first bombing in my life. It took place in the Kidderpore docks, thus not far from our dwelling. The newspapers are telling us that very few were injured and next to none died, but from the sounds that day I doubt they are telling us the truth. Surely, a significant number of lascars must have been wounded if not killed. It was the Japanese who bombed. It seems like they want to occupy Calcutta the way they have occupied Singapore. It was an awful feeling, knowing the bombs could hit our abode at any time. When the house started shaking, we took shelter under our bed. We thought we had prepared enough by curfew and blackout. How is the situation in London? I wish I could say I hope you will never experience anything like that, but something tells me that you already have, considering that you are in the epicentre of this unholy war. No matter what I hope, you and your family are safe, wherever you are.

Yours sincerely,
Debu

Tanushree clenched the thin envelope, knowing this was only the beginning of the World War II story. She and Joshua sat on the stairs of the Gedächtniskirche, where she had suggested to meet after only reading a few lines of the letter. The church had stood there with its oxidised half-bombed copper roof since the last world war. A beautiful and sunny afternoon had turned gloomy. It began drizzling, and in only a moment's time, she could smell wet pitch blended with something metallic. After studying her face, Joshua grasped her hand.

"Let's take one step at a time, OK?" he said.

Two cars passed by on the high street.

"I wonder how it must have been for your grand-parents, considering how much the city was destroyed during the war. Weren't they scared?" she said at last.

"I know they moved out to Buckinghamshire for a few years, but they still kept their house in Golder's Green," Joshua answered.

A little boy jumped in a puddle in front of them, upon which his mother gripped his arm tightly and led him away.

"Subhas Chandra Bose definitely has good rhetoric. I think he'll be able to recruit many people to the German Free India Legion. Similar work is already being undertaken by The Indian National Army and I'm convinced he will want to collaborate with them," Shilpa told her Aunt Debapriya.

"I'm not very fond of his collaboration with the Axis powers. Did you know the INA was actually the brainchild of a Japanese man and not an Indian? I think they just want to occupy India like they are doing with some parts of East and Southeast Asia," said Debapriya.

"Yes, I'm also an advocate of non-violence but we might have to make many compromises to free India in the way Gandhi wants to."

It was early October 1941 and close to Durga Puja. The 52-year old Debapriya had travelled from Rangoon to Calcutta for the festive season. That evening she had brought her 24-year old niece to College Street to buy silk saris for the female family members.

"What do you think about rani pink, Shilpa? Would that be a good colour for your mother?"

"I don't know if she's into wearing bright colours."

The shopkeeper took out one sari after another. Debapriya's eye twinkled. She picked up a light blue sari with golden diamond patterns on it.

"How is work? It must be nice to be teaching in the same school as your husband."

"I'm quite enjoying it, thank you. Yes, Aditya and I spend all our waking hours together. He's teaching me tricks to get the students' attention. My voice is too soft, aunty."

"I knew from the beginning you would do well Shilpa. You with all your interests! I'm sure you will become a headmistress one day. Oh, how I had wanted to become a teacher. Who would have thought I would become a businesswoman instead and trade teak side by side with my college Mathematics lecturer?"

The middle-aged woman smiled to herself.

"Life certainly has its mysterious ways."

"Your life seems so good in Rangoon."

"We're afraid the Japanese will strike one day! Sometimes we think of moving back to Calcutta but our sons have never lived outside Burma and the inhabitants of this city are quite a handful. Aren't they?"

"They're just elated by the freedom fighters. Everyone wants independence. We would be so happy to have you near us."

"Oh, all these beautiful buildings. Do you think Calcutta will be bombed?"

"No, why would you say something like that?" Shilpa answered her aunt Debapriya.

"It's difficult to think otherwise with all that is going on in Rangoon." Her face looked and for the first time, Shilpa could clearly see the fatigue and worry. She grasped her aunt's arm.

"Do you really have to go back for Saraswati Puja?"

"I wish it could all be like in the olden golden days, but who will take care of my husband?"

"Oh, just leave him there. It was his own choice not to tag along."

"Oh!" For a moment, there was a surprise in her aunt's face, and then then they both began laughing, but very shortly, Debapriya's face turned into one of worry and scare again.

"I'm sorry, I shouldn't make blunt insensitive jokes in times of these," Shilpa said and touched her aunt on the shoulder.

"It's OK. I'm just extremely worried about what is to come."

At that moment, Shilpa realised how little she knew about the happenings of Rangoon even though her blood relatives lived there.

Chapter 24

A December evening in 1941, Chandramukhi had taken her three youngest sons Amit, Dhanesh and Alokesh to see the Christmas lightings in Park Street. Before returning home, they stopped by St Paul's Cathedral to listen to carols. The moment she entered her parents' home that evening she was met by a worried look on her husband's face, a look she had seldom seen.

"What is the matter, dear?"

In the background, she could hear a male voice on the radio.

"The Japanese have bombed Rangoon. I have sent a telegram to Debapriya to know if they are alive."

The next couple of days, tension hung in the air in the Tollygunge house. Debendranath woke up every morning and prayed. Chandramukhi had never seen her husband praying openly before. Two days after getting the news about the bombing, he sat on the veranda and reminisced about his childhood. He remembered how he and his sister used to play tag and how every day when he came back from school she came to meet him at the gate with a smile on her face. He was one of the few who could make her open up. Someone knocked on the front door. He walked out in haste to see if there was a message from Debapriya but to no avail. He had even called Sathananda's office but there was no connection.

"You have not eaten all day, dear," Chandramukhi put a hand on her husband's shoulder.

"I made an omelette. Please have it or you will fall ill."

When he looked up, she could see he had been crying. They had lived together for 36 years but she had never seen him so devastated.

"Father, you must eat. We have to keep our hopes up."

He turned around and looked at Shilpa. As she touched his shoulder, he covered his face and cried. She thought about her last conversation with her aunt and bit her lip. She had no more words of consolation and inside she was feeling empty. She knew the chances of seeing the woman again who had been her role model from childhood were small.

A month later, Debendranath returned to Hazaribagh for a few days and his wife and children stayed in Calcutta with his in-laws. Chandramukhi tutored young children of the neighbourhood to make her ends meet. She did not want to be dependent on her parents and tutoring gave her something to occupy her mind with now that her life companion was far away.

Almost two months later as she was tutoring she heard a loud knock on the front door.

"Just a moment, please."

She put on her blue Hawaii sandals and walked up to the front door. As she unlatched the door, she was met by a bearded face. The man's hollow cheeks had streaks of mud on them. His skin was tanned as if he had spent days at a stretch in the sun. His worn-out suit spoke of more prosperous days. The eyes were sunken.

"Boudi, don't you recognise me?"

Chandramukhi's heart palpitated as she realised who the man was and she gasped for air.

"Come in, Sathananda!"

He stepped into the house and as he bent down to touch her feet he began to howl.

"I'm sorry I couldn't bring back your sister-in-law and my sons. My darling wife and my precious sons are gone."

She bent down and put her hands around his cheeks to keep his face up. Then she embraced him and helped him to stand up on his feet again. Chandramukhi's mother-in-law came out and stared in awe at the broken man who had always been so well-dressed and eloquent. The pampered child who had been sent to study in England and never seen hardship. The two women led him to a chair on the veranda.

"You need to rest, Sathananda. I put clean clothes on your bed to wear after taking your bath."

He quietly drank his water from the steel mug and the two women still shocked to see him did not find the words to say. Chandramukhi called her husband to come home that afternoon. Sathananda slept until early evening the next day. At times, they heard an agonised howl.

"You are skin and bones!" Debendranath exclaimed. He looked as if he had seen a ghost after setting eyes on his brother-in-law. Sathananda said nothing but walked up to the dinner table without raising his eyes from the floor. He sat down with the rest of the family. After a moment's silence, he opened his mouth without any explicit request as if he knew they expected him to speak. He spoke in a mellow tone.

"I was in my office and when I came back in the evening it was all gone. Our house was shattered. I didn't even find their bodies and I could not bear looking for long. I knew they were at home when the bomb fell."

It was the first time he had described it in words to anyone. The other refugees he had trekked with were not in a state to talk about what they had seen in Rangoon and there had been no need of explaining.

"We began our journey that evening, eating rice porridge when we needed to fill our stomachs. Many people fell sick on the road and never made it to Calcutta."

"Have you heard about our parents' latest project?" Dhanesh exclaimed.

"Yesterday, when I came home from school, the children were still playing in our garden," said Amit.

"I asked Ma and apparently, the whole thing was Father's idea. The old man really took me by surprise. He had some kind of epiphany after visiting a shanty town," said Alokesh.

"Well, I think it's great that he's finally doing something instead of just sitting and reminiscing," said Dhanesh.

Amit gripped the ball between his fingers and gave it a spin pretending to be a real bowler.

"Come on, throw it already. You'll twist your wrist one day if you continue doing your tricks!" Dhanesh and Alokesh laughed.

"And…hit! Run!"

"I didn't even know he had a heart," said Amit.

His brothers laughed.

"The only thing he ever tells me is how badly I'm doing in school. Otherwise, he just sits there on his rocking chair with his newspaper staring out in the air," continued Amit.

The three youngest sons of the Roy Chowdhurys were mainly brought up by Chandramukhi. For the first decade or so of their lives, their father had been living in Hazaribagh and only came home on holidays apart from when he worked in the law practice in Calcutta. They rarely spoke to the old man and as a result, had never seen the dynamic and enthusiastic person he used to be before the bombings of Rangoon and the freedom struggle.

Amit took the position of the batsman and prepared for hitting the ball.

He had suspected it that evening he heard about the Japanese bombing in Burma. Debapriya was dead. She was dead! Still holding the light green aerogramme in his hand, and his face completely still, he did not know what to do next. His body did not know how to react. Instead of waiting for it to make a decision, he stood up, went to the little hallway and took on his winter overcoat, chequered scarf and brown loafers to avoid the cold after walking aimlessly for a few hours. He had already planned it. He was going to walk aimlessly through Hampstead Heath in the drizzle. He tied the shoelaces and gently pushed down the door handle and walked out in the crisp January air. His face was still not showing any emotions, and he had left the Debu's letter on the kitchen table.

Dear Isiah,

I hope this letter finds you in good health. I have some bad news for you. My sister Debapriya has passed away. We received a telegram from Burma saying that the whole family was missing, but a week ago, Sathananda came and knocked on our door miraculously with a dirty face wearing wretched clothes. The poor widowed man had walked all the way from Rangoon to Calcutta. Isiah, I know how much you cared for my sister, so please do not take this message too badly. On this note, I end, and please send our greetings to Esther.

Yours sincerely,
Debu

After walking for hours, he finally came home past supper time. A shiver went down his spine as he saw the letter on his dinner table again. His wife, Esther, sat at the table waiting for him.

"What's the matter, Isiah?" she asked.

"Debu's sister died in the bombings in Burma," he replied.

At the moment those words came out from his mouth, he was no longer able to muffle the cry he had been suppressing for so many hours.

"Were you close, Isiah?"

It was an awkward situation because he had rarely spoken about Debapriya since he got married. Now, she was dead and he had to explain what type of relationship he had with her to his wife.

"Yes, in our youth we used to be very close."

He let everything else be left unsaid. She would be able to put two and two together. He could still not believe he was dead. He took out the handkerchief from the right chest pocket and dabbed it on his eyes. He excused himself from the table, went upstairs and lay down on their bed. He thought about the few months they had been close in his youth. It felt odd that the young doll-like girl was no longer.

Ten days after the bad news about Debapriya reached them, a white envelope arrived from England. Debu was still in bed, but when Chandramukhi came in, he jumped up.

"I thought he was dead!" he said in a high-pitched voice.

"See, at least God has been merciful to us about one thing."

She wrapped her arms around him and her forehead against his.

"I'll let you read it in peace and quiet," she said.

Dear Debu,

I hope this letter finds you well. I cannot even begin to describe how life has been for us for the past few years in Europe. Yes, I'm mentioning us because I was finally allowed to marry my life-partner Esther after her father passed away three years ago.

Half of London has been bombed, so to live in a more secure place, we rented a little cottage in Buckinghamshire.

With best wishes,

Isiah

After folding the letter and putting it on the bedside table, he thought to himself for a short while how matters would have ended up if Debapriya had only dared to marry his friend.

Part IV

Chapter 25

The fresh smell of the antiseptics sprays hit Tanushree in the face. It was one of those things that were customary when they were about to land in Calcutta. She seized Joshua's hand as the plane slowly began to descend towards the ground. She tried to look out, but to no avail, it was in the middle of the night. The only thing she could see were the street lamps of nearby neighbourhoods of the North. Suddenly he grasped her hand as if he had seen through her excitement. They both walked slowly down from the flight, suddenly hit by the warm wall and damp air.

"This almost reminds me of the letters from your grandfather to my own."

Tanushree smiled at him.

Joshua carefully picked out the bones from the hilsa fish with the fingers of his right hand as she had shown him. Beside the hilsa fish lay a heap of pulao and on another side of the plate some raita. He was exhausted from the long trip and struggled to keep his eyes open. They sat at Threesixtythree at Grand Hotel on Chowringhee Road in the hub of Calcutta's commercial centre, where Joshua was staying.

"What did your family say about you and Akash breaking off your engagement officially?" he said neutrally.

"My mother took it very badly. I assured my parents this was my final decision the first thing I did upon the Senguptas' arrival in Gothenburg and Akash was there too. I think it was all for the better."

She avoided saying what else Akash had told her parents. It would just make him nervous.

A feeling of utter excitement went through Joshua's veins. She could sense it.

"So, here I am, sitting in the heart of Calcutta, the city I have always dreamt of visiting, with the woman I have fallen in love with. And she is not getting married! That calls for a toast!"

"Fallen in love with?" She wanted to make sure she had not misheard. She knew her eyes showed anticipation no matter how much she tried to hide it.

"I couldn't stop thinking of you, Tanu. Yes, I think I might have fallen in love with you. Would that be a problem?"

She sat paralysed.

"I'm speechless."

She wanted to make sure she had taken the right decision before uttering a word. For a moment, she felt bad to think that she was responsible for shattering another man's dreams of a happy future. The next moment, she was filled with gratitude and joy. She grabbed his hand and like that first time when they met she let her eyes rest on him a little bit longer than he was comfortable with. The only difference was that this time he allowed her to. But after a while, his face began to crumple in disappointment. She knew she had to open her mouth before it gave him the wrong impression.

"I love you, Joshua. No one has ever understood me like you do despite your ups and downs."

His worried and agitated face burst out in a smile. She leaned forward and kissed him fleetingly. They both looked around them, because they knew showing affection in public was not necessarily approved of in this country. The waiter looked down at the floor avoiding their gazes. They had obviously made him uncomfortable.

"Come, I know a place we can go for dessert."

They walked along the long hallway with green marble floor lined with windows on one side. A few guests sat by the outside pool. Upon leaving the hotel, they nodded to the guard who put his palms together in the traditional way to bid them goodbye. Together they walked through the big black gates of the hotel into the bustle of Chowringhee Road. She grabbed Joshua's hand and led him through the busy streets to New Market. She had lost count of how many people they had brushed shoulders with during the short walk. Some of them stared at him as though they had never seen a white-skinned person before. She could hear him telling himself under his breath that it was out of sheer curiosity and that their gazes meant nothing bad.

A girl in a muddy ragged dress pulled his finger and when he looked down on her she put out her hand to ask him for money. Sweat dripped from Joshua's forehead. The crowds, smells and noises made him dizzy. She could see it in his face. Then they finally entered the pink Victorian Gothic building and as they walked through the narrow corridors lined with stalls of women's garments, trinkets and food, She could sense that Joshua felt a bit relieved to have left the crowd. A few minutes later they stood in front of one of her favourite confectioneries. Through the glass window, they could see all sorts of sweetmeat. He looked up. It said, "Nahoum and Sons" in golden letters. They went inside. On a mahogany cupboard lay paper boxes with 'Rich fruit cake' written on top in green.

"They are famous for their Christmas cake, but I'm going to make you taste something different."

She went up to one of the employees in the shop. The man took out a white paper box with blue writing on it, went to the glass window and put chocolate rum balls in the box. She paid at the counter and then came back to Joshua. She took out a rum ball from the box. It had a swirly pattern on it.

"Here, take a bite."

Joshua took a bite and then she put the rest of the ball in her own mouth. It was chocolatey and succulent just like it looked. The rum ball melted in Joshua's mouth and for the first time that day, he told her he had tasted something his taste buds could remotely relate to.

"You can ask them if it is possible to visit the Maghen David synagogue if you want to. Don't you want to see where your grandparents got married?"

"Yes, I do. Do you think that the owner remembers my grandfather?"

She could see he became full of expectations and was once again reminded what had brought him to the city. She knew it made him even happier to think that the other reason that had initially brought her to the city, her planned marriage to Akash, was not going to take place and that he had her to himself. He stroked my cheek and tucked my hair behind my ear.

"Thank you for bringing me here, Tanu."

She ran down the stairs from the third floor to have a chance to enter the gardens of Victoria Memorial before sunset. The Maidan area was the only place where she could find some peace and quiet in this bustling city. She walked all the way from Park Circus along Shakespeare Sarani, getting drowsy by the strong sunlight and the exhaust from the cars, but she told herself that she was better off walking than getting stuck in the traffic jam in Park Street. She had promised to take Joshua to the place where lovers meet in secret. He was there at the gate looking rejuvenated just like that day she saw him on the platform at St Pancras station. He smiled broadly as she approached.

"Did you get some rest?" she asked.

He leaned down and kissed her cheek.

"Yes, I did. I slept for fourteen hours straight. This city certainly takes its toll on your energy. Did you have a nice lunch with your family?"

"Joshua, I told my parents you are here and uncle Amit told them whose grandchild you were. They don't seem as upset anymore now that they understand me. Let me introduce you to them tomorrow."

He looked concerned. Small droplets of sweat appeared on his blushed face.

"Are you sure I'm good enough for them?" he said in a husky mellow voice.

"How can you even ask that?" Her voice sounded a bit agitated, but she could not help it. She wanted him to believe in himself.

"Did you even hear how happy my uncle seemed to welcome you into our family?" she asked.

He nodded in the way he usually did when he didn't believe in himself. She grasped his hand and got her fingers intertwined with his.

"Do you know what? That day our eyes met in London, I dreamt of doing just this. I wanted to walk with my fingers entangled with yours. But never would I have dreamt it would be in the city our grandfathers met more than a century ago. I was so afraid I would never see you again that evening that I came home and cried, Josh."

His face showed compassion. He smiled shyly and clasped her fingers harder, and looked at her with pride. They walked hand in hand along the gravel path to the whitewashed building of the Victoria memorial. Around them in the park were other couples walking hand in hand. It was that time of the day, just before dusk.

"Joshua, tell me what kind of impression you want my parents to have of you."

She had to figure out what made him so doubtful about the meeting.

"I want to be dependable in their eyes, Tanu. I want to be someone who can take care of their daughter at all times."

"Do you not think you're dependable?"

"You know I have my ups and downs."

"So do I, Joshua, and I have chosen you knowing you have your ups and downs. I will try to take care of myself when you struggle and if you let me in,

I can be there for you. I have taken care of myself for more than a decade. I don't think it will be a problem. I am ready to give up consistency for someone who can understand my emotions most of the time without explanations. What else would you want them to think of you?"

"I want to be able to talk with them about their interests and get to know them. I hope we have some common interests."

"I'm sure you will find common interests as long as you just be your insightful self. But I have to warn you mine is a very rowdy family. Everyone is loud and likes to take up a lot of space. I know that's scary sometimes, but you will always have me by your side."

She clenched his hand and stroked his fingers. He felt more at ease. The initial social anxiety had subsided; she could feel it. They walked into the monumental building of Victoria Memorial to see the exhibition about the history of Calcutta.

"My parents are really not that horrible. It's just that I lost faith in romantic love for some time and allowed them to arrange a marriage for me. They were upset that I broke off the engagement, but if I bring someone home whom I really love and trust I'm sure they will be happy. Don't worry, just join us for lunch tomorrow. Let's go to Calcutta Stories. They serve dishes from the diverse Calcutta of the past. Have you ever had Armenian, Parsi or Jewish Indian food?"

Chapter 26

For some years now, Debendranath had been working from Calcutta, and the school-aged children lived with him. They alternated between their dwelling in Tollygunge and the house in Dhakuria, and this August in 1946 there was a peculiar air. It was smokey as he set out to the High Court. Suddenly, someone bashed him on the head – it was so hard he was unable to get up for a good few moments. Those good few moments showed out to be longer than an hour. As he finally forced himself to stand up on his two legs, he saw bodies everywhere. Or at least he assumed they were dead. They were of different religions he could notice on the clothes of the victims. Walking down along the street, he even saw a young woman who had been knocked off her cycle. It was the first time he had seen so many dead bodies before. He ran to the Sealdah train station, afraid to become noticed by the mob. He ran as fast as he could, only stopped to catch his breath at the station entrance. He was so eager to get on the train to Vikrampur he almost forgot about his children.

"Oh, Father, there has been a curfew in Calcutta. Didn't you know?" Shilpa said upon opening the door.

"I left home far too early," Debendranath responded.

"Oh, I cannot imagine what you have been through? Is that dry blood on your forehead?" she asked.

He walked up to the stainless steel bucket and the little mirror in the bathroom. After seeing the many victims along the road, he was hardly shocked by the crack and the blood on his face. He took up a piece of cotton and dipped it in his cologne.

The two men who guarded the main black gate to their estates in Vikrampur, opened it carefully. It was still early morning and like the day before, smokey. On their way from the station, they had passed by the horse cart. While they entered the premises, Debendranath looked at his eldest daughter's face. It was sunken and her eyelids wrinkled, but the adrenalin from yesterday's sights had forced him to make this journey to see his wife and his children.

"Baba, eschechen?" he heard his youngest son Alokesh shouting. Debendranath heard the hasty footsteps on the marble floor.

"Look at you!"

There was horror in Chandramukhi's eyes. She gently touched the wound on his temple, which was dry by now. He knew she had read the morning news.

"Oh, stop worrying about me, you have no idea what I witnessed yesterday."

"Then pray do tell."

Once the children were out of sight, she hugged him and kissed him on the neck.

"Yesterday, I witnessed a massacre. The streets were full of dead bodies. Sometimes I wonder if I will follow the fate of my brother."

Albert Hall, where Debendranath had spent countless hours with his party colleagues as a young student, had turned into a coffee joint. The place was often visited by the most ardent of revolutionaries. He was no longer active in politics, but still felt inspired by the environment.

Debendranath Roy Chowdhury lit another cigarette. Smoking gave him the dopamine kicks his monotonous life had stopped giving him long ago. He had become a chain smoker despite his wife's daily pleads to start thinking about his health. He was on his daily visit to the bar library of the Calcutta High Court where it was customary for him to sit and read during the days. He was hoping to get in contact with other solicitors. It was the second month in a row he had been spending his days there but to little avail. He had recently lost his post in Hazaribagh and had joined his family in Calcutta, but age and the events of yesteryears had caught up with Debendranath. The wrinkles that used to appear next to the corners of his eyes when he smiled had turned into lines of worry and anxiety. The now 59-year old man knew it would be difficult to re-establish a career in Calcutta at this age. But he also knew he could still not retire from his profession. It would be impossible for the whole family to live on the savings he had inherited from his family. As he sat there surrounded by lawyers from all echelons of life, his mind wandered off. After coming to Calcutta, he had felt alienated. The city had changed greatly since his student years.

It had become the base of thousands of men from the Allies. Soldiers could be seen everywhere. In 1943, when Kidderpore docks were bombed, his family visited his wife's parents in Tollygunge. He had felt the shaking from under the bed, where he and his wife sought shelter. The second world war had ended now, but in the midst of it, all Debapriya's family was killed in the Japanese bombings of Rangoon. A year later his older brother was slaughtered in the streets of Dacca by a Muslim mob. Sitting in the bar library, he could not hold back his tears as he thought about the siblings he had lost. The zeal of his past was long gone. He still dreamt of returning to peaceful Vikrampur sometimes but the longer time that passed the more impossible he knew it would be to return.

"You are such a greedy old man," his wife would say.

"You ought to be grateful that we have a home and a beautiful family here in Calcutta. Forget your zamindari. There is no difference between us and the people who are trekking barefoot from East Bengal. Have you even looked at the conditions in the colonies they are building for the refugees? They too are people who have had to leave their homes Debu."

Sometimes, he would be deeply impressed by Chandramukhi's benevolence and ability to put things into perspective. He agreed with her and felt proud to be married to such a wonderful woman. Yet it still felt unfair to become expropriated and lose something that was so close to his heart.

She had noticed her husband's recent vices and she knew very well he tried to compensate for his losses. Deep down, she felt his sorrows. She too had been close to her sister – and brother-in-law and she too was a child of East Bengal. She was still traumatized by the nocturnal flight to Calcutta. But she tried to keep a calm facade for life to progress in their new home.

It was hard for all of them to see how the man had changed character overnight. From being a very dynamic and people-loving person, he had turned into an agonised soul with sunken eyes the day he learnt about the bombings in Rangoon. Sometimes Chandramukhi would wake up in the middle of the night hearing her husband wailing and screaming Debapriya's name or that of his older brother Ritendra. In the beginning, she had believed time would heal all wounds, but quite on the contrary, his mental state became worse for with each day that passed.

It was 1946 and the now 56-year old Chandramukhi woke up with her body trembling from the loud bangs on the front door. The gate guards had come to warn the family of the fierce Muslim squad that had gone ballistic and now attempted to kill all Hindu inhabitants of Vikrampur. Loyal peasants of the village had come earlier during the evening to notify the family's servants. It was yet another gesture from the followers of the future state religion to those who would be in a minority of the new nation.

"Madame, you have to leave now! Your lives are in danger," the guards shouted in a panic-stricken tone.

Chandramukhi had seen this coming and was prepared. A teak almirah, the carved dark wooden frame of the bed gifted to her on her wedding and a showcase were packed on a carriage. Three of her children were already in Calcutta with Chandramukhi's parents and Debendranath was still in Hazaribagh. Her oldest daughter Shilpa and her husband Aditya were both working as teachers in Calcutta. Her oldest son Nilesh was studying at the Medical College and Amit went to Hare school. Her two youngest sons Dhanesh and Alokesh who were now 12 and 11 were with her in Vikrampur., Chandramukhi could feel the sweat caused by tension and nervousness trickling down her neck. She stood up from the provisional cot she had slept in by the entrance to the building to be on guard. She felt nauseated, but she knew she had to keep it together for her children. Her eyelids closed for a while and she lost balance. Seconds later she woke up on the cold white marble floor. She ran up the stairs to the children's bedroom and shook the two boys to wake them up and held both their hands down to the carriage she had prepared for the occasion. This was it. She knew it would be their final journey from Vikrampur and also from East Bengal. The night was sombre but the air was soothing. She avoided lighting the gasoline lamp in fear of being discovered. The adrenalin pumped in her blood and her pupils were wide open. Once in the carriage, she pinched herself hard in the arm. She had hoped it would all be a bad nightmare. What would happen if someone noticed them? She could feel her heart pumping the blood through her body hard through the sari. She gasped for air and drew a few breaths to keep herself calm. The carriage began its bumpy ride towards Calcutta.

"What's happening, Mother? Where are we going?"

She let the questions of her young children go unanswered. The truth to be told, she did not know the answers herself. Who knew if they would still be alive in the morning?

"Shhhh, darling. I'll tell you in the morning. Try to get some sleep now." She stroked her son's cheek and kissed it.

"Mother, your forehead is full of sweat. Are you doing well?"

Amit took his handkerchief and dabbed it on her forehead. Then he fell asleep with his head against her chest. In the middle of the horror, she felt grateful for her family. Such was the temper of Chandramukhi. She would from that moment fill the role of the optimist in the Roy Chowdhury family in a time when many felt disheartened due to loss of family members and property. This was only the beginning. In a way, this journey was a blessing to the elderly woman. Her body was no longer fit as a youngster's, but she had stayed in Vikrampur in hope that the situation between Hindus and Muslims would get better even though deep down in her heart she knew this day would be inevitable. She longed to be with her husband and children in the safety of their newly built home in Dhakuria in the southern fringes of Calcutta. She knew how lucky she was. Many refugees would leave East Bengal with nowhere to call home. They would not have the luxury of going by flight, but many would rather go on foot. She would leave her packings on this side of the Padma river to have their own journey over the water on a freighter to Calcutta, while she herself would board a flight from Dacca. The air company was partly owned by Shilpa's in-laws. They had dedicated the enterprise to saving refugees from both sides making frequent trips between Calcutta and Dacca. Like many men in those days, Shilpa's father-in-law too was an ardent swadeshi follower. Chandramukhi knew deep in her heart it was naive to think of Calcutta as a sanctuary, especially in the middle of a roaring war. Who would know when the Japanese would drop another bomb? Maybe it would not cause damage to the docks this time but even more human lives. She had felt the quakes of the first bomb under her bed in her parental home in Tollygunge clenching the hand of her husband in terror. The lump in her throat felt thicker and thicker. Now that the children were fast asleep, she could let the tears of despair gush down from her eyes. She heard herself shrieking in fear but muffled the sound with her cotton sari. As she glanced back on the marble mansion she had just left for the last time in her life it looked ghostly. Her body shivered. Being accompanied by another adult would have been comforting. She needed to cry on somebody's shoulder but instead, she tried her best to act stoic to her young sons.

Chapter 27

Joshua and Tanushree boarded the boat close to the arched marble gate at Prinsep Ghat. He jumped on before her and took her hand to help her cross the gap between the land of the boat quay and the small vessel. She put the bag with the cheese and tomato sandwiches she had made in the space in the middle of the boat that was covered with a canvas. They chose to sit in the shaded area because of the strong sunshine. It was only 2 p.m. and the sun was high in the sky. The oarsman sat outside with his back against them looking out on the water. What she assumed was daily tanning had made his skin dark and shiny. His leg and arm muscles were firm and visibly strong. Joshua drew her nearer and she let her head rest on his chest. For the first time, she felt safe and not preoccupied with negative thoughts of losing him. She closed her eyes. He put his arm around her waist and kissed her cheek. The three of them were silently aloof in their own thoughts, the oarsman rowing in his own world. All she could hear was the splashing sound of the river Hooghly caused by the oars. The air was serene. The sun rays made the water glitter like silver and the ores made rippling water rings.

"Would you like to have a sandwich, Tanu? You dosed off. Are you feeling hypoglycaemic?"

Sometimes, it was far too obvious he was a scientist but she loved his nerdy side.

"No Joshua, I think it's just the emotional roller coaster ride I have been through the past couple of months that's made me so tired. I fell asleep because I felt safe in your arms."

"I'm happy to be at your service, Dr Roy Chowdhury," he said and reminded her she had finally defended her PhD thesis. He smiled his cheeky smile at her. Those moments of confidence had become more and more common and she felt proud of him. She unwrapped a sandwich and handed it to him. It was a perfect day to have cheese and tomato sandwiches in Calcutta.

She was not sure she could handle another of the heavy rich lunches of the past week. She could have easily fasted for a week, even though she still had not had enough of *rasgullahs* of course. They were slowly travelling northwards along the river.

"So after I have shown you Belur Math, the holy grounds of the only Hindu denomination which has ever resonated with me, where would you like to go next?"

"I want to see the college where our grandfathers met. Where our lives first intertwined decades before we were born." He had the ability to move her with his words.

The boat approached the Belur Math where the religious leader Vivekananda several decades earlier had founded a mission in the name of his teacher Ramakrishna. The reason his philosophy reverberated with her was that he emphasized the value of all castes and how there should not be differences between them. Ramakrishna had taken inspiration from Muslims and Christians. Her grandfather had been one of the early social liberal followers of this Vedic school of thought and he had passed it on to his progeny. They disembarked and walked into the garden. She saw men clad in orange attire everywhere. The premises were calm and quiet in a way one seldom experienced in the surroundings of Calcutta. She always felt at peace when she came here.

"I can't wait for you to move to London. Because you are coming, aren't you?"

"Of course, I am, Joshua." This time, her answer was heartfelt and none of that doubt she had felt the first day was there anymore.

They entered the pompous temple, which was a mixture of Muslim, Christian and Hindu architecture.

She made Joshua walk through the Calcutta streets convincing him it would be the best way to discover the city. It was unusually hot for Mid-December, and the scorching heat from the sunburnt the skin on his nose slightly. They walked past the lightly red-coloured police headquarters in Lal Bazar, the previously Anglo-Indian Bow Barracks and old China town in Tiretti Bazar. Not once did she let go of his hand along the way. It made her a bit proud to feel needed by someone who was so independent. Someone who had taught her so much about herself in such a short time. For once, she led his way. When they finally reached Ezra Street, he looked exhausted. It was a crowded street, more crowded than the already bustling places he had been to in Calcutta so far. In the middle of the street right among the people walked a cow. Joshua felt the dizziness coming over him again. She looked at his face and the pearls of sweat covering his forehead.

"This is Ezra Street, Joshua. We're almost there. Just a few more minutes," She tried to comfort him.

The street was full of hardware and electric stores. They walked in through a narrow doorway and climbed three floors up on steep red coloured stone steps. There it was! On top of the dark brown mahogany door hung a light green board saying 'Cohen, Huq and Roy Chowdhury solicitors'. It was evident it had been there for many years because the borders had turned yellow and slightly brown in some places. She knocked on the door.

"Come in," said a deep male voice from inside. She recognised that voice very well.

She pulled the little round metal handle and the door opened. In the first office sat a slightly obese elderly man with a moustache behind his over-sized wooden desk full of papers.

"Tanushree! What brings you here?"

"Joshua, this is my father's elder brother. Uncle Amit, Joshua's grandfather was Isiah Cohen. He has come to Calcutta to trace his footsteps."

She avoided the other reason that had brought Joshua to Calcutta, but still wondered to herself whether Uncle Amit had heard the news about her and Akash.

Her uncle startled at first as if he had seen a ghost and then he moved back his chair, stood up and moved toward us. He took Joshua's hand.

"Very pleased to meet you, Joshua. I can hardly believe I have the luck to meet Isiah Cohen's grandchild. Come with me, I will show you his office. My father was very particular about keeping his things in place. I think he hoped until his last day that Isiah would one day return to India and join him in the firm again."

They walked into the next room. Big binders and books lined the bright light green walls on both sides. The walls were in the same tone as the board above the entrance door. The furniture was in solid mahogany and very ornate. At the far end of the room by the window stood a large desk.

"See, the old man even kept Isiah's feather pen," uncle Alok said with a smile.

Uncle Amit picked up the pen from the desk and put it in Joshua's hand. He took a firm grip and looked scared that he would break or drop it. Then he turned and looked around the room with the pen still in his hand. On the back wall hung a large black-and-white portrait of his grandfather, Abdul Huq, and Debendranath Roy Chowdhury. He clutched her hand in reverence while his eyes filled with tears.

"My grandfather was also very careful to keep Debendranath's letters and pictures. I have always been wanting to meet that man, Mr Roy Chowdhury, but I knew he passed away many decades ago. Meeting Tanushree has been my way of meeting this enigmatic man I have only seen in photographs and read letters from."

She handed the letters Judith had given her to her uncle. Joshua looked out the window in his own dreamy way. Uncle Amit reacted similarly to her father after reading.

"You knew about the fate of your uncle Dhanesh, didn't you, Tanushree?"

"I vaguely remember my father telling me, but I had no idea what he was like as a person. Uncle Amit, I have read so many of my grandfather's letters sent to Isiah. I got a whole new impression of him because Joshua's family had kept all the memories. I wish someone had told me earlier about how he felt after the Partition. It would give me a new perspective on life."

"Tanu, I suppose people wanted to carry on with their lives. Our scars are still fresh and it hurts to talk about our many losses even though 70 years have passed since the Partition."

"But you are a lawyer, uncle Amit. Does the next generation not have the right to know the truth?" she asked insistently. Her uncle looked down at his shoes where he sat at his desk and nodded. She could tell she had made him guilty.

He asked them to sit down and have tea with him.

"Of course, I think you should have the right to know. We live in a funny culture, which might be hard to understand for those who were brought up in developed countries. Our people have been deprived for so long that now that we are going through development the focus is on glittery malls, modern multi-storey apartment housing and cool restaurants. Few people think of preserving what has been there for centuries. Let bygones be bygones is the prevailing attitude in our society."

Joshua opened his mouth for the first time.

"But then if you don't let the past teach you, you have to reinvent the wheel over and over again. Do you really find that efficient Mr Roy Chowdhury?"

Her uncle smiled.

"I agree with you Joshua, we just have to convince the rest of our people."

A man came by and handed each of them a clay cup with tea. Her uncle lifted his cup to simulate a toast.

"Welcome to Ezra street, Joshua. You were always a part of our family."

Joshua looked up. He and her both looked at her uncle in awe.

"You are a couple, aren't you?" They glanced at each other and smiled.

Oh, Indian street food how she had missed it! *Papdi chat*, *paubhajji* and *pani puri*. She did not know if she was allowed to feel this euphoric about something so trivial as food when her future happiness was at stake, but she still relished it. There was a long silence of munching, filling *pani puris* with tamarind water and lip-smacking.

On the car ride from the airport the previous day, she had tried to imagine the looks on her parents' faces when she told them. Akash's parents had made a case out of her last-minute decision to reject their son. She felt like she was going for a hearing in court. She had tried to warn her family in the car from Landvetter airport that she had made up her mind, but they too seemed convinced it was possible to save the situation.

"Akash is not coming to Calcutta with us," she had announced in the car without being asked.

Alokesh Roy Chowdhury had turned his head from the front seat and looked at her with a puzzled expression on his face.

"His parents will come to meet us tonight. Let's continue discussing this then."

She could hear on her father's overly self-convincing tone that he understood she was not going to give her childhood friend a second chance.

Then the wall of damp air and wind hitting her when she came out of the car relieved her of her worries for some time. There was a moment's joy and a homecoming much longed for. Then they had that beautiful moment when they read her grandfather's letters. The worries for what was to come had returned when she saw her father's smiling face and her mother's anticipatory eyes in the restaurant. Beside them sat the backboneless Akash. At the other end of the table sat Mr and Mrs Sengupta. Before she could say anything, Akash sighed, but did not say anything. He did not know she could use the powerful weapon of blackmail because she had not uttered a word about Ute.

They continued their feast. She took another *pani puri*, cracked a hole in it with her fingers and filled it with tamarind water and mashed potato. Then she realized now was the time. She took a deep breath.

"Father and Mother, Akash is not coming to Calcutta with us next October because we have decided not to get married. We will not give it a second chance for reasons we both are aware of."

There. She had uttered the words. Everything stopped. Even Akash seemed surprised by my sudden announcement. Her mother choked.

"Tanushree, don't be foolish. Relatives from both sides are expecting you to get married."

Menakshi Roy Chowdhury put her face in her hands, but it only made me more insistent and impatient. She knew she would meet resistance and especially from her mother. But who could blame her? After all, she had waited until the last minute to tell her. Mr and Mrs Sengupta seemed unmoved.

"Mother, Akash and I have already talked about this. We both think it's better we go our separate ways. His parents have already cancelled all arrangements, but I wanted to wait to tell you and Father face to face about my final decision. I knew you did not take my call the other week seriously."

Her father, who had not been warned, was awestruck and from her chair, on the terrace of the Indian street food restaurant, he only observed what was going on without saying a word. Akash opened his mouth for the first time that day.

"Your daughter is in love with another man, Mrs Roy Chowdhury."

She glared at him. She was not sure she was ready to drop that bomb, but now he had done it for her. But for once she kept silent and had no intention of outing him. He really was backboneless and it was such a joy to know she would never have to be his homemaker.

"Tanushree, is this true?"

"Yes, it is true, Mother."

Her father's face shifted from deeply concerned to curious. Her mother's face was red as a cherry in anger.

"How long has this been going on? Is this the reason you have broken the engagement? What will our relatives think? Think about poor Mr and Mrs

Sengupta and how much trouble they have gone through to make arrangements." Akash's parents nodded.

She looked down on the brownish tiles. What had started out as a feast of food and joyful recognition of flavours had turned into mourning of a marriage that was not going to take place. She thought hard about how to reply. Both Akash and she knew very well there was another reason why we had called off the wedding, but she had promised to keep it to myself. She had never seen Akash so nervous before.

"Yes, Mother this was the reason. It was entirely my own fault."

Surely, a little white lie couldn't hurt. Akash looked at her with gratitude. He knew she lied to protect him. Her father looked at Akash's face with contempt. He could tell from her voice that she was lying. The rest of the afternoon was spent in silence. No one asked about Joshua and she kept it a secret that he was there. No one had to know. Not yet.

"Well, Tanushree, this of course comes as a shock to us but you seem to be determined about your decision," her father said before anyone else had the chance to talk.

"I hope this will not affect our relationship Mr and Mrs Sengupta. "

"We are going back by the early flight tomorrow Mr Roy Chowdhury. We need to rest," Mrs Sengupta said. She was shocked at how little resistance she had shown and still seemed upset.

Maybe she finally knew her son was just as much at fault as she was.

That evening, she met Akash for a drink at the hotel in the old GPO building.

"Oh my God, I'm so relieved. Let's never do this again," he said.

She laughed. It felt nice to relax and just be friends again.

"So, what are you going to do about Ute? Will you introduce her to your parents?"

He looked up at my face in awe.

"I know everything. I had lunch with her with Elodie. She seems like a really sweet girl. Judged her way too fast the first time."

"I'm sorry," he said quietly and looked abashed.

"I'm obviously upset with you, but you should apologize to yourself. From now on, try to be honest to yourself and other people. OK?"

He nodded and took a sip of his strawberry margarita. We sat on bar chairs by a high round table.

"Do you want me to talk to your mother or are you intending to do it yourself?"

Her voice sounded strict. He sighed and looked concerned. After some time, he looked up at her again and opened his mouth.

"I promise I will, Tanushree."

Chapter 28

A train from East Pakistan arrived at Sealdah station. People gushed out from the station building. At that moment, Debendranath felt someone tugging on his shirt from behind. At first, he ignored it, but when he felt it a second time he turned around. He saw a young filthy girl carrying an infant. Her hair was tangled as if she had not combed it for several days. The red and white flowery dress she wore was dirty and on her nose was a streak of mud. She was barefoot. She put out her hand and begged him for money. He squatted and looked into her eyes. They were full of expectation. He put a coin in her hand.

"What is your name?"

"Shanta."

Debendranath immediately recognized the accent. The girl was from the other side of the border.

"Where are you from, Shanta?"

"I am from Barisal. This is my little brother."

She held up the infant to show Debendranath.

"Did you come on the train from Barisal today?"

"We came some time ago. Now we live in the slums behind the station."

A woman in a printed nylon sari approached them.

"What are you doing, Shanta? Did you just ask that man for money? I don't know where you are learning these things. Apologize to him and return the coin he gave you. At once!"

Debendranath reacted over the woman's words. Something told him the girl was not an ordinary beggar. Maybe the family had been dispossessed and forced to the slums. The woman took Shanta's hand and led her away.

"Dirty immigrants! Go back to where you belong. You are destroying our city," an elderly man bellowed at the sight of the little girl. He pointed his walking stick in Shanta's direction.

Debendranath closed his eyes and tried to pretend he had not overheard. The man was right in some ways, Calcutta was a place under constant change. The size of the city had increased by millions of people since the second partition of Bengal, and the southern suburbs had become gentrified into large parts. But where did he want the immigrants to return? To the mouth of the lion? He had heard this type of comment many times since he moved to the city and he tried to ignore them every time. Still, at the bottom of his heart, it bothered him deeply. Were these people beasts with no sense of compassion? Didn't they understand that most refugees would give anything to return home? These kinds of comments made Debendranath harbour mixed feelings about the city, mainly because of the bias that existed toward East Bengalis. He ran after the woman and Shanta.

"Madame, please wait a moment, I want to talk to you. Let me buy your children some food."

"We have enough food at home, babu." Her emphasis on the word 'babu' made Debendranath think she felt patronised.

"Please don't misunderstand me, I came from the same part of Bengal as yourselves. I want to hear your story. There's an egg roll stand over there." He pointed towards a hawker's stall not far from where they stood.

He was a bit surprised over his action, but the contempt of the old man and the innocence in Shanta's eyes made him take it. The woman looked away and if he was not mistaken he had convinced her.

"Come, Shanta." Debendranath took her hand.

The eggroll man handed over rolls to all three of them. They were piping hot.

"If you want to understand our story, babu, you should come to our home."

Debendranath had never visited a shantytown before. It smelled of a mixture of latrine and cooked food. Now he did what his wife had asked him to when he sat at home and reminisced over Vikrampur. The woman led him through an area full of simple brick buildings with tin roofs. People bathed in the streets. They stopped in front of a small room with three cots. There was not even a collapsible gate, instead but a canvas drape cordoned off the bedroom. She had taken him home to show him something, he was sure. Her husband came in and they greeted each other putting the palms together in the traditional way.

"These are my parents, Mr Roy Chowdhury." She handed him two black-and-white pictures. They did not live to see Calcutta.

It was their dream to come here one day. This city has saved us, babu, but we will never regain our homes. Hearing the woman expressing gratitude for the city made Debendranath feel bad. He was in Paris of the East and still he could not fully enjoy it. He saw Bengali literature in the shelves and realised the woman had been schooled.

"I share your sentiments Madame. I too left my home behind."

"But you didn't end up in the slums. This is the difference." He wanted to help them more, but he could not bring himself to open his mouth after her comment.

"Now, please leave, Zamindar Babu. I brought you here so you could see what wretched conditions other people live under. I knew by the way you are dressed you had never set foot in these types of areas before. Look at it as a lesson. Think of our children and how they may never be lucky enough to go to school."

Her eyes turned fierce. For a moment, he felt like she was a ghost and he was Ebenezer Scrooge. He was too ashamed of himself to say anything.

"Here's the door." She lifted the drape to give way to him.

Debendranath opened the gate to the front porch with a smile on his face when he recognised Shanta's mother's face. The young woman looked as stern as that day in their shantytown. But she had come surrounded by a group of children.

"Thank you for joining us, Madame!"

"Aditi Kirtania."

"Mrs Kirtania, this is my wife Chandramukhi." She nodded towards the elderly woman.

"I've brought some of the children from our slums and a nearby colony. Most of them have come from the other side of the border and their parents have not had the money to send them to school. Our new life is hardly a bed of roses as I tried to explain to you last time we met, Zamindar Babu."

"I'm no longer a Zamindar, I would prefer if you called me by name." For the first time, the woman looked at Debendranath with sympathy. It occurred to her he might not be as conceited and haughty as all the other babus she met. Maybe he did have a heart.

"We will teach English and Mathematics to begin with. Would you do us the honour of teaching Bengali Mrs Kirtania?"

Aditi Kirtania's jaw dropped.

"I know you're not illiterate. I spotted the Geetanjali and the works by Sarat Chandra in your bookshelf." Her face crumpled.

"My father taught me how to read and love literature, Mr Roy Chowdhury, but I have never been lucky enough to go to school."

"How old are you?" asked Chandramukhi.

"I'm 23."

"What does your husband do for a living?"

"He's a rickshaw puller. In East Bengal, his ancestors have been fishermen for generations and we could always afford our daily bread without any problem. We had a decent home and we would have even sent our children to school."

Her eyes closed for a moment and she looked away. She avoided mentioning her husband's vices and how they decreased his daily net income to close to nothing. But the Roy Chowdhurys both noticed the suppressed worry in her face. The couple had taken a liking to the zealous woman.

The children sat around the dining table. Chandramukhi distributed exercise books and pencils.

"We will begin by learning the numbers in English and Bengali." She began to write down the number one in both languages on her large sheet of paper.

"Please copy this to your exercise books. Shanta, please pick out ONE guava from the bucket."

She walked up to Chandramukhi and plunged into the bucket to pick up a fruit.

"Now we continue to the next number. Swarna, could you please come and pick up TWO guavas?"

The little boy was shy. He smiled but did not dare to leave his seat. Chandramukhi went closer and put the bucket at his feet.

"No one will watch you, Babu. Close your eyes, everyone!"

When she opened her eyes again, her shy student smiled at her broadly with a guava in each hand. That morning they were taught all the numbers between one and ten in both Bengali and English. Debendranath peeped in through the door which was ajar and looked at his animated wife with pride. He saw her light brown eyes radiating. At the age of 62, she still enthralled him. Chandramukhi had worked very few days after finishing college even though she had tutored her children almost every day. It gave her a new sense of satisfaction to help others.

When it was time for lunch the cook served the children rice and moong daal with spinach and rohi fish on steel plates. The mouth smacking from the table told Debendranath the food had been to their liking.

Aditi was preparing to leave for the day when Debendranath stopped her.

"Have you ever thought of becoming a teacher? I mean getting a university degree."

"I have not even gone to school, Mr Roy Chowdhury."

"We can do something about it. I have enough funds to send you to university but you have to clear all other exams first."

From that day, Chandramukhi and Debendranath began their decade long drilling of Aditi. Every afternoon, the children would play in their garden while she was taught everything between heaven and earth from Shakespeare to differentiation. At the age of 33, the same year as Shanta finished year 10, her mother gained admission to the Basanti Devi college for a BA in Bengali. A couple of years later Aditi finished her teacher's training from Hastings House. The Roy Chowdhurys' helped her in all the ways they could both financially and morally.

Chapter 29

"I hear Tanushree has already met your mother Judith. After my father's death, she began writing to my own mother, Debendranath's wife, to ask about her memories of Debendranath and Isiah. I think Judith wanted to remind her father of his old days in Calcutta. It is such a wonder the two of you came across each other," my father exclaimed. He seemed sincerely happy for us but my mother sat quietly with a scrutinising facial expression.

"Yes, Mr Roy Chowdhury, we were invited to my parents' place a few weeks ago."

"Judith has saved all of grandfather's letters to Isiah and most of the old pictures as you know. There is so much you never shared with me," she said.

A waiter brought in a bowl of *aloo makalas*. Joshua's eyes fixed on them. He recognised them immediately. 'I adore these. We used to have them at home all the time,' he explained. She smiled because she loved to see him excited. He said it in a way that even made her critical mother burst out in a smile.

"Joshua, tell me more about where you met my daughter. We want to hear the whole story," said her father. She blushed. She never talked about these things with her parents.

"There was a concert in Cadogan Hall two and a half years ago…" he began.

"To be more precise, he performed there with his choir," she filled in to make her mother's rigid heart melt.

"I was introduced to Tanu that evening, but we did not really begin talking until Rohini set us up a few months ago," he finished his sentence.

"From the way you fill in each other's sentences, it seems like you have known each other for years," said her father. It was the first time they had done anything like that, but they both noticed it too and smiled at each other.

"How did you meet your wife, Mr Roy Chowdhury?" Joshua asked.

"Ours was an arranged marriage, Joshua. I didn't have the guts of my daughter and thinking back I must say I made a good decision. But you never know what had happened if we were completely free to make our own choices. Maybe my wife would have chosen someone much more handsome and accomplished. What do you say?" He turned towards her mother and smiled cheekily.

"Don't talk nonsense!" Her mother had opened her mouth for the first time. She was an introvert in character but could be very strict at the same time.

"We were introduced by our parents and met a couple of times before the evening of our wedding."

Joshua looked down on the table, a bit concerned. She knew he was thinking about my broken arranged marriage, and he did not like the idea of shattering another man's dreams, no matter how many times she told him how wrong the whole thing had been. She looked at him from the side to make him lift his gaze from the table.

"There are times in life when one has to compete, Joshua, and if the competition is about one's soulmate, giving up is a very stupid decision." Joshua looked up at her father with wonder. He had looked through his personality.

"So, do you think it's okay that Tanushree broke off her engagement to be with me?" The question was asked in the most unassuming way in a quiet humble tone. She noticed he did not dare look into her mother's eyes. Her father had already won over, it was clear from the beginning. Now she stared at her mother for her to open her mouth and her father did the same. She cleared her voice.

"I was not too happy when I heard what had happened to the engagement to Akash, but if being with you makes my daughter happy then so be it. You have all my blessings."

"Thank you, Mrs Roy Chowdhury." Her mother nodded towards him with the reticence of someone who did not want to express her inner thoughts.

For a moment, there was silence at the table.

"I'm sorry about the broken engagement, Mr and Mrs Roy Chowdhury. It must have been a lot of hard work. But if you don't mind I would really like to be part of your daughter's life."

"Let's not mention the engagement again, Joshua. Let bygones be bygones," she said quietly. Suddenly, everyone's eyes were on her and there was compassion in their faces as if I had told them the whole story.

That evening, Josh and she sat at the dinner table in Dhakuria, which was often mentioned in his grandfather's diary. The night between the 14th and the 15th of August 70 years earlier, their grandparents had been sitting around it listening to Nehru's freedom speech. The very same table had witnessed Sathananda's face in 1942 when he told his wife's family of the bombings in Rangoon. In 1951, the dining room had been the first classroom of ten curious students who would never have had the possibility to be schooled without it.

So much had become clear within the past couple of months. Not only could she tell people about her thesis on musical modes and our moods, but the questions she asked herself lying on the bathroom floor in Berlin half a year earlier had been answered. She knew how the loss of close family members and dispossession had affected her grandfather because of half a century old letters and diary entries kept by the family of the first man she had been able to explain herself to. The first man who had ever made her feel safe in his arms and asked the same questions she did. She knew how traumatised her grandmother had been the night she had left East Bengal for the last time and how she had kept it together for her children. She could explain how a man went from being happy and successful at everything to becoming a wreck because of the atrocities life had brought him. She could tell the world about the beautiful friendship between two men who kept looking out for each other for almost seven decades no matter where life brought them. It suddenly dawned on her that if she had not dared to disappoint her parents by rejecting Akash, she would have still been ignorant about these events and so had the rest of her family.

Later, she brought out her violin and the little tabla machine played teental beat for me. She improvised a composition based on raga Asawari. Joshua watched her mother's face brighten up with pride. She had told him how similar their backgrounds were and the self-doubt that had made them give up on music. Her father served them samosas and rasgullahs they had bought from Mouchak. They had Makaibari tea with milk but no sugar.

"We are not here to celebrate India's independence like our relatives before us, but we are here because the past months have taught us about their difficult journeys in life and we owe it to them never to forget. We are also here to welcome the grandchild of our father's best friend into our family," uncle Amit said. She looked at him with gratitude.

"Come, Josh."

She took his hand and led him to the front porch. The sun was setting but the street was busy as usual with people walking, rickshaws and loud vendors. Just like her two youngest uncles and Father did the day they discovered the true character of Debendranath, there were children playing cricket in the street. As she sat on the rocking chair with her fingers intertwined into Josh's, she silently hoped no one would ever muffle their voices and that they may continue playing for the rest of their lives.

Chapter 30

It was just at the moment that the sitarist began playing the fast-paced jhala of raga Malkauns that Debendranath thought about Isiah. The collaboration between the tabla player and the sitarist was intense where they sat behind the white ornate columns. They played at a high pace and Debendranath was ecstatic to see the sitarist striking the strings up and down. He thought about the days he used to learn the instrument himself. After minutes of playing the intense jhala, the instrumentalists finally finished.

"Tell me, Abdul, how is Isiah? I have not received any news for a long time. I even wrote him a letter some time ago, but got no answer."

The handsome Abdul Haq, who by now had many grey hairs, wore a blue salwar kameez in raw silk. He had returned to Calcutta after a few years in London training as a barrister of the inner temple.

"He is doing really well, I hear, especially with his research studies. At this old age, he has even managed to find himself a romantic partner."

"Is that so? He finally found the woman of his dreams after all these years." Debendranath always felt bad about what had happened between his sister and Isiah. He could not help but think Debapriya would still be alive if she had dared to commit to his friend. Debendranath ran his fingers over the jute mat on which they were sitting in the middle of the courtyard of Shovabazar Rajbari. The evening was dark, but in the two corners at the front by the stage two fire torches lit up the courtyard. The ambience reminded him of the days in Vikrampur when his own family used to organize all-night concerts in their courtyard and music salon.

"Yes, before returning, a few months ago I went to hear Isiah play the piano. I saw his eyes were constantly resting on one red-haired young woman in the audience. I also noticed that the young woman could not take her eyes away from him. So, after the concert, I had to ask Isiah whose face he had been staring at throughout the concert. He was certainly coy about it, but later on, I heard that the girl used to be Isiah's student. She has been with him for a long time now, and the talk of the town was that they were going to get married soon. But her father seems to be critical about it, so we'll see. These are words heard from Hannah's husband Avram."

As positively surprised as Debendranath was about the news, he became a bit disappointed at the same time. Why did Isiah have to be so awfully secretive about everything? He wished he could have written to him. He also felt sad to hear about the resistance Isiah got from the girl's family.

"And how did you find the climate in England, Abdul?"

"Well, it had its drawbacks and advantages. In the beginning, I used to visit a mosque in south-west London every Friday. I wore my cap as usual when I went to pray in God's house. But there were multiple occasions on which I was ridiculed in public for my headgear. I stopped wearing it outside. That was my first encounter with racism in London."

Debendranath thought about Isiah. His letters had been unusually cheerful in the past. He never mentioned the downsides and probably so because he did not want to make his friend worried. But the letters had made Debendranath suspicious.

"Were there more occasions, Abdul?"

"There were times when people mocked me for my accent. It was also common that people stared at me in the street," he replied.

He thought about his argument with Debapriya's husband Sathananda many years ago when he had hinted his brother-in-law knew nothing about hardships and felt bad. The man had never complained to him, but Debendranath wondered how life in England must have been at the beginning of the century for Indian students. As he was thinking quietly to himself, the sitarist began playing another alaap.

Walking home early the next morning, he began getting flashes from the visit to Shanta's place the previous day. He had an idea and could not wait so he woke up his wife the first thing he did when he got home.

"Debu, it's still early. Let me sleep."

"Chandramukhi, would you like to teach the children of the poor with me? We could invite them to our home and provide them with one meal a day?"

She smiled. It was the first time she had seen him so zealous in a long time. She sat up with her legs dangling from the elevated bed still unable to open her eyes properly.

"From where did you get this idea, Debu?"

He asked their servant to make a pot of tea for them and began telling his wife about the incident at Sealdah station.

Debendranath choked at the sight of the red communist flag in his home. Dhanesh, his second youngest son, had become more and more fervent in his attempt to fight the class war. He was sent to school in Jadavpur, where many of his newly arrived classmates had similar sympathies. This was years before the Naxalites, he called himself a Marxist and read the Communist Manifesto by Karl Marx secretly. As much as Debendranath was proud of his son's independence of mind, the communist party of India was one he had difficulties accepting. He had already lost all land and taxation rights in 1950. Was that not enough power to the people? Never dared he utter those words to his wife, because he knew she would call him greedy. Rightfully so.

"Dhanesh, I did not see you in the office this afternoon."

"I had homework, Father."

"And how did the banner get here?"

"It's something we made in college." Debendranath sighed. He had wanted to send his youngest son to a convent school in town, but he was out of funds.

"Every era has its own issues. In your days, the question was how to become free from the crown and your party did a good job. But you have to agree your comrades fought in the interest of gaining power themselves. They were mostly middle-class men and often lawyers."

"I don' t agree that that was our aim, Dhanesh." He had never discussed politics with his son before and enjoyed Dhanesh's way of instigating an argument.

"What voice did the labourers and farmers have, Father?"

"We would have certainly welcomed them."

"They didn't feel welcome and they still don't feel they're our equals. This is why we need a class war."

"I believe in socio-economic equality my son, but it has to be well-deserved. Equality should come from mutual understanding. No one should judge you based on your economical background no matter which layer of society you are from."

He could see in his son's face that he enjoyed their discussion. There was a smile on Debendranath's lips, a smile Dhanesh had seldom seen.

"Father, I'm going to meet some friends by Dhakuria lake but I'll prove you wrong when I come back."

"Don't be away too long, Dhanesh and do bring a torch. It's already dark outside."

Debendranath dosed off on the rocking chair on the front porch. He woke up a couple of hours later by a knock on the front gate.

"Debendranath Roy Chowdhury?" The police officer was stony-faced.

"Yes." He opened the gate to let the man into his house.

"We have some very bad news." The old man's body and mind could not take another tragedy but he acted indifferently.

"We have found your son's body. He was hit by a car, Mr Roy Chowdhury. I'm very sorry."

"What? I don't understand. Dhanesh has been killed in a car accident?"

The officer nodded solemnly.

Debendranath's face became sweaty and the colour turned pale. He sat down on the chair again. At the same time, he could not help but think twice about what had happened. His mind played with all kinds of thoughts. Had he fallen victim to a mob or members of the opposite party? Had he committed suicide? He didn't seem like that kind of character. If only he had taken the time to get to know him before.

"No!" Debendranath screamed at the top of his voice. "Lord, please have mercy!"

"Can we see the body?" he was shocked to hear his voice asking.

"Was he taken to the hospital?"

Tears gushed out from his eyes as the initial shock subsided.

"It was too late, Mr Roy Chowdhury. I'm terribly sorry."

Chandramukhi came running into the room. She looked into her husband's eyes.

"Mrs Roy Chowdhury, your son…" The police inspector began a sentence but could not bring himself to finish as he saw the face of the elderly woman becoming more and more distorted. Her pupils dilated and the complexion of her skin became pale just like her husband's. She felt a type of nausea she had not felt since that night in Vikrampur seven years earlier when she had fled East Bengal in fear of her life. Her eyelids closed while her body fought to keep its posture. Then her fingers reached for something to hold on to but her vision was too hazy. She fell down on the floor and lost consciousness. The back of her head left a trace of blood on the concrete floor. When she woke up hours later, she was at the hospital. Her head had been bandaged. She called for the nurse.

"Sister, I would like to see my second youngest son, Dhanesh." She was still in denial of what had happened and wished it all to be a bad nightmare, just like she had with that night in Vikrampur.

"I am afraid your son has passed away, Mrs Roy Chowdhury. You had a minor heart attack and hurt your head when you fainted."

"He can't be gone." Chandramukhi cried. "He's just a young boy."

"I am afraid there was a car accident, Madame." The nurse held the woman's hand and stroked her warm forehead. She cried loudly now and the tears she never let out in front of other people streamed down her face unsuppressed.

Epilogue

The crooked old man sat and sipped tea on his front porch in Dhakuria, with a cigarette in his right hand, and a copy of the Statesman newspaper on his lap. As he read the news about the atrocities in East Pakistan, his eyes filled with tears. Hundreds of thousands of people had so far fallen victim of the genocide. India supported the Bengali nationalists, and Hindu East Pakistanis gushed in through the border in order to live better and safer lives in West Bengal. He remembered his own final journey across the border thirty years ago. It had not been as traumatic as that of his wife's but he had suspected it would be his last journey and he was scared for what was to come.

"Oh, Debu, I cannot stand to see you like this," his wife Chandramukhi said as she touched his shoulder with her hand.

Since retiring, fewer and fewer words had been exchanged between the two of them and he often sat on the porch reminiscing in his solitude. His daughter Shilpa and her husband Aditya had taken over her parents' project of teaching the children of the poor. Debendranath's only joy in life had become the morning walk to the grocery shop where he fetched the daily yoghurt and milk bread, the evening walk to the nearby Lake Market and his frequent visits to the Ramakrishna Mission library. Apart from that, he sat at home counting the hours between the meals. Their third youngest son Amit who was unmarried had lived at home until the late fifties, but for the past years both he and Tanushree's father Alokesh, their youngest child, had been abroad. Some of the friends of their sons had fallen victims of the Naxalite movement, and Roy Chowdhurys knew it would be safer for their own children to stay abroad. Less and less for each day that passed did they expect them to return home. Amit eventually did return back from New York where he studied for his JD degree.

In the afternoon, Debendranath decided to make a trip to Jyotish Ganguly in Barobazar in North Calcutta. He used to be a frequent visitor of those parts of the city in his student years and while he still worked as a solicitor at Cohen and Roy Chowdhury solicitors. He and Jyotish had their differences, but Abdul had passed and Isiah returned to England with his young wife a few months after they got married. In 1905, a short while after the first partition of Bengal, he had first met Jyotish Ganguly and learnt about their differences in opinion. For many years, Jyotish had cut him off, but after the demise of his wife he had missed the companionship and had looked up Debendranath and Chandramukhi's address. Today, as often before, the old friends and adversaries, Jyotish Ganguly and Debendranath Roy Chowdhury were engaged in deep political discussions over a cup of coffee and an egg roll at the Indian Coffee House in College Street.

"What do you think about the situation in East Pakistan, Debu? Are you not happy you made the decision to move to West Bengal before all hell broke loose?"

"I am grateful of course that we came here in time, but I am saddened to know how the inhabitants of East Pakistan have been treated. Bengali is not recognized as an official language even though it is the mother tongue of large parts of Pakistan and people are being persecuted based on their religion and position in society."

His family, for the sake of their sanity, had given up all hope to find back their property in East Bengal the very day India left the British crown in 1950 and Zamindars left their property and taxation rights. Neither had they set foot across the border since 1944.

"I hope they will not come here and spoil our city." Debendranath sighed but refrained from speaking against Jyotish. It was not the first time he had heard that type of remark. Times had indeed changed in Calcutta. Many foreign companies had moved out and refugees moved in, leaving the streets full of beggars and hawkers. After talking to Jyotish, Debendranath realised he could no longer sit at home. He wanted to help the refugees from East Pakistan that experienced the same fate and perhaps worse conditions than he had decades earlier.

That evening after his visit to the Ramakrishna Mission library, he passed by the neighbouring Bedi Bhavan. It was an ornate building from the thirties which housed many refugees. He left two bags full of fresh vegetables at the doorstep he had bought at the Lake Market. Coming home in the evening he found large portions of his exposed skin covered with a thin layer of dust from the streets and the smoke and exhaust made him cough. The cough did not stop.

He went to the bathroom and saw the basin becoming stained with blood. When it finally stopped, he gargled with water from the tap. He went out to the kitchen to tell the cook to prepare dinner for twenty people. Then he packed the food in boxes and walked out again in the late evening to distribute them to the beggars under the bridge in the market area Gariahat. Chandramukhi had overheard the conversation between Debendranath and the cook while preparing the spices in the kitchen garden. Her face lit up in a proud smile. But she had no idea of the bloodstains her husband had left in the bathroom. There was a light drizzle that evening and her beloved Debu came home with wet hair. The cough continued as he went to sleep.

"Your body is trembling, Debu." Chandramukhi put her hand on her husband's forehead. It was burning. "You should not have gone out in the rain yesterday. But I'm proud of you. I don't know where you got all that energy from but what you did was a beautiful deed." Debendranath smiled but he could hardly open his mouth to speak anymore. He was drained of all energy as he lay there being nurtured by his wife as a little child.

Shilpa put the back of her hand on her father's forehead. He had been lying in bed over the past day. At times, he opened his eyes but he struggled to keep his eyelids up and his voice was feeble. Debendranath made a gesture for her to lean closer. With a heavy breath, he began to whisper.

"Tell me the name of Israel's prime minister, Shilpa."

"It's Golda Meir, Father."

"And who was India's first female prime minister?"

"It was Indira Gandhi." Tanushree's aunt understood that he took her as a child.

"Yes, and do not forget the name of Srimavo Bandaranaike."

The voice resembled the one he used when she was a young learner. She was the girl who was going to show responsibility and good leadership skills as the eldest sibling. He smiled up towards her like a mischievous child. He must have been struck by some type of dementia. But at the same time, he reminded her of her childhood dreams. She had admired the early female leaders of the Congress Party. As a teacher of History and Philosophy, she had tried to make her female students at the convent school critical towards society and its many presumptuous inhabitants. Being allowed to grow up as a tomboy she was also a strong proponent of the idea that it does girls well to practice any sports. Their minds should question hierarchy and patriarchy but never had she dared to lead outside the classroom. She had not had a true outlet for her political ideals. What had made her sink? Was it societal expectations? Was it the depression after the demise of her little brother and the aunt who always encouraged her in life?

Shilpa sat on the bedside and watched her father's body languishing slowly. Chandramukhi stood by the door and shed tears. She cried because something told her Debendranath would not survive the night.

"I wish I could bring him back to Vikrampur, Shilpa. That's all he ever dreamt of."

"No, Mother, he is at home now surrounded by his family. This is the town that saved us. We have no right to long for the other side. That life was a fairy-tale. This life is reality." She spoke with a strict tone to her mother, a tone that reflected how tired she was of her family longing back to East Bengal year after year. When was life going to progress? She was so adamant about it that even her father opened his eyes but kept his mouth shut. Instead, he took her hand in his own and held on to it in a loose grip. His body was shivering and sweating at the same time.

"The last thing your father did yesterday was to feed twenty beggars. On his way back from the market yesterday, he left two bags of vegetables at the refugee camp in Bedi Bhavan. I believe that was his way of paying back to this city, Shilpa. He had some kind of epiphany after talking to Jyotish."

The doctor came, measured Debendranath's pulse and examined his heart and lungs with his stethoscope.

"His pulse is low and he's having difficulty breathing Mrs Roy Chowdhury. You know his cancer began spreading almost a year ago now. With someone of his condition, the pollution and dust of this city are not ideal. On top of it, his yesterday must have been strenuous. I will not lie to you, Mrs Roy Chowdhury. This might be the last day of his earthly life." He gave the old woman a compassionate glance.

Chandramukhi nodded. Nothing the doctor said came as a surprise to her.

She spent the whole night chanting religious songs and watching over her husband. A little kerosene lamp in the corner of their bedroom was lit on a low flame. She heard his breath becoming heavier and heavier. Then she grasped his hand. It was cold. She leaned down to stroke his cheek and kissed it.

"Thank you for battling by my side every day for the past 66 years. I don't know what I will do without you. But I saw what you tried to do yesterday and

I promise you to keep up that spirit. You have no idea how happy I was to have you back. You will always be that elated and benevolent man that I married in my heart."

The tears gushed out and she was muffling a shriek much like that evening in Vikrampur when she fled. But it wouldn't matter now. The bedroom door was locked. Nobody would hear her.

"I know I seldom express my emotions but I love you, Debu. When you leave me for your heavenly life, I will keep you in my heart and think about you every day until our paths cross again."

She let her lips touch his forehead and then disentangled her fingers from his and walked towards the door. She knew he was gone now.

The next morning, Debendranath's body lay cold in bed and his hollow eyes stared out in the open. Chandramukhi put her hand over his eyelids and closed them. She had no more tears to spare. Instead, she called all her children to tell them the sad news. In the evening, they took the body to Nimtala. There the flesh of a man once so highly principled whose heart had drowned in disillusion and sorrows and partitioned into two states was burnt into ashes and poured into the Hooghly river.